full flight

~

also by ashley schumacher

amelia unabridged

full flight

ashley schumacher

WEDNESDAY BOOKS
NEW YORK

First published in the United States by Wednesday Books, an imprint of St. Martin's Publishing Group

FULL FLIGHT. Copyright © 2022 by Ashley Schumacher. All rights reserved. Printed in the United States of America. For information, address St. Martin's Publishing Group, 120 Broadway, New York, NY 10271.

www.wednesdaybooks.com

Library of Congress Cataloging-in-Publication Data

Names: Schumacher, Ashley, author.
Title: Full flight / Ashley Schumacher.
Description: First edition. | New York : Wednesday Books, 2022. | Audience: Ages 12–18. |
Identifiers: LCCN 2021042264 | ISBN 9781250779786 (hardcover) | ISBN 9781250779793 (ebook)
Subjects: CYAC: Marching bands—Fiction. | Dating (Social customs)—Fiction. | Grief—Fiction. | High schools—Fiction. | Schools—Fiction. | LCGFT: Novels.
Classification: LCC PZ7.1.S3365545 Fu 2022 | DDC [Fic]—dc23
LC record available at https://lccn.loc.gov/2021042264

Our books may be purchased in bulk for promotional, educational, or business use. Please contact your local bookseller or the Macmillan Corporate and Premium Sales Department at 1-800-221-7945, extension 5442, or by email at MacmillanSpecialMarkets@macmillan.com.

First Edition: 2022

10 9 8 7 6 5 4 3 2 1

For my Michael, for everything.
And for Chris, because life is for the living.
Thanks for catching the stars with me.

chapter 1

⸙

weston

I'm learning a new piece on the piano when she happens. That's how she feels: like a Happening. One minute I'm awash in a sea of notes, the next the practice room door flies open, hitting the stopper with a dull *thud*, and she's there, her saxophone dangling from its strap around her neck.

The last note I played is ringing in the air and waiting for the run that follows, when Anna James rounds the bench to stand close to my face, her brown eyes pleading with me before the words leave her mouth in a torrent.

"Look," she says, "I'm going to level with you because I have no choice. If I screw this up, it's literally the end of the world. My parents will be sad. The band will be sad. *I* will be sad. Just *promise me*," she says gravely, "that you'll agree with everything Mr. Brant is about to say."

She might be a Happening, a tornado with feet, but she looks normal. Brown hair, brown eyes, white skin, a shirt that

{ 1 }

looks like it can't decide whether to accentuate her curves or hide them, and . . .

Christmas socks? On the first day of school. In *August*. They're peeking out from beneath her jeans, faded yellow pom-poms atop ornamented trees.

"Do you even know who I am?" I ask, staring at the socks.

It's a loaded question, an accusation. In a town the size of Enfield, you can't help but recognize everyone in the hallways of EHS. More often than not, you know the limbs of your classmates' family trees as well as your own, the same grand-parents and parents and aunts and uncles showing up at every forced singing program and school play you've been in since childhood.

Enfield is one of those absurdly small Texas towns, the kind that claims to be Christian and has a church on every corner. Except the biggest cathedral of all is the football field in the dead center of town where—from August to December—everyone comes to worship the god of cowhide and metal bleachers and congealed cheese nachos from the cash-only concession stand.

So, she knows me. She probably knows my full name and my GPA, and she's definitely heard the town "scandal" that my parents divorced and the "shocking" news that I ran away to Bloom because of it.

And I vaguely know *her*. I know she's first chair saxophone this year by default. I know that instead of joining band in the fifth grade like everybody else, she joined her freshman year—my sophomore year—before I went away to Bloom. I know she has parents that are still married, because most every-one in Enfield does. I think she has a little sister.

But that doesn't mean anything, this kind of knowing. We were at band camp together two weeks ago, for Christ's sake, and she didn't speak to me *once*. Not that she was an exception; hardly anyone except Ratio and—occasionally, when he seemed to suddenly remember we were friends— Jonathan spoke to me, except to pry about *why* I had gone to Bloom and *why* I had come back. Like they didn't know. Like they wanted me to talk about Mom and Dad's divorce out loud, just to hear me say it.

But none of them are standing too close to me in a practice room either. Only Anna James.

She is watching me, her head cocked as she presses down her saxophone keys in a drumming rhythm, the rubber pads clicking against the metal in a strange tattoo.

She says nothing, and I feel fuzzy and hollow. Dreading what she's about to say. *Never mind. I have you confused with someone else.* Or worse, *Sure I know you. You're the freak that wears the black leather jacket.*

She doesn't, though.

When she speaks, it's almost a whisper, and chills run up and down my arms.

"I know you, Weston Ryan."

It's ridiculous, but I almost believe she means it, despite years of parents and teachers whispering behind cupped hands that I am "gifted but strange," great with music but not so great at fitting in. I can almost pretend that my two best and only friends haven't always seen me as their social pity project.

Suddenly, I wonder if Anna has heard the rumor that is *still* going around, a whole year later, that *I'm* the one who took a hatchet to the high school's stupid Memorial Memorial Tree.

I'm sure she did. It made the front page of the Enfield weekly paper and everything: "Tree Representing Hope for Future Chopped Down." Town police were searching for the culprit, the article said. It used words like *malicious, vengeful,* and *pernicious,* words not seen in the paper since ninety-year-old

Mr. Summers refused to participate in the student-versus-faculty Thanksgiving basketball game.

> The sapling, fondly referred to as the Memorial Memorial Tree by students, was planted only one month ago by the student council after the original Memorial Tree was struck by lightning last spring. The council held bake sales throughout the year to pay for the new tree and the original's stump removal, never imagining their hard work would end in tragedy. The last Memorial Tree had a rich history, presiding over the center of the student parking lot since the days when the lot consisted of posts for horses; this Memorial Memorial Tree lasted under a month.

I didn't touch that *fucking* tree. The only reason everyone thinks I did is because someone overheard me telling Ratio "Good riddance" when he told me the news, which, for the record, was only because the replacement tree looked like it wouldn't even last the mild Texas winter. *Twig* is too generous a term. It probably shriveled up and died of embarrassment.

It didn't help the rumors when I transferred to Bloom for the next school year.

But Anna isn't looking at me like I'm a tree killer that skipped town after murdering important vegetation. When Anna looks at me, I can almost, almost, *almost* believe she sees through everything—the whispers, the tree accusations. All of it.

We're interrupted by the door opening as, in a much softer fashion, our band director enters. The tiny room is now over-crowded with a piano, my mellophone case, my backpack, Anna and her saxophone, and Mr. Brant.

"Weston Ryan," he greets me. "I'm surprised to find you here after school."

I gesture vaguely at the sheet music atop the piano. "Practicing, sir."

Avoiding my mom's empty house, sir.

Mr. Brant nods, his eyes jumping between us. "Good. Anna has informed me that you're going to help her with the duet you two share in the production number. Is this true?"

Anna scoots to stand beside Mr. Brant, and I can't decide if it's harder or easier to breathe now that there's an appropriate distance between us. Her eyes are begging as she stares meaningfully at me, her hands closed in a choke hold on her saxophone, and something about the way she is looking at me—like I'm the answer to all of her questions—makes my insides shift.

I don't have the luxury of time to decide if it's a good or bad shift.

"Of course." The words leave my mouth without my brain hearing what it is I've agreed to.

If I thought Anna's eyes were bright before, it's only because I didn't know that eyes could look like hers do when she smiles at me. Luminescent. Like unexpectedly stumbling across the first fireflies of summer.

It almost makes me want to smile back.

"Excellent. Good," he is saying. "You need to get it down. And soon, understand? Or Anna's part goes to Ryland. He'll need time to work it up before the regional contest."

"Yes, sir," Anna says. She's trying to get me to look at her.

"Fine," I say.

Mr. Brant raises an eyebrow.

"I'm not sure what the good town of Bloom let you get away with, Mr. Ryan, but the Enfield Bearcat band does not say *Fine* to their director in that tone."

Bloom. Long, long hallways with no Jonathan or Ratio, band members in the wrong color of uniform and with different faces calling me Speed Racer, coming home to a house with one parent instead of two.

It's the last part that makes me shrink back. I should feel grateful for the reminder that Anna James is better off not being anywhere near me. If Mom and Dad couldn't stick it out, there's zero hope for me. Ever.

The thought makes my chest feel empty.

"Yes, sir," I tell Mr. Brant.

He nods again, almost apologetically, like all the teachers have since I came back to Enfield for senior year.

"Good," Mr. Brant says. "Good. I'll check in periodically over the next few weeks to see how it's going. It's a state year. We can't afford any mistakes on the field."

With that, he returns to his office, leaving the heavy wooden door open behind him and pushing Anna and me into a silence that we both expect the other to break.

"Thank you," she says finally. She's not as close as she was when she first happened, but she takes a step toward me. "I didn't think you'd say yes."

Her smile is tentative, and even though I should keep my distance, I want to see her eyes light up again, so I say, "But you know me, Anna."

She laughs. A full-bodied, too-loud, too-wonderful laugh.

"I do," she says. "I do."

I can't help myself. "Tell me something you know about me," I say, making my voice soft so that the few people loitering in the band hall don't hear me.

"Just one thing?" she asks.

"Just one."

She is doing that staring thing, the one that makes me feel like there are sparklers in my blood.

"Your hair looks better longer," she says.

I rub a hand over my close-shaved scalp. Cutting it had been a poor life choice, thanks to an afternoon of boredom, hair trimmers Mom used on the dog, and wishing that everything could be different. I might not be able to control my parents' marriage or how everyone treated me at band camp, but I *can* decide what to do with my hair.

Maybe can and should are two different things.

"It's okay," she says and smiles. "It'll grow back, right?"

We're only talking about hair length, but the air between us is crackling so loudly I swear I smell smoke.

Whatever God is in charge of the six churches that line the one road through Enfield must be on my side today, because Anna's phone chimes and rescues us from this weirdly intimate conversation. Or maybe God really does know what's best and has a plan or whatever and is trying to get Anna as far away from me as possible.

"Shoot," she says. "I've got to go or I'll be late for dinner. It's chicken nugget night. See you tomorrow?"

Like it's a question. Like we aren't required to be on the practice grid every morning at six o'clock sharp.

"Tomorrow," I say, making my voice a little harder, but she smiles.

There are two wolves fighting inside me: one that wants to push her away and one that wants to see if I can make her smile.

They'll tear me to pieces.

I flinch.

I can't help her.

Ratio can teach her the duet; he plays the mellophone. It'll be just as good. Better, even, because Ratio is the golden boy of Enfield.

But as I pack my things to leave, she stays in my thoughts. The practice room, previously a quiet sanctuary, now seems too empty and lonely to be a hiding place.

I tell myself I don't need another distraction. I should coast through senior year until I can get out of Enfield, go somewhere new. Somewhere that no one cares if your parents are divorced or gives you pitying looks because they remember what it was like when they were together. Somewhere that gossip isn't the lifeblood of a town.

I ignore the dark mass in my stomach as I drive home. Tomorrow I'll get Ratio to help Anna. And everything will go back to normal.

Mom left on another business trip this morning, which means the house is too cavernous and hollow to bear when I walk in. The wildfire that has burned beneath my skin since the divorce has space to roam here, dragging itself from room to room, blackening the piano she and Dad bought me when I was seven, blazing through her paintings hung in frames Dad made in the shop behind the house, the inferno razing my childhood memories one after the other.

I can't decide if it hurts more or less to have them burn.

Mom always leaves a stock of those annoying food delivery service meals in the fridge, but the thing is you have to cook them yourself. "Easy!" the lemon chicken ricotta box promises. "Quick! Fun!"

The instructions look anything but. I grab instant noodles from the back of the pantry and put them in the microwave.

There's a note on the island, written in Mom's perfect, narrow handwriting:

> *In Cincinnati until Friday. Let me know if you go*
> *stay at your father's. Clean your boxes out of the attic.*
> *Bulk trash coming next week.*
> *To the moon and back,*
>
> > *Mom*

She hasn't said she's selling the house, but it's coming. The rooms are too neat, the cupboards inching toward bare. The living room smells faintly of paint, and I can see where she's been touching up the walls.

I take my noodles upstairs, forgetting about the attic boxes. Mom must have known this would be the case, because she's lined them up in front of my bedroom door, blocking my way.

Seriously?

I fold back cardboard flaps. Mostly old Scout uniforms, piano trophies from elementary recitals, and less-than-stellar drawings of handprint turkeys and finger-painted trees. I find a plastic-covered report from freshman year biology, the cover page proudly proclaiming, "The Kaua'i 'ō'ō, by Weston Ryan," with a large pixelated drawing of the bird beneath.

It opens in my hand, and I'm about to return it to the box, when my eyes snag on the last page:

> The Kaua'i 'ō'ō was last seen in 1987, a single male bird thought to be the last of his species after his mate died in a hurricane. When scientists played the Kaua'i 'ō'ō's song near the last known location of the male bird, he came flying toward them. He thought the scientists were another Kaua'i 'ō'ō. He thought he wasn't alone, that his family was still alive.

I push the rest of the boxes toward the stairs—I'll sort and carry them downstairs later—but I keep the report about the Kaua'i 'ō'ō.

Later, when I can't sleep, my thoughts swirl into an obsessive loop about the lonely bird in the Hawaiian forest. Did it know it was the only one? Did it mourn? Was there a flash of hope in its bird brain, a flash of recognition, when he heard his song played?

I think my dreams will be haunted by the Kaua'i 'ō'ō, but instead they are clouded with Christmas socks and the girl who wears them in August.

chapter 2

❧

anna

When we first moved to Enfield, I hated it.

"I don't have any friends," I told Mom while she unpacked pots and pans and Dad unwrapped the newspaper from our plates. "What am I supposed to do?"

Mom shot Dad a Your turn *look*. He gave my shoulder a squeeze and smiled.

"Why don't you take Bear-Bear out and show him the backyard?" he said. "He's probably scared and needs you to explain that we're here because it'll be a better life for us all."

I told him it was a stupid idea, but I waited until my parents were distracted by Jenny to slip out the door.

I took Bear-Bear out to the fenced-in half acre and walked him around the perimeter, whispering stories of moving trucks and tearful good-byes, but telling him it would be okay. That this new place was going to be even better than the one we left behind.

And my chest began to feel lighter and lighter.

I didn't have friends in Enfield, but I had someone who lis-
tened. It was just as good. Maybe better. Or at least that's what I
told myself.

I keep catching Weston staring at me in morning rehearsal.
The first time it happens, right after the warm-up mile, I smile
at him. He *almost* smiles back, a blip of something lighting up
his eyes, but he smothers it and looks away.

We're on the blacktop practice grid, the one marked up to
look like a football field, with yard lines and end zones. It's
how we navigate our places in the show, individual ship cap-
tains who map by number of steps off of white sideline dashes
instead of stars.

Mr. Brant is twenty feet above us, on the director's tower,
Ratio is far below, on the three-rung drum major podium, and
both are flipping through their big orange binders to try and
figure out why the final set of the opener looks lopsided.

The forty-three of us with instruments stand at loose attention, ready to spring into action at the first command.

My stomach is in knots, and not just because Weston Ryan
can't keep his eyes off me.

If Mr. Brant can figure out why our ginormous arch looks
lopsided, that means it will be almost time to begin the production number, and soon it will be time to play the duet.

With Weston Ryan.

My duet partner.

The one who is not smiling around me on purpose . . .
probably because I basically attacked him in the practice
room yesterday.

I look across the grid to where he stands. We're supposed to
be exactly opposite each other, the two endpoints of the arch,
but Weston is at least four steps behind me, and if I had to
guess which of us read their dot wrong . . .

"Anna," Mr. Brant calls. "You're too far forward. Check your dot."

My cheeks are burning as I wrestle the index card booklet from where it dangles at my waist. The string hangs from my neck, messenger-style. At my frantic movement, it twists awkwardly around my sax's neck strap, and for a moment I'm certain I'm going to accidentally strangle myself.

"*Gilligan*," somebody in the woodwind section to my left whispers, and my blood boils. I am *not* a Gilligan. Not this year.

It's my third year of band, which sounds like a lot until you realize that everyone else joined when they were *nine*. While the handful of us fifth graders that *didn't* join were shuffled through a series of cliché art projects and myriad busywork assignments, my friends were in the intermediate school band hall, learning the intricacies of quarter notes and treble clefs and dynamic markings.

"Why won't you *join*?" Lauren pestered relentlessly. At ten, she was already too talented for her own good, quickly climbing the ranks to second chair flute. "You'd be great! And you'd get to hang out with me and Andy and Katherine during fifth period."

She wasn't the only one. As we got older and band kids were excused midclass for some contest or another, teachers who had known me for years would look at me expectantly.

"You'd better get going, Anna."

"I'm not in band, Mrs. Thomas."

"Oh. Are you sure?"

"Positive."

Their confusion was understandable. I hung out with band kids. I went to all the concerts. I was respectful, polite to a fault—something most band members were, due to the fear of God Mr. Brant instilled in them should they act otherwise. I made good grades and *liked* school, to the point that I thought being called teacher's pet was a compliment.

But I wasn't a band kid. Instead, I waited like a faithful retriever outside the band hall for Lauren to grab her case, Andy to grab his mallet bag.

Band and I were like the couple in a Christmas movie that you *know* will end up together but keep meeting at the wrong time, until—after the kiss and the snow flurries at the movie's end—you wonder how they ever existed apart.

But we had to be apart. My family's money status was a pendulum, swinging from *Not much at all* to *More than enough* and then back to scrimping and saving.

Dad was constantly working after Jenny was born. After the news started using phrases like "economic downturn" and "unemployment rates," I knew things were tight. We used to eat out every weekend, go on vacation once a year. Dad used to sneak me twenty dollars for ice cream at school, for trips to the movies with Lauren and Andy, for whatever I wanted.

Except, even with Dad always working and Mom's secretary checks, there were nights we ate wilted leftovers at home. We went to the local water park in the summer instead of driving to Colorado or Florida. Dad—always Dad—still snuck me money, but it was ones and fives and came with a *Don't tell your mother*, and this time he meant it. We never went hungry, but I knew.

By the time Jenny was a toddler and I started fifth grade, things had started to look up. Dad found a job at a new printing company. His paychecks were smaller than before, but I heard him and Mom whispering that they would grow as he brought in new customers to the business.

When band sign-ups came that same year, and the high schoolers came to our school and played for us and offered to let us try their instruments, I was excited. I loved the shiny instruments. I loved the warm feeling in my chest when I imagined myself making music next to Lauren or Andy or any of my friends. I loved the idea that I, Anna James, with my lips and air and finger movements, could make a melody come from nothing.

But then they handed us a bright orange information sheet with fees listed for instrument rental, music warm-up books, concert attire, and private lessons. On and on the numbers went. I didn't bother to add them up.

We were doing better, but not Anna-can-join-band better.

At lunch that day, after the high schoolers had left, I told Lauren and Andy that I wanted to do art class instead. When I got home and told my parents that it was band sign-up day and I didn't want to do it, they asked if I was sure.

"Yes," I lied.

They exchanged a look of relief when they thought I couldn't see.

But band was patient, always waiting, always whispering from the wings that maybe, just *maybe*, it would someday be music's turn.

The whisper became a roar in the spring of eighth grade, when we had to sign up for our high school extracurriculars. The James family was taking vacations again. We were eating out twice a week, Dad occasionally bringing home BBQ sandwiches and fries from Fixin' Burger *just because it sounded good*.

So I talked to Mr. Brant—who was and always is looking for suckers stupid enough to sacrifice their entire high school lives at the altar of music—and I signed up for band.

This is what I've been waiting for since I was nine. And now that I'm finally here, I can't screw it up. Especially when it would be a slap in the face to my parents, who dutifully pay my private lesson fees, my rental fees, because they're *so, so proud* of me. Especially during a state year. Especially when failing at the duet would mean dragging literally everyone else down with me.

Feedback from the amplifier at the back of the field pushes me out of my head, and I pretend to find the correct page in my dot book—I don't—and step forward until I'm even with Weston. He's looking at me intently, his gaze prickling on my left side. When I look up, he ever so slightly nudges his head to the right, and I take a half step farther away from him. Another twitch. Another half step. A very slight nod.

Maybe he's not avoiding me.

"All right, band. This needs to be wrapped up by Friday's game, are we clear? Now, let's do a quick stand-and-play through the production number before showers. Everyone should have their music memorized, yes?" Mr. Brant doesn't wait for an answer. "Good? Great. Stand in place, but practice your step-offs for the first half of the number. On your cue, drum major."

My stomach drops. Thunder cracks above my ship's drooping mast. Mr. Brant *knows* I haven't got the duet down. It's why he called me into his office yesterday after school and made me play through the whole thing, note after agonizing note—why I lied about Weston agreeing to help me before I had even *asked* him.

Did Mr. Brant really expect me to fix anything overnight? I didn't think I'd have to play in front of the *entire band* so soon.

But the duet comes, and as the other woodwinds and brass fade away to make room for me and Weston, the flowing stream of his music is met with a solid rock of wrong notes. Not too-sharp or too-flat right notes. Wrong notes. All jumbled and sticky and . . . wrong.

I can't seem to hit a single one.

When Mr. Brant yells for us to stop, Ratio has already

stopped conducting and everyone else has dropped their play-ready postures.

After calling for check, the formal command to break from attention, Mr. Brant stares down at me.

"Two weeks," he says, his voice dreadfully ominous.

The whole band is looking at me. I'm standing in the waves of their disapproval, and I tell myself I'm a rock, one of those sturdy ones that's been there forever, with barnacles on every exposed surface. My insides don't listen. They feel like a turtle tangled in a net, tossing in the surf.

Sometimes, when I feel like I'm underperforming, when I'm not being the Anna James I'm supposed to be, the one people expect, the shadows come for me, thick as heavy clouds and with human silhouettes that try to cover my mouth so I can't breathe.

They are coming for me here. My chest is too tight. It doesn't ease when Mr. Brant repeats, "You have two weeks to fix this. Get a copy of your music to Ryland by rehearsal tonight. Ryland, be ready to play it on a moment's notice."

I have to look across the wide-eyed stares of Terrance and Samantha, the freshman saxophones under my dubious leadership, to see Ryland. He's first chair clarinet during our marching and concert seasons, but he's also first chair sax in the jazz band.

He shoots me an apologetic look.

Everything is too close, too pressing, and I feel my chest start to buckle beneath the weight of my embarrassment, the shadows gripping me tighter.

This was supposed to be the year I did not fail. This was supposed to be the year I belonged, that nobody could call me a Gilligan.

An eternity passes before Mr. Brant calls, "Band dismissed."

Everyone scatters, rushing for the showers. It's too early in the school year for wet hair and baggy sweats—some upper-classmen already entertaining thoughts of "Best Dressed" and "Most Put Together"—but these things take time, and time is in precious small supply in the crowded morning locker rooms.

Lauren doesn't stop to talk with me, only cocks her head in a silent question from where she's collecting her sheet music and piccolo. It's best friend body language, her asking *Are you okay?* and my small smile an answering *Yes.*

And I am okay, mostly. But I take more time than I should in the shower, standing beneath the lukewarm water and reminding myself that this is where I want to be, that band and I are meant to be together, no matter the odds, no matter what the shadows whisper.

My wet hair drips water down my back all the way to second period.

"It wasn't *that* bad," Lauren says at lunch. "I mean, it's nothing like last year, when Timothy beaned Lydia in the back of the head with his trombone slide only two days before the area contest, remember?"

I pick at the crust of my sandwich. "Who could forget?"

"And you have *weeks* to get it right. Not days, you know?"

Normally I'm the one trying to point out silver linings, so it's weird to hear them come from Lauren.

Without asking, Andy reaches over and takes my regular yogurt and replaces it with his Greek yogurt and, a second later, an apology Oreo. It's been our long-standing agreement since Andy's mom insisted on sneaking Greek yogurt—or as Andy calls it, "reek" yogurt—into his lunch bag.

I've already filled them in on my despair—on practically forcing Weston to help me, and his unreadable behavior, on the complete embarrassment that is Mr. Brant's ultimatum of giving my piece to Ryland, and how the *entire* band knows.

"I can't wait to see how you get on with Weston," Andy says. "That guy is an odd one."

"What do you mean?" Kristin asks. She's the only freshman at our lunch table, but everyone allows it because she's the band's one oboe and needs to be kept happy. Oboes are hard enough to tune without their players sitting alone at lunch. "He seems okay."

"He always wears that leather jacket. Which, fine. But even during *the dead of summer*? The guy thinks he's Phantom of the Opera or something. It's weird," Andy says, taking a bite of yogurt. "We had the same piano teacher until he quit last year. Can confirm that he is stupid talented but also stupid antisocial. The kid. Is. *Weird*."

"Definitely weird," Lauren agrees, and annoyance flickers inside me that she so readily agrees, even though I'm willing to bet all the money in my piggy bank that she has never spoken to Weston. "Why don't *I* help you?" she asks, turning to me. "You don't actually need him to learn your half, you know."

Weston Ryan. I didn't mean it to be a lie when I told him I knew him, but I *don't*. Not really. Not in the concrete way that is knowing Lauren or Andy or just about anyone else in school. Weston is like the low-lying mist that hovers over the crop fields in the early morning, present but never once settling.

I know enough, though. A few flashbulb, out-of-context memories of him from my freshman year, before he left for Bloom: Weston sitting in the corner of the band hall reading his book during the long summer two-a-day practices. Weston, a distant planet orbiting the sun that is Ratio's and Jonathan's loud jokes and ready smiles. Weston, taking the time to catch a gecko that had wandered inside during the hubbub of game-day packing chaos and carrying it outside to safety in gently cupped hands.

Weston, after the last Tuesday night rehearsal of my freshman year, leaning against his old forest-green Explorer in his
leather jacket, blond hair longish and dangling in a defeated
downturn of the head, his cell phone loosely held in a pale,
slack arm.

I had been one of the last ones in the parking lot that
night, after my group took its turn staying late to put away
the equipment. I should have asked him what was wrong, but
I didn't. I had to walk past him to get to Mom's waiting car,
but I didn't say a word.

I know that the reason he wasn't here last year had to do
with his parents' divorce and that he spent it at Bloom High,
Enfield's next-door neighbor and rival in every activity, including marching band. I heard the jokes at band camp two
weeks ago, people calling him a traitor.

He didn't laugh.

But, most important, I know that with the exception of
Ratio and Jonathan, everyone believes Weston Ryan is someone to be tolerated or avoided. And I wonder if the seasick
feeling in my stomach is because I know—I *know*—that if
people ever knew about the shadows that hovered outside the
happy-go-lucky personality outfit I put on every morning,
they would think I was unfriendable, too.

So I tell Lauren, "Y'all are busy. I've got it covered."

As if summoned by our conversation, Ryland appears at
the table, and Lauren, Andy, and Kristin are suddenly deeply
involved in a conversation among themselves.

"Anna? I wanted to say sorry. I swear, I didn't say anything
to Mr. Brant about taking your duet. Really. I don't want it."

He has his tray in hand, feet pointed away from the table
like he might need to bolt from my anger, which is ridiculous. Ryland gave me rides to practice countless times before
I got my license. He's constantly joking under his breath in

woodwind sectionals to make me laugh, or trying to drag me into joining jazz band.

Being mad at Ryland would be like being mad at a puppy. A very talented puppy.

"I know you didn't," I say, slipping my Oreo onto an unoccupied square of his tray. "But if Weston doesn't work out, I might need your help."

Ryland snorts. "Hate to say it, but Weston might be your best shot. The guy's odd, but he's a beast at all things music. If anyone can help you get it done in time, it's him."

"Hey!" Lauren says, leaving her fake conversation much too quickly to join ours. "I already offered to help her!"

Ryland smiles at her over my head. "Yeah, like she wants help from a piccolo. You're the only one for a reason: nobody could stand to hear two of those *things* at once."

"I'm the only one because I'm the *best* one." Lauren steals the Oreo from Ry's tray and pops it into her mouth.

Unfazed, Ryland drawls, "Want to know how to get two piccolos to play in tune?"

Lauren glares.

"You have to kill one."

"Ha ha. Very funny. Hilarious. At least I didn't have to go to the nurse for getting a splinter in my lip."

Ryland rolls his eyes and walks off toward his table, calling behind him, "At least my instrument can be heard from more than ten feet away."

Lauren turns to the table, "*I* don't play loud enough? My section has four people. Four. His has *seven*, and Mr. Brant *still* tells them to play louder every rehearsal."

"Don't you and Ryland go to youth group together at First Baptist?" Kristin asks timidly.

"Yes, fortunately. Only God can help that boy, bless his heart," Lauren says.

"Um, they also *dated*," Andy says, putting another Oreo in front of me.

"So, you hate each other?" Kristin asks.

Lauren snorts. "Oh, honey. If we started hating everyone we dated in band, there would be no friends left. Andy here is working his way through the brass section like it's his job."

"Excuse you. I'm promoting intersectional relations," Andy says. "It's a burden, but somebody's got to do it."

"What a hero," I deadpan.

"He's also the sole reason for the mono outbreak last year," Lauren says, popping a baby carrot into her mouth.

"Yeah, no. That's from you gross wind instruments dumping saliva on the floor and flinging spit particles everywhere. There are *no* human liquids involved in drum lines, other than blood, sweat, and tears."

The banter loosens the knot that has been in my stomach since rehearsal. All through history and Spanish, I had turned the morning over in my head, magnifying it into a huge Godzilla-like monster that squashed everything else.

But here, with Lauren and Andy sparring and Kristin looking afraid to laugh but doing it anyway, it doesn't seem so bad. The year is only beginning. There's plenty of time for me to fix things. No need for shadows.

When the bell rings to end lunch, I've almost convinced myself everything is okay. Then, I feel the tingling sensation of being watched, and there is Weston Ryan, leather jacket slung over his arm, leaning against the brick wall of the student stairwell.

Something unfamiliar tightens in my stomach when my brown eyes meet his blue, and I don't entirely mind it. I don't mind it at all.

"Um, I need to go talk to him," I tell Lauren, inclining my

head toward Weston. "I'll see you in class. Grab my pre-cal book from my locker for me?"

Lauren is also looking at Weston, but her eyes are narrowed. "He is *weird*, Anna. So weird. Are you sure you don't want me to come with you?"

I break my gaze from Weston and angle myself slightly away so he can't see my lips moving. "Why does everybody keep saying that?" I'm surprised at how exasperated my voice sounds, how defensive. "Is it because of the jacket?"

"It's because of his *him*-ness. You know how everyone loves Jessica instantly without even knowing her?"

I think of the pretty, bubbly trumpet and nod. "Yeah? So?"

Lauren lowers her voice into a pointed whisper. "*That's* how everyone feels about him, except it's weirdness instead of adoration."

The way people talk about Weston strikes me as supremely unfair, even if I can't put my finger on why. And so what if he wears a leather jacket? He also reads books and escorts geckos to safety. And he didn't toss me out when I barged into his practice room begging for help.

He can't be all bad. I'm convinced he can't even be *mostly* bad.

"I'm weird," I point out, and Lauren makes a frustrated sound in the back of her throat.

"You're socially approved weird. The weirdest thing about you is the Christmas sock thing, and maybe that your family is charmingly ridiculous."

I have nothing to say to this. Lauren is easily my closest friend. We've known each other since third grade. But even after numerous sleepovers and hours spent together on the band bus, I wonder if Lauren has time to really know anybody. She is involved, and brilliant, in *everything*—band, cross-country, academic competitions, dance team—and she still finds time to swim competitively outside of school.

She is always *going*, and sometimes it feels like our friendship is an afterthought when her activities for the day are done. It's why I don't take her up on her offer to help, because even if she means it now, she won't have time later.

The thought rubs me the wrong way, but it gives me my voice. "I'll be fine. I'm just going to talk to him for a minute. Grab my book?"

Lauren rolls her eyes, plucking my lunch box from my hand. "Fine. I'll put this in your locker, too, but only because it'll make it easier when your parents have to come collect your things after you die of weirdness."

"Just *go*," I say.

We have five minutes between classes, and our whispered argument has already taken up two.

I know Weston is still waiting before I turn around because I can feel that his eyes haven't moved. When I face him, I see his gaze drop—just once—over last year's blue church-mission-trip shirt and my favorite jeans down to my tennis shoes. And back up.

I have the absurd thought that I wish I was in my first-day-of-school shirt with the fluttery sleeves. As if boys notice things like sleeves.

My face is on fire when I come to stand before him. He doesn't straighten from his lean, and I'm grateful because it gives him the appearance of being shorter than his much-taller-than-me height.

I don't know what to say. My brain is short-circuiting. I'm simultaneously playing a loop of today's disastrous rehearsal and the way Weston's eyes widened when I came into his practice room yesterday.

I say the first thing that pops into my head.

"Are you going to grow your hair out?"

Internally, I cringe. *Well done, Anna. Way to make literally every conversation starter about his hair.*

His face clears, the sun peeping out from the clouds on an overcast day when you thought there would be only darkness, and he tilts his head. "Do you want me to?"

Something about his eyes and the way he is staring makes me overly aware of the backpack strap scraping against my shoulder.

"What I want is for you to tell me when we're going to meet to work on the duet," I say.

His face clouds. *Tut, tut,* I think. *Looks like rain.*

"I can't help you."

My heart falters. "You can't or you won't?" I ask.

He opens his mouth to answer, but I say, "Don't lie," and he closes it.

"Everyone lies," he says after a while.

The one-minute warning bell clangs between us, but we don't move.

"What if we agree not to lie?" I say. "Like, what if we promise to tell each other the truth, even if it sucks?"

When I was little, I had a crush on an animated pirate from an educational children's TV show that Jenny watched. He was supposed to be the bad guy, the villain, but something about the way his mouth slowly changed from a smirk to a smile had excused his insistence on kidnapping letters of the alphabet or squashing perfect shapes.

That's what Weston's slow smile reminds me of: a pirate's smile. A rogue's. It makes my legs question whether they remember how to be legs.

"Do you want me to grow out my hair?"

His voice is too deep to be playful, his eyes too earnest.

"You can do whatever—"

"You promised," he says. "The truth."

I'm fumbling for an answer when the final bell rings. Saved by the bell, indeed.

"Class." I gesture aimlessly toward a hallway. "I can't be too late to Mrs. Benson's."

"Wouldn't want that." His voice is *so* deep. "But Anna?"

I stop midturn. "Yeah?"

"My hair? You like it longer?" Weston raises his brows.

I take a tiny step forward. "What if I do?"

He shrugs. "I'll grow it out."

I'm going to be late, but I have to ask. "Why?"

"Because I know you, Anna James," he says.

And then he's gone, walking toward the senior hallway.

I don't realize until halfway through math class that he never definitively said if he would help with the duet.

chapter 3

weston

I'm a Grade A idiot.

When I left my teacher assistant period—which is a complete joke, since mine is in the band hall with Mr. Brant—early to catch Anna after her lunch and tell her I couldn't help her, I knew what I would say. I was prepared. I had rehearsed it, even: *I can't help you. You will thank me for it when I don't make everything worse.*

But her eyes were sparkling, and something about the glint in them, the way she was unafraid to be seen with me, batting off the concerns of Lauren Anderson, made my stomach hurt. I couldn't say anything.

And then she acted half interested in my hair again, like she had noticed me before, like she cared enough to have a preference, and I couldn't stop from smiling.

What happened after lunch can't happen. I can't be taken in by how her ears reddened when she realized I was watching her, or how she looked at me like she was trying to memorize my face.

Ratio can help her.

And I *definitely* can't spend any more time thinking about her hair . . . or the way her thighs fill her shorts during rehearsal or her jeans during school . . . or how cute her ears are, even when they aren't red.

Shit.

It's the first Tuesday night rehearsal of the season, but more important, it's my first time in the Enfield stadium since everything that happened last year.

It looks and smells exactly like I remember. Floodlights flicker on overhead in anticipation of the dying light, bringing little clumps of artificial turf into stark focus beneath my shoes. There's the lingering smell of football player sweat, their after-school practice cut short to give the marching band time on the field.

The metal stands that stretch toward the sky are blinding as they catch the sunset and the stadium lights, reflecting more heat onto the already hot field. They're empty, but when rehearsal starts, band parents will fill the first two rows to watch us run the same sets over and over.

The field is vacant, except for Ratio and Landon standing side by side and peering down at a dot book.

Of *course* Ratio is here early to help a Gilligan.

"I just don't understand how I am supposed to get from the fifty-yard line to the"—Landon pauses to glance down at his field placement—"the thirty-yard line in that amount of time. What am I supposed to do? Take freakin' huge, monster-sized steps?"

"Yes," Ratio and I say in unison.

Landon groans as Ratio flashes me a grin.

"Better start stretching those quads before practice," Ratio says, handing Landon back his dot book. "You're going to need it."

As Landon makes his way back to the band hall, I help Ratio set up the drum major podium, the two of us working in the comfortable silence that I missed at Bloom last year.

Ratio, Jonathan, and I had bonded at an ill-fated dodge-ball game in first grade, and while nobody can say we've been inseparable ever since, we have an understanding built on weekends spent playing video games, riding four-wheelers, and—once or twice—playing our instruments as loudly as we could in the woods surrounding my house, two French horns and a euphonium blaring into the night and silencing even the persistent wail of the coyotes.

Mom's house, I remind myself. Dad lives in Bloom now, and nobody would call the scraggly trees around his trailer a wood.

"Speed Racer," Ratio greets me formally.

"I told you not to call me that, *Hor*atio."

"Fair enough." Ratio laughs. "But you've gotta admit, those Bloom kids might not be able to march but their nicknames are catchy."

"So is ringworm, but nobody wants that," I say.

Speed Racer. The moniker I'd earned from running back to set after the Bloom director called for another attempt at whatever part of the show we were rehearsing. On Mr. Brant's tightly run Enfield ship, jogging back is a requirement. It saves time. It improves cardio. If you're caught not complying, it means an extra lap around the track added onto your next morning mile, or push-ups for the entire band and the resentment that comes with them.

It was so ingrained in me that I hadn't been able to break myself of it, even though Bloom kids just ambled back to their spots. It gave a new bunch of classmates the opportunity to snicker at me behind instrument bells and raised hands.

"I'd prefer you not bring up highly contagious diseases," Ratio says. "You missed the mono outbreak last year. It was brutal. Half of percussion was down, the trumpets were dropping like flies, and the woodwinds always look kind of sickly anyways, but they were especially pallid. They looked like the wraiths in *King's Reign*."

"Too bad I missed that," I say around a grunt. The metal of the podium screeches loudly as it latches into place. "Shouldn't Jonathan be the one helping Landon? He's the euphonium section leader."

"Jonathan had student council after school," he says, leaning down to rub his ankle. "Besides, as drum major, I couldn't let Landon keep missing his first mark of the production number. Speaking of which, he didn't even know what the production number *was*."

"Like, the music?" I ask.

"Like, that the production number is synonymous with the second piece of music in the marching show."

"Christ."

"Don't curse," Ratio says. "*Especially* to take the Lord's name in vain."

If I had a nickel for every time Ratio has told me not to curse, I could buy us both handmade Holton French horns.

"Fuck off," I say without malice, and Ratio laughs.

A minute of silence passes before Ratio pushes on the top of the platform with an experimental hand to make sure it's latched on both sides. "So . . . are we going to talk about it?" he asks.

I rub podium grime from my fingers onto my shorts. "About what?"

Ratio gives me a *Don't be stupid* look, but I'm really not sure which "it" he is referring to. Bloom? My parents?

"About Anna."

Oh. That.

"What about her?"

Now Ratio is giving me a *You are actively being an imbecile* look.

"*What about her*," he parrots. "I saw you flirting with her after A-lunch, Wes."

"I wasn't flirting. We were talking about the duet."

Ratio climbs the steps to the podium and sits with his legs dangling, elbows balanced on his knees. "I know you love music, but I've never seen you smile that much over a solo, forget a four-line duet. Spill."

Ratio's pose is so achingly nostalgic, I'm not sure whether to laugh or cry.

When we were younger and summers weren't spent at band camp and two-a-days and special sectional rehearsals, Jonathan, Ratio, and I would spend long afternoons in my tree house.

It wasn't actually a tree house. It was a wooden platform Dad built about ten feet off the ground with a ladder in the middle, but it was perfect for battling off the stormtroopers that hid behind the trees, shooting us with their blasters. We were vigilant young Jedi, well trained in the art of deflecting their attacks with our lightsabers.

We were always victorious.

Junior high brought an end to our Jedi training but not our long hours spent on the platform, often silent, lying flat on our backs and looking at the branches above.

But then there were feelings that demanded sorting, and Ratio would sit on the edge of the tree house with his disproportionately long legs stretched toward the ground and his chin rested on his bent arms, Jonathan would sit cross-legged and run his hands over the worn planks, and I would stay on my back to stare at the trees.

We would talk about parents and how they didn't hide their moods from us anymore. We would talk about girls at school and wonder why some smelled like cotton candy while others smelled like brown sugar and what it meant if they said *you* smelled like Axe body spray. (Was it good? Bad? We never figured that one out.)

We would talk about band and our worries of sucking at marching in high school—*ha*—or our fears of what lay beyond high school in the shadowy land of college and the future and time. Always time.

"I wasn't flirting," I tell Ratio. "She's funny. I smiled. End of story."

Ratio raises an eyebrow. "I'm calling bullshit."

I can't hide my surprise at his language. "Call it what you want. It's the truth."

"Bull. Shit. You like her. And for the record, I approve. She'd be good for you, honestly."

I'd been leaning with my back against the podium next to Ratio's legs, but I turn to stare at him, looking up into his smile-crinkled eyes to drive the meaning home.

"I can't have her, and you know it." Saying the words aloud burns my throat.

"Well, for starters," Ratio says smugly, "you can't *have* a person. But I don't see why you can't pursue a mutual, healthy relationship with her."

"You know why," I grit out. Is he really going to make me say it?

"Tell me anyway."

Fine.

"Because," I say, "she's perfect, and I'll ruin her. Or worse, I wouldn't get the chance to ruin her because we would get two seconds into . . . whatever it is people do, and she'd realize how messed up I am and run for the hills."

We turn our heads as laughter interrupts the field's silence. Through the gaping main entrance to the stadium, the band is trickling out the back door of the school and making their way toward rehearsal.

I'm too busy trying to spot Anna to hear Ratio.

"Wait, what were you saying?" I ask.

Ratio looks to heaven like God himself might intervene on his idiot friend's behalf. "*Firstly*," Ratio says, stretching the word out to show his irritation at repeating himself, "it's called 'dating,' that thing people do when they like each other. Secondly, that's awfully presumptuous of you to assume you can ruin a person. And thirdly, there aren't any hills in Enfield, so Anna would have to be particularly motivated to run for them. Besides, I don't think that's going to happen."

"What makes you say that?"

Ratio claps his hand on my shoulder and smiles. "Because you're a moron, but you're also a great person. That's why. Even if you do suck at *King's Reign*."

"Will you help her? Please?" My voice sounds all the more frantic in my rush to get the words out before we're no longer alone. "Just a couple days a week. As a favor."

Ratio is already done with this conversation, his eyes focused on the approaching band members and his mind racing to the rehearsal ahead.

"I'll do you a favor," he says, and I don't have time to figure out if it's relief or sadness that ices through my veins before he finishes, "I'll do you a favor by *not* helping Anna."

And then we are enveloped by the sound of forty voices laughing and tumbling over each other as the band spills onto the sidelines.

I can hear Anna's laugh above the rest. It's like music.

Rehearsal is demanding enough to temporarily douse my restless mind. There are too many things clamoring for my attention.

We are rehashing the problem spots in the opener, smoothing out the rough edges so we can perform it well at halftime this Friday and move on to fully concentrating on the production number next week.

Mr. Brant is beside himself in the announcer's box above the field. The band has forgotten how to read dynamic markings. The flutes need to be less quiet. The trumpets need to learn what *ff* means, because they are playing excessively loud and out of tune at a *ffff*. The tubas are slightly off beat. Freshmen are pedaling, and worse, sophomore Gilligans who should know better are pedaling, their legs frantically propelling an invisible bicycle instead of marching from heel to toe in a smooth glide.

Each repetition, something goes wrong. Mr. Brant switches off the metronome pinging its rhythm from the back of the field. "Again," he says. "Again." And we run back to set.

With enough *again*s strung in a row, you can almost hear the origins of the Gilligan moniker: *Again and again. Gill-again. Gilligan.* We run back to formation with legs and backs and brows pouring sweat as the sun droops into the horizon to give the stadium lights center stage.

Rehearsal isn't all pomp and severity. Mr. Brant accidentally says "No more booties bobbing" instead of "No more bodies bobbing," and he has to cut to an early water break so everyone—including the parents, assistant director Mrs. Taylor, and Mr. Brant himself—can contain their wheezing laughter.

My real distraction is Anna. We are on opposite sides of the field in the opener, and over the grueling three-hour rehearsal we barely move toward each other. Each time I look at her and she doesn't look back—because she's helping her section, laughing with nearby woodwinds, or studying her dot book with a furrow between her eyebrows—it feels like mashing as many piano keys as I can down at once.

We only lock eyes one time, and when we do, she smiles and waves at me from across the field with her pinky finger. By the time I decide smiling back would not be an implicit promise to help her, she's turned away, her lips holding her smile as she laughs with Lauren, but it doesn't stay in her eyes.

When rehearsal is finally over, everyone forms a tight circle on the sidelines. Instruments are held at awkward angles to avoid dents. Woodwinds squawk at careless brass elbows and hands for fear of chipped reeds. Percussionists thump mallets on the weary shoulders of their bandmates until they are slapped away like mosquitoes. Instruments are an extension of our bodies, expensive limbs made of metal and wood instead of blood and tissue.

We are circled for final dismissal, a tradition reserved for games, contests, and Tuesday night rehearsals. It's a formal ritual, a call-and-answer chant that Mr. Brant instated at Enfield long before any of us were born, and even the Gilligan-iest Gilligan knows the commands.

On Tuesdays, dismissal is the punctuation mark of Mr. Brant's speech, which is always about what needs to be done by the next rehearsal, how the parents in the stands need to make sure their students are practicing at home until their lips are chapped and their fingers bleed, and how pride in everything we do will be what earns us straight ones—the highest possible honor—at contest.

It's the drum major's job to call out the dismissal commands. The previous drum major stood on the podium to issue them, but not Ratio. Instead, he stays on the ground, and the band circles even tighter around him, our instruments in the down position but our bodies at attention as we wait.

Ratio's voice is strong, cutting through the distant sound of cicadas, the quiet murmurs of the parents, the dull white noise of the speaker.

The band's answering voice is stronger.

"Drill positions of atten-*shun*! Feet."

"*Together!*"

"Abs."

"*In!*"

"Chest."

"*High!*"

"Head."

"*Up!*"

"Eyes."

"*With pride!*"

"Eyes!"

"*With PRIDE!*"

"EYES!"

"*WITH PRIDE!*"

There is a long moment of silence. Everyone's eyes are trained upward. Everyone is so, so still.

"Band! What is our name?"

"*Bearcat band!*"

"What are we about?"

"*Pride! Trust! Respect! Go Cats!*"

It's the last command, but nobody moves. The energy is palpable, coursing among us like a web.

Later, we will complain about how long rehearsal lasted, make fun of the players that were singled out tonight, and even mock our sections, but for now, we are one.

Another moment of silence.

Another.

"Band dismissed."

The spell is snapped as the silent whole becomes the boisterous many. Instead of searching for Anna in the sea of faces, I make myself focus on twirling my mellophone in a slow circle, trying to rid it of spit and the hint of water I heard on my high D.

I want to find Anna and tell her I can't help, that Ratio—despite what he told me—will be happy to assist. But I also want to avoid her, to have one more day where the possibility of knowing Anna James can twinkle in the back of my mind like a sparkler.

The fire is a dull crackle in my ears, but this is not how I expected to feel after my first Tuesday night rehearsal back at Enfield. The final dismissal had felt exactly right, but this, avoiding an alto saxophone—a *girl*—by escaping to my car at the edge of the senior parking lot while everyone else takes equipment and instruments to the band hall, feels exactly wrong.

My backpack is on a band hall shelf, but I don't care. My car keys are attached to my case handle by a lanyard, so I don't need the pack. I have history homework to do, but what's one zero of what will surely be many?

I have a long night of quests in *King's Reign* ahead of me.

I'll have Ratio tell Anna that I'm not helping, like the coward I am. After our lunch conversation, I don't trust myself to look her in the eye and tell her anything.

I can't even make it through one perfectly normal rehearsal without the fucking melancholy breathing down my neck; I'm not going to drag her down, too.

"Hey!"

Great. I'm hallucinating Anna's voice. Wonderful.

"Weston Ryan, I know you can hear me."

She is out of breath when she reaches me, a conjured daydream stepping into my reality.

"Hey," she huffs out, and I can't believe how *here* she is. "You can't . . ." She pauses, setting her saxophone case on the ground so she can run agitated fingers through her ponytail. She must have skipped going to the band hall to follow me. "You can't offer to help me with the duet and say you'll grow your hair out for me and *then* say you *won't* help me and avoid me at rehearsal. You just can't."

I'm flipping through all the memories I have of Anna James, and I'm not sure if I've ever seen her angry. Her eyes are still glittering, but now they're stuffed beneath thick, scrunched eyebrows.

I don't know what to do with my hands, so I fold them into my elbows.

"I'm sorry," I say, because I can't think of what else *to* say.

When I don't offer up more words, Anna's eyes roam my face before mirroring me, crossing her arms.

"What is it?" she asks. "What's the problem?"

How can she be so much shorter than me and I still feel cowed?

"I'm not good for you," I say.

Anna's mouth falls open like a cartoon character's, and I briefly worry a mosquito will fly down the back of her throat.

"*This* is why you've been acting so weird?" A beat. "You're serious?"

I nod. "Yes."

Anna rolls her eyes.

"Are you a hundred-year-old vampire that likes the smell of my blood?"

Her tone is so startlingly businesslike that I'm sure I've heard her wrong.

I blink. "What? No?"

"Is that a question?" Her mouth twists and I can't help but follow its movement.

"No, I'm not a vampire."

"Are you a serial killer?" She takes a step closer, dropping her arms and sidestepping her case beside her feet. Does she know she still has the saxophone strap dangling from her neck?

"I'm not a serial killer," I say, looking at where the clip that attaches to her sax falls on her sternum. I unfold my arms and half reach for the neck strap before I realize what I'm doing and shove my hands into my pockets. "Or a onetime killer, if that was your next question."

My voice is warming in the back of my throat, the closer she gets to me. It feels like my entire body is ablaze, and I'm not sure if she is going to put me out or douse me with gasoline.

I'm not sure which option I prefer.

Anna takes another step forward. She is close enough that I can feel her breath on my neck as she tips her head back to look up at me, mouth tilted. "Last question?" she asks.

"Shoot."

The slant of her mouth turns impish. "Do you wear the leather jacket because it's how you hide your shame of killing the Memorial Memorial Tree?"

I can't stop the laugh, the loud bursting kind that fills my entire body. So she has heard the rumor, but that she would dare to ask what nobody—even the school counselor—has ever bothered to ask to my face . . . I kind of love her for it.

"Are you going to turn me in, Miss James?" I tease.

Her grin is relieved. "No," she says, and her smile fades. "But . . . if you aren't a vampire or a tree villain, what makes you think you're such a menace to society?"

"Not to society," I say, though there's no confidence behind my words. "To you."

Anna looks like she wants to laugh, but she doesn't.

"I can take care of myself," she says. "I'm better at that than I am duets. I promise."

"I doubt it," I say.

God, she's making this difficult. And how does she still smell this good after a three-hour rehearsal? She's making the thoughts clog in my brain, and I'm quickly forgetting all my arguments for giving her space.

"There's only one way to find out," Anna says, "and it's to help me with the duet and stop not-smiling at me."

My whole world is quiet in the spaces between her words. Even the sound of the crickets and cicadas fades away.

There is only Anna. There is only us.

"I can take it," she adds. "I'm very capable, you know. *Loads* of people have smiled at me and yet somehow I manage to go on living."

"Ratio will help you," I say, the practiced words stale on my lips. "He's a French horn player, too, you know."

"I don't want Ratio's help," she says. She takes another tiny step closer to me, like she hopes I won't notice if she moves slowly enough. "I want yours."

I'm quiet, but Anna's face doesn't change. Her smile doesn't falter.

"It's called being friends. I promise it's not scary." Her smile gets bigger. "I'm not going to bite you."

I drop my head and squeeze my eyes shut so I don't have to look at her.

"I'll help you," I concede, "but we can't be friends."

An owl hoots above us in the silence that follows, probably chasing bugs drawn to the stadium lights. In the distance, the band hall door slams open, the sound clattering across the parking lot. We won't be alone for long, and I wonder idly if adulthood has as many interruptions as high school.

I'm still standing with my eyes shut when I feel her hand barely brush mine. My eyes fly open, but she is already reaching for her case, and I'm not sure if I imagined it.

"Okay," she says, but her voice is all wrong. "I'll see you tomorrow, Weston."

She sounds so tired. So . . .

Lonely.

The flare of recognition sears my insides, and though I didn't think it was possible to watch her any more closely, I do. She's walking to a blue car with a short yellow paint streak on the front, and her ears are red in the car light as she worms her case into the backseat.

The Kaua'i 'ō'ō from my report comes flying back to me, perching on my shoulder.

Probably not another of your kind, he chirps, *but you'll fly like hell to find out.*

"I'm sorry," I say.

I don't yell it. Car doors are beginning to open and slam around us. We're out of time, but Anna stops and softly closes her car door.

The last Kaua'i 'ō'ō leaves my shoulder to fly into the night.

"I've worked on our duet since the beginning of summer, you know," she says, slowly walking back toward me. "As soon as I got the music, I started practicing. It's the only part of the entire show I'm struggling with, the only part I can't nail down."

Anna doesn't seem to mind that parents and the entire band are beginning to funnel around us to get to their cars, so I ignore them, my eyes never leaving her face.

"Do you think things happen for a reason?" she asks. She doesn't give me time to answer. "Because I do."

I'm tempted to agree. *Someone* must be pulling the strings to continually interrupt our every conversation at the exact moment I want to see what comes next.

"*Anna.*" A younger, narrower, whinier version of Anna appears at her side. "You didn't say good-bye to Lauren *or* Mrs.

Anderson *or* come get your backpack, and now Mom's mad at you. Like, *really* mad."

"Oh, that's enough, Jenny. Nobody's mad." This comes from Anna's dad, balding, round, amiable. He is smiling Anna's playful smile as he comes to stand beside me, Anna's polka-dot denim backpack hooked over his shoulder. "She's trying to make you lose your good behavior bet so you can't pick this week's movie, Bagels."

Mr. James turns to me and, like Anna, has to look up at me to smile. "Anna said they could go a week without arguing and nobody believed her. Now family movie night is on the line."

"It's not 'on the line,' Martin," Mrs. James says, pulling up the rear. "You're being overly dramatic."

"It is too," Jenny mutters. "Nobody wants to watch *Elf* when it's hot out."

Anna pretends to zip her lips. "I'm not arguing with you," she says. "This week's movie pick is *mine*."

I'm stunned into blankness as they talk over and under each other, verbally poking and jabbing and playing too quickly for me to process.

Seeing the James family from a distance at rehearsals or games is different from this up-close display of Anna's features scattered across four different faces. Anna has her dad's smile. She and Jenny share twin noses that don't belong to either parent.

Mrs. James's dark brown eyes look like they have been copied and pasted onto her oldest daughter, but they hold no sparkle when she looks at me. She is even shorter than Anna, but I've never felt smaller than when Mrs. James dismisses me with an Enfield-patented fake smile.

"Time to go home, Anna," she says. "It's late."

"I'll be right behind you. I just need to tell West—"

"It's *late*," her mom repeats, and even though her tone is *almost* playful, there is no room for argument.

"*Ooh*," Jenny taunts.

"Oh, whatever." Anna shoves her. "Like you're going to break me that easily."

"Please, please, please don't pick *Elf*," Jenny says. "Please."

"Begging is a surefire way to get her to pick it," Mr. James says. He rubs his hand on Jenny's head, ruffling her hair. Jenny jerks her head away, and the three of them squabble about movie nights and hair maintenance on the way to their SUV.

Mrs. James glances over her shoulder to ensure Anna is going to her car.

"I think I'm the only sixteen-year-old with a strictly enforced bedtime," Anna tells me under her breath.

"*Anna!*"

"I'm going, Mom. Sheesh." Anna sounds aggravated, but her smile is indulgent. " 'Bye, Weston," she says too loudly, a show for her mom. "I'll see you tomorrow!"

I hold up my hand in a good-bye but don't say anything, and then get in my car. When she drives past me on her way out of the parking lot, our eyes connect over our dashboards and she smiles, sparkle and all.

Ten minutes, I think on my way home. We must have talked, collectively, for at least ten minutes. I let myself smile over the jazz radio humming through my speakers.

Even if Anna's mom looked at me like I was a bug.

Even if my dad's door is already shut and his bedroom light off when I come home and eat a sandwich over the sink.

Even if this will never work, I will let myself smile at the possibility that is Anna.

Before I fall asleep, I decide to push my luck. Tomorrow I will try to talk to her for twenty minutes.

chapter 4

anna

The summer before seventh grade, Lauren invited me over for a sleepover. It was nothing unusual. But the swim party that came before in her backyard pool was new. Girls and boys in bathing suits covering sleek swimmer bodies glided around the pool, shoved each other beneath the small artificial waterfall, and lounged around the pool's stone edges with their long legs kicking through the water.

"I want you to meet my other friends!" she said, gesturing to the members of her swim team.

It was the first time I'd felt self-conscious in my swimsuit, my newly arrived boobs wildly larger, more noticeable, more every-thing *than the thinly muscular people before me.*

I refused to let it bother me. I swam. I chatted. I smiled. I even started to enjoy myself.

But at one point, I sat on the hidden bench beneath the water-fall and looked out at the kids with their Gatorade and smiles and thought maybe it would be better to hide there for the rest of the evening.

It was better, I thought, to be alone by yourself than to be alone surrounded by people.

After showering, I count the stars on my ceiling in an attempt to coerce my wired brain into exhaustion. So much of marching season feels like this, as if the only quiet time I have to myself outside of school and rehearsals is in my bed, staring at my glow-in-the-dark constellations.

My room might be an artificial night sky, but my brain is an ocean, full of disconnected thoughts that wash up on the beach like flotsam and jetsam, begging me to poke them with a stick.

It's especially true when I'm tired, and after a long Tuesday spent replaying my conversations with Weston Ryan over and over in my head, I am *very* tired, even if my brain hasn't gotten the memo.

The ocean in my head spits a rough piece of driftwood onto the shore, gnarled and sun-bleached, and begs me to examine it. Here. Now.

It washes up often, no matter how many times I hurl it into the sea.

It asks why I joined band in the first place.

It asks why I stay, why I try so hard.

My heart pumps faster and my hands are clammy as I tell the driftwood the same thing I always do, shoving the memory of my very first marching performance into its bark-stripped face.

It was a Friday night, between the second and third quarters, right after the cheerleaders and dance team performed. We played the opener, a fast, crowd-pleasing number that relied heavily on the drum line. I only managed to play part of the time—my saxophone still only a hunk of metal and a reed instead of a natural extension of my body—and the time I *did* play was filled with quiet, hesitant wrong notes.

But at the end of the performance, when the music hung in the air and the crowd's restless murmurs were a distant, dull hum, I played one note. An E. Perfectly in tune. Perfectly timed. I could hear it settle just beneath the trumpet line's music and into the crevice created by the other saxophones.

Everyone else played the right notes, too, and for the first time, I felt it, the high that comes from knowing you did exactly what you set out to do. It was a stalwart, heady thing. Accomplishment and a swelling feeling mixed together in my bloodstream like a shot of adrenaline, amplified by the certainty that we were all reveling in the moment together.

In the stands, I could see my parents on their feet and cheering. Mom already had one of those cheesy buttons the band parents wear, a picture of me and my marching shako atop my head.

That's why, I tell the driftwood, as I banish it back into the deep ocean floor of my mind. *I can't stand the thought of living without that feeling.*

My heart has slowed with the memory, so I settle in and resume counting.

I make it to five stars before the ocean tide returns, full of Weston and his smile and how he always smells faintly of leather and pine. I consider pulling out my journal—black and nondescript, it could be a school notebook—from where it hides beneath my mattress, and writing by the light of my phone, but my limbs feel too heavy to move.

I make it to sixty-three stars before Mom comes in without knocking.

I startle when the door opens, and a ludicrous part of me wonders if Mom can sense that my thoughts are a whirlpool of band and Weston.

"Whatchya doin'?" Mom asks. "Asleep already?"

"No," I groan. "Unfortunately."

I move my legs to the side of my bed to make room for Mom to sit beside me.

Nobody in the James family is small. Like the teapot song from elementary school, my family is uniformly short and stout.

I don't usually mind that my jeans are easily twice the size of Enfield's largest cheerleader or that I'm not as thin as the models that grin at me from magazine racks. And I still don't. But I *do* wonder what Weston sees when he rakes his eyes over me like he did after lunch today. I know I shouldn't care, that I'm more than my body and it's perfect the way it is . . . but I wonder if he likes what he sees.

The dark is my best friend. If Mom *can* hear my thoughts, at least she can't see my cheeks turn crimson.

"Did you just drop in for a nightly chat?" I ask.

Mom pats my knee through the purple bedspread. "Sort of," she says. Her tone makes me scoot up in bed to lean against the headboard.

"What's up?"

Mom breathes in deeply. "I talked to Lauren's mom tonight. At rehearsal."

And the sky is blue, I think, but I say, "Yeah. So . . . ?"

Meeting Mom's eyes is like staring into deep brown mirrors that are backlit, even in the near-dark. Dad calls it her Eyeball Magic. He claims that's why he fell in love with Mom when they were fifteen.

It's disgustingly cute.

But in the light trickling in from the hallway outside of

my and Jenny's bedrooms, Mom's eyes are concerned, and her head is tilted with worry.

"She told me about your snafu this morning."

With Weston swimming circles in my brain, I had *almost* managed to forget the disaster that was the morning rehearsal. I hate that Mom knows.

"I've got it handled," I say. "Lauren offered to help me. But it was only a touch of stage fright. No biggie."

"Mrs. Anderson also said you turned down Lauren's help. That Lauren said you were going to work with that Ryan boy."

I freeze, and immediately force myself to relax, hoping Mom didn't catch it. I usually tell her everything, but I want to keep Weston and his pirate smile to myself, at least until I figure out what it means.

It's not time . . . not yet. And I don't like the way Mom says his last name with a tinge of accusation, like she's borrowing Lauren's tone from lunch.

It makes my arm hairs prickle.

"Um, yeah," I say feebly, trying to sound nonchalant, and maybe a touch tired so Mom will leave. "He's my duet partner. What about it?"

"We don't know this boy, Anna," Mom says, like that settles anything. "Mrs. Anderson said he was kicked out of Enfield last year. Is that true?"

I know better than to roll my eyes where my mother can see, but it's a struggle.

"He didn't get kicked out, Mom. Mrs. Anderson is being dramatic, as usual. That's what happens when you have the talent-hoarder as a daughter. You get bored and make up stuff about other people's kids to pass the time. And you can't get kicked out of school and brought back the next year. That doesn't make any sense."

Mom shifts on the bed.

"Mrs. Anderson doesn't lie, Anna. She says he's the one who is responsible for the new Memorial Tree fiasco." I open my mouth to argue, but Mom cuts me off. "The *why* doesn't matter. Why don't you let Lauren help you? Oh! Or maybe William! You know he'd be more than happy to help."

This time I turn my head so I can hide an eye roll in my pillow. It's a physical need; my eyes will cramp if I don't.

Our moms have been trying to set me and Will up since the dawn of time, or at least since they volunteered to bring cupcakes for Enfield Elementary's Western hoedown and discovered they accidentally dressed their offspring in matching outfits.

It's such old news, it was probably written on a scroll by one of those witches burned in early America: *Because on the first of October they will both wear blue bandanas, Anna James and Will James are destined for eternal love. So sayeth their mothers.*

It doesn't matter how many times we tell our parents that you can't date someone with the same last name. There is zero chance we're related—William was born a Thomas and took the name James when his stepfather adopted him in grade school—but we agree it's still too weird.

It's also the only thing we have in common, really—our last names and our insistence that we like each other as friends but nothing more.

Mom is mostly kidding, and I understand the impulse. Really, I do. William is every mother's dream for a first boyfriend for her daughter. Handsome, smart, a talented guitar player in the worship band at his church, a star on the baseball team.

If there were postcards for parent-approved boyfriends like there were for places, William James would be on one, front and center, probably with a halo around his head.

"Mom, I'm not going to ask William for help, okay? He's

not even in band. And it's not like I'm going to *date* Weston. He's just helping me out with this duet."

Mom looks like she is about to argue, so I hurry on.

"I've gotta get it right or it goes to Ryland, and I really, really, *really* want to prove I can do it, you know?"

Mom is quiet for so long, I wonder if she knows the way my tongue tasted like copper when I said the bit about not dating. Is it really a lie if you don't know the answer?

"I'll talk to Dad about it," Mom finally says and sighs. "I trust you, Anna. I just want you to be careful. Okay?"

I force a huge fake yawn and lean across to hug Mom around her middle.

"I'm always careful," I say. "It's like my superhero power."

Mom rolls her eyes. It's so unfair that my parents can do that and it's funny, but if I so much as flick my eyes in the wrong direction, I'll be grounded for sassing.

"Tell that to the yellow streak on your front bumper," Mom says.

"I thought there was room! And I needed an ice cream cone. *Why* Fixin' Burger needs neon-yellow poles between their *three parking spaces* is a mystery somebody should investigate in a documentary."

Mom hugs me and kisses my cheek before gently pushing me back onto the pillows.

"Nobody's going to watch that documentary, hon. Not even Dad."

"He watched that whole mockumentary on sea cucumbers and it was *two hours long*. Two hours, Mom."

Mom is already closing the door behind her. "Don't act surprised. You know the lengths your father will go to when he's avoiding the lawn mowing." She chuckles. "Good night, Anna. I love, love, love you."

"Love, love, love you more," I say, and then she's gone.

He may not have a postcard, but I can't stop thinking about Weston as I drift in and out of sleep.

My late nights of counting stars and beach combing do nothing to improve my lesson with Mrs. Itashiki when Thursday rolls around.

"You are biting your reed again. Drop your jaw. Lower. *Lower*, Anna."

The air escapes from the side of my mouth and my saxophone squeaks angrily.

Mrs. Itashiki flinches.

"You're not concentrating," she says. "When you don't concentrate on your embouchure, you clench up."

My stomach is rumbling, dissatisfied with the protein bar I scarfed down between my locker and the band hall. Thursday lunches are now sacrificed at the altar of marching band, my thirty-minute private lesson making it almost impossible to eat a full meal.

"You need to have a nice, full sound," Mrs. Itashiki says, tapping her pencil on the duet music. "That mellophone is going to eat you alive in volume. Your job is to round out the bottom notes, but you can't do that if your tone is this poor."

I rub my hands down my face, letting the saxophone dangle from its strap as I take two seconds to try to remember why I thought joining band so late was a good idea.

"There's also the problem of your counting. That is a full quarter rest. You gave it maybe an eighth."

"I'll be able to take my cues from my partner," I say. "He's solid. He's got it."

Mrs. Itashiki looks disapproving. "You must be able to play the duet as if you're the only one playing," she says. "You need to be able to play around the silences."

She makes me play through the duet once more, circles with a pink highlighter an already-circled accidental I missed twice in today's lesson—"*C sharp, Anna.*"—and bustles off to her next school, her next set of woodwind victims.

A headache buds between my temples as soon as the door closes behind her. I don't have the energy to put my saxophone away. I can't even imagine going through the rest of my classes. The ocean in my head roars angrily, the waves casting shadows on the beach that escape from my head and crawl up the walls of the practice room.

I let them. I don't bother to push them back.

The shadows only come when I'm alone. They know better than to come for me when people are around. It's the one thing I have: the certainty that no one needs to worry about me. Anna James is cheerful and kind and optimistic. She has no shadows.

And if she does, she traps them in a notebook where they can't get out.

They're always a variation of the same thing: my fear that I'm going nowhere, that I'm running as fast as I can into the unknown, that I'm disappointing everyone.

I wish I was the kind of person who finds uncertainty exciting, an adventure. I wish my tumultuous insides matched my bright outsides.

They don't. Not always.

I decide the best use of what remains of lunchtime will be nudging my case into the wall repeatedly, making a satisfying *thump* that echoes the pounding of the waves in my head.

When the door opens, I stop in shock. I half think I'm hallucinating as Weston crouches in front of me to look up into my eyes, his long legs bending beneath him.

"You okay?"

There is no sign of the rogue smile. Weston Ryan is all

concern, scrunched blond eyebrows, full downturned mouth, blue, blue eyes.

We haven't spoken since Tuesday night rehearsal. Mostly because Mr. Brant suddenly realized we needed to practice stand tunes for tomorrow's game, and that meant the last two mornings have been in the band hall instead of on the grid, but it's not the only reason.

I've been avoiding him, too tired from the first week of school and rehearsals and duet stress to sort through the feelings that pop up like daisies when he's near. He tried to talk to me yesterday—I saw him coming toward me after rehearsal—but I was a chicken. A tired chicken. I pretended I had to go to the restroom so I wouldn't have to talk to him, wouldn't have to hear him tell me *again* that we can't be friends.

I make myself sit up straighter. "I'm fine," I tell Weston, and because he and everyone else in the world expects me to always be smiling, I do. "Just messing with my case."

It takes all my effort to banish the shadows from the practice room.

Weston tilts his head. "Isn't this your lunch period?"

"My new schedule with Mrs. Itashiki," I say as explanation, making my voice purposefully cheerful. "Private lesson times during band class booked up before I remembered to choose a slot. She's doing it as a favor on her way to her lessons in Bloom."

Weston doesn't react to the mention of Bloom, but he does lean forward, slowly, like I'm a butterfly that might take flight at the slightest movement.

"May I?" He gestures at my saxophone.

I nod, my smile slipping. Can he see the shadows trying to worm their way back onto the walls?

His hands are a whisper at my belly as he moves to unclip

my instrument from the neck strap. I watch as he unscrews the ligature, gently removes the reed and places it in its box, and separates neck and body, before putting them in their foam beds. His movements are reverent, like he's handling a sacred object, or playing the piano.

The locks clank happily as he closes them. *I like him better than you*, my traitorous saxophone murmurs, and I know it's remembering all the times I've jammed the mouthpiece onto the cork without greasing it first.

I know, I think. *I don't blame you.*

When he's finished, Weston stands from his crouch and drops onto the piano bench Mrs. Itashiki sat on during our lesson, but because he's much taller, his knees bump into mine. Despite my headache, shooting stars flood my bloodstream.

For once, he's the one to break the silence.

"What are you thinking?"

I look down at his sloppily tied black Vans. They look like our marching uniform shoes. I decide I have nothing to lose by being honest.

"I'm thinking it would be better to give the duet to Ryland."

Weston makes a noise somewhere between a sneeze and a scoff. "You're not serious," he says.

"It's a state year," I say, meeting his eyes. "I'm not going to be the one who screws this up for everyone. Ryland could have the music perfected by tomorrow. It's going to take me at *least* the two weeks to get it right, and even then it won't be as good, if it's good at all."

If he were someone else, one of my friends perhaps, Weston would put his arm around me or—more likely—swat my knee and tell me lovingly but firmly to buck up, to stop being pathetic.

But this isn't Lauren with her low tolerance for emotion or

Andy with his eagerness to always be moving, never settling in one moment too long.

This is Weston Ryan. The boy everyone whispers about. The boy my mother warned me against. The boy with the leather jacket who keeps insisting we can't be friends.

"Do you really want to give it to Ryland?" Weston asks. I open my mouth to answer, but he interrupts. "Be honest."

"I don't want to give it to Ryland," I say, "but I also don't know if I can do it."

He'll never know how much it costs me to admit that last part. Anna James does not *do* failure.

"You can," Weston says.

"How do you know?"

He's quiet, it's a thinking silence. I can almost see him turning words over in his head, sifting through his thoughts to put them in the right order.

"It's a call-and-answer," he says finally. "Our duet? Do you know what that is?"

His voice doesn't hold an ounce of condescension, so I say, "Sort of."

Weston inhales. "In this case, throughout the entire piece, our sections take turns playing altered versions of the same melody, or melodic phrases that finish the other's thought. It's kind of like finishing each other's sentences."

"And?"

"*And,*" he says, "our duet is the ending to that. Both melodies are wound together to resolve any questions the music asked throughout the piece."

"What does that have to do with anything?" I ask. "My calls will sound like dying geese and my answers like screeching cats. Ryland would be a much better partner."

"I don't *want* Ryland to be my partner. I agreed to help *you.*"

"You didn't, though," I say, and the pounding in my head makes way for incredulity tinged with exasperation. "I mean, you did, but you took it back."

"Well, I un-took it back after Tuesday night rehearsal."

"But why?" I ask. "And don't say it's because you don't want to be partners with Ryland."

"Call it curiosity," Weston says.

"Be honest," I remind him.

I'm not firing on all cylinders, but anyone could see he's holding back. I want to know what he's afraid to tell me.

"I want to see if things really do happen for a reason," he says. "And . . ." Weston takes a very deep breath, like he's about to plunge under water and isn't sure when he'll breathe again. "And because you called, and I answered."

Stupidly, I think about Mom and how my tongue felt heavy when I promised not to date Weston. With anybody else, it would be easy to keep a promise I've had no trouble adhering to for sixteen years, but with Weston, I feel myself crumbling around the edges.

Our shared curiosity burns between us.

"So you'll help me, then?" I ask.

This time, Weston doesn't pause. "I'll help you," he says.

"When?"

"Tomorrow?" he says. "Before school?"

We don't have morning rehearsals on Fridays on account of staying up so late at the Friday-night football games, and I'm relieved I won't have to wait an entire weekend to be in the same room with him again.

"Yes," I say.

He pulls his phone out of his pocket to check the time. "Ah. Almost."

"Almost what?"

He smiles a full smile at me, the pirate smile. "I owe you five minutes."

I have no idea what he means, but I say, "I'll hold you to that."

"Tomorrow," he promises, and I smile back as the bell ending lunch rings.

When I slip away to class, the shadows don't follow me. They don't show up for the rest of the day.

chapter 5

weston

When I told Jonathan and Ratio earlier this summer that I was officially coming back to Enfield for our senior year, they weren't surprised.

"Took you long enough," Jonathan said. "Shocked you made it a whole year in Gloom 'n' Bloom." He clapped me on the back with his controller, accidentally unpausing our quest on *King's Reign*. The dog we'd picked up in the last village barked a greeting before Jonathan managed to repause it.

Ratio only smiled his tilted smile at me, nodded once, and said, "You'll have to challenge Darin for first chair, you know."

"Unless they amputated all of Weston's fingers in Bloom, there's no way on God's green earth that Darin could beat him in *anything*," Jonathan said, laughing. "Especially mellophone. Especially music."

I didn't hang out with Jonathan much after I went to Bloom. He always had less time than Ratio, a careful if not deliberate stepping aside from our group of three, but his praise warmed me through. (As did his bashing of that Goody Two–shoes asshole Darin.)

"Look, I'm drum major," Ratio said. "I'm not going to bad-mouth members of the band."

"There's no one here!" Jonathan gestured around at Ratio's perfectly clean bedroom. "Not even a dust bunny to gossip."

"The air in Enfield has ears," Ratio argued, with the learned reverence of somebody who had grown up in a town too small for its own good.

"Well, can you tell the air our drum major is an ass who has mentioned he's drum major sixteen times in this conversation, and see if it can make him stop?" I asked.

"The air has ears, not miracle-working abilities," Jonathan deadpanned. "Be glad you weren't here last year, Wes. Ratio was *insufferable*."

I'm tempted to retroactively agree with Jonathan as I pull into student parking Friday morning and see Ratio's car in the lot. He's in the uniform closet when I find him, shuffling through bright orange garment bags and counting to himself.

"Why are you here so early on a game day?" I ask.

Ratio jumps a little, mutters under his breath, but keeps counting.

"Fifty-three, one hundred, six," I say.

He is not amused. His eyebrows lower, but he keeps counting, sliding the bags from right to left as he numbers them.

"Worried someone came in and stole a bunch of orange and white marching uniforms from 2001?"

"Forty-three," Ratio finishes with a glare. "And what are *you* doing here so early?"

"I'm going to help Anna with the duet, like you said I should."

Ratio's entire countenance changes when he smiles. "Atta-boy. Fill me in at lunch about how it goes. And hey, did you finish the English homework last night? I was going to see what you thought of question nine," Ratio says, flicking the closet light off behind us.

"Forgot," I say. "I'll get it done before class."

"English is *third period*, Weston. And they're short essay questions. *And* today's periods are condensed because of the pep rally."

"I'll get it done," I promise. "It's fine."

Ratio sighs and looks at me meaningfully.

"What?" I ask. "Out with it."

"Your grades," he begins. "I know you didn't get to perform at a couple games in Bloom because you fell below passing, and Mr. Brant will have a fit if you—"

"My grades will be fine," I say. "Last year was different. I'm not going to fail in Enfield, okay? I mean, I'm not going to make straight As, but I'm not going to get suspended from band."

"But you *could* make straight As," Ratio says, mystified.

I don't argue. Instead I say, "It'll be fine. I swear."

"You better swear," Ratio says. "It's my head that will be mounted on Mr. Brant's wall alongside yours if you can't per-form during a state year."

"At least if my head is mounted you'll have a fair chance of beating me at *King's Reign*."

Ratio snorts. "Don't you have a girl to impress? A duet to teach?"

"Don't you have shoes to shine? Uniforms to recount?"

"I am *not* recounting them. Once is plenty."

I keep my face as straight as possible and say, "I think I saw you double count a bag."

Ratio holds my gaze. His eye twitches. "You are a real ille-gitimate love child, you know that?"

"Have fun recounting, you bastard."

I hear Ratio begin to count aloud as I close the practice room door.

I'm at the piano when Anna comes in, but since she isn't barreling in to beg for my help this time, I don't stop playing. I can't resist adding some flourishes that aren't on the sheet—octave reaches to make the music swell, grace notes between runs.

I think Anna won't notice, but as soon as I reach the double bar, she claps softly and whispers, "Show-off."

She sets her case on the ground next to my backpack, the unfinished *Hamlet* short answer questions peeking out through the gap in the zipper, and moves to take out her saxophone.

"Wait," I say, and she straightens. Her hair isn't in its customary ponytail. It's loose and free, a chocolate river with streaks of caramel running over her white band polo. For a second, I'm lost in it, entertaining all kinds of illicit thoughts of it streaming through my fingers.

"You promised," she says, and her voice is a touch panicked. "You said you would—"

"I'm not backing out," I say. My own band polo, stiff and wrinkled from a year shoved in the back of my closet, scratches my shoulder when I shrug. "You just don't need that, yet."

Anna looks more than doubtful. "I don't need my *saxophone* to work on our *saxophone and mellophone duet?*"

I scoot to the side of the bench, hoping she'll sit without me asking. She does, and I'm worried she'll somehow feel the goose bumps that pop up on my arms through my jacket when she settles next to me.

"Am I so bad that it'll be easier to teach me a new instrument?"

I snort. "Honestly? It's crossed my mind."

She shoves my arm playfully. "I retract our honesty agreement."

The entirety of my wildfire is now concentrated where her hand touched my arm. Ignoring the burn is impossible, but I say, "I think this will help."

I pull out the sheet I worked on last night, our individual parts stacked on top of each other on my unevenly hand-drawn music staffs.

"I was thinking about the silences in our duet," I say. "I thought maybe it would help to see it on paper and hear it on the piano. That way you can focus on how the notes fit together first, and how they'll sound later."

I worry none of this made sense, but Anna nods, leaning forward. Her leg presses into mine with the movement.

"I didn't realize you had a rest here where I decrescendo." She points.

I nod, quickly playing the notes on the piano. "It's the last lull before the push to the end, see?"

"You're not going to make me play my part on the piano, are you?"

"It's easy," I say. "Just play the first note of your two runs. The rest are whole and half notes. You know which notes belong to which keys, right?"

She nods as I take her closest hand in mine. Anna James has rings on two of her fingers, a rose and a tiny Christmas tree.

"What's with you and Christmas?" I can't stop myself from asking.

"What?"

I tap her ring gently. "This, the sock thing, choosing to watch a Christmas movie in September."

"Honestly?" she asks.

"That's what we agreed."

Anna's voice is hesitant, and though no one would dare call her meek, her voice is quieter than I've ever heard it.

"At Christmas, the world feels like it should, you know?" She inhales deeply. "Like, there's a whole world trapped inside me, and most of the year it doesn't match up with the outside world. But Christmas feels different, like maybe I belong in this world after all." She looks at me like she's trying to make me understand by using only her eyes. "Bad things don't seem as bad, and good things seem amplified, so I try to bring Christmas with me however I can. To make the world more . . . Anna friendly."

I must stay silent too long, because she says, "That's stupid. Sorry. Next time I'll just be a different kind of honest and say my dad bought the ring for me and I really love snow or something."

Her cheeks are crimson.

"It's not stupid," I say, my heart pounding. Outside the practice room, I hear the ruffling of feathers, a lone bird resting on a marching trophy from his journey traveling the world in search of his kind. "It's not stupid at all."

I know exactly what she means about the world not being friendly, though I'm surprised that bubbly, smiling Anna knows what it's like to feel the resistance between what you see and what you wish *could* be.

Neither of us wants to break our heavy stare, but when we finally do, I reluctantly release her hand and point to the keys, refreshing her memory of middle C, of the A key sandwiched between the second and third black keys.

"Ready?" I ask, half wanting her to say no so that we can keep talking.

"Yeah," she says. "How do we start?"

"That's the easy part. It's the same as being on the field. We breathe together."

And then, easier than should be possible, we inhale as one and begin to play, our hands naturally reaching over and under each other to wind our music together. It's not perfect; on top of going slower than tempo so Anna can count out the keys, she plays into a rest and I accidentally bump her hand and cause her to play a wrong note. But we make it to the end of my hand-scratched notes and sit in awed silence.

"It's beautiful," Anna says. "It sounds like Christmas."

"It does," I agree, not looking at her. It's enough to see our hands resting side by side in our laps.

"Maybe it'll be okay," she says. "Maybe I'll be able to play it."

"You will," I promise. "I'll make sure of it."

I feel her shift beside me.

"You're as different as everyone says you are," she whispers. "I'm so glad."

Sometimes I think the wildfire is a kind of homesickness. When my room is dark and a certain piece of music comes on my headphones, or when the sun hits the lake just right, I'll feel homesick for a place I've never been.

But you don't tell people that, not even the Ratios or Jonathans of the world, because they'll think you're being melodramatic or too much of whatever it is that people are afraid of having too much of.

Instead, I quietly collect them, the moments that make me hungry for something I've never tasted, hoping that someday I'll be able to piece them together into a map that will lead me to a place where wildfires make sense and the people you love don't change or leave or break.

Anna's warmth at my side makes me reconsider that the homesickness is an unknown place.

Maybe it's a person.

Maybe it's her.

"Do you want to try playing on the saxophone?" I ask.

She doesn't turn her head, doesn't look up from the piano keys. "No," she says thoughtfully. "Not today."

"Okay."

"Play me something, instead?"

So I ignore the distant chime of alarm bells—the ones that warn of divorce and forgotten homework and the way Anna's mom and everyone else looks at me like I'm an obstacle instead of a person—and I play Anna the beginning of the melody that started forming when she happened, the one I can't get out of my head.

The music thumping full volume through the hallway speakers is almost loud enough to drive Anna's melody from my mind, but not quite. I can feel the bass of "Eye of the Tiger" in my chest.

Fridays are a blur of orange and white streamers decorating the hallways and of classes shortened to accommodate the weekly pep rally. Band kids are in matching jeans and polos, cheerleaders twirl in skirted uniforms accented with crisp white tennis shoes, and football players wear jerseys that look comically large without pads.

I tried once to explain to the other French horns in Bloom the concept of weekly pep rallies, the madness that grips Enfield every Friday and doesn't let go until the bleary-eyed Saturday mornings. But it's difficult to convey the equal parts tolerance and artificial excitement that Fridays bring if you've never had "Another One Bites the Dust" blaring at you from the school's speaker system in between classes, never had teachers chanting Enfield cheers from the 1970s to start their classes, or walked into the school gym to find rows and rows of chairs set up in front of the bleachers for the football team like they are visiting dignitaries.

Despite only finishing half my *Hamlet* homework and not being allowed to wear my jacket over my band polo during school, it's hard not to feel the thump of energy coursing through the halls, to stand a little taller when I follow Ratio to the set of bleachers reserved for the band during the pep rally.

The clamor—the blaring music, the yelling and laughter of students of all ages crammed into the wooden bleachers, the tuning of instruments—is loud, but not loud enough to erase Anna's song.

It hums quietly in the back of my head, where it has been playing since this morning, a little beam of sunlight that illuminates the dust motes. Anna's melody has taken on a life of its own since I played it for her after our abbreviated lesson. I wonder if I should write it down. I wonder if she'll want to hear it in its entirety if I do.

Very soon, we will have to *actually* work on the duet, and we will have to go through the painstaking, precise dance of throwing the same notes together over and over until they meld. But how was I supposed to turn her down, to be a strict tutor, when she asked me to play for her and her hair fell down her back like that?

Her song crescendos into a full roar when her hand touches my knee from the seat one step below me on the bleachers.

She grins up at me—at *me*—as her dutiful saxophones file in behind her, legs bumping into high wooden bleacher seats that have needed a new coat of paint since before I was born.

"Hi," Anna says.

"Hi," I say.

Her saxophone strap is tangled in her polo collar, and if we were in the practice room instead of in front of the entire school, maybe I would straighten it for her. Instead, I stare at it and at the tiny little brown hairs that have come loose from the ponytail she's corralled her hair into since our lesson. Even partially bound, the strands strain to wrap around her collar, her ear, her forehead, like overly adventurous twists of ivy that can't stand to be in one place.

Anna is still looking up at me, her eyes bright and her mouth teasing.

I think maybe she's waiting for me to say something, to stop staring at her hair, but she says, "Lucky for us, huh? That mellophones and saxophones sit next to each other at games and stuff?"

"Yeah," I say. "Lucky."

"For strictly duet purposes, of course," she says.

I nod. "Of course."

"Lest you thought I enjoyed your company and your un-orthodox duet teaching methods."

I can't stop the smile. "Wouldn't dream of it."

"Good," she says. I expect the conversation to continue, but she turns to Terrance and Samantha and starts to tune her section.

I let myself feel disappointed, even though it's ridiculous to *miss* her when she's right in front of me.

In gross juxtaposition to Anna, Darin Leonard is beside me, his too-big nose and too-small eyes peering at me over his mellophone bell.

"Shouldn't we be tuning, too?" he asks.

The terrible thing about Darin—the terrible thing about Enfield as a whole, really—is people are *really* good at the bullshit southern talent that is being an absolute dick while making it sound helpful or kind.

Teachers *love* Darin. He turns in his homework on time and above par, his manners are impeccable, and he is always smiling in the way that adults can't see through but makes every student want to barf. Even Mr. Brant, usually more perceptive than the average adult, loves Darin and was more than a little apologetic when I won back first chair in our playoff at band camp.

Technically, Ratio is first chair, and he will be again when concert season rolls around and his conducting prowess is no longer needed, but for all intents and purposes, I'm section leader during football season.

And no small part of me enjoys that his being second chair, and eventually third, is driving Darin *mad*.

"We'll tune as a band in a minute," I say. "Always do before pep rallies, right? Unless you need the extra time?"

Darin smiles and claps me on the shoulder. "Nah, just checking with you, O Great Leader," his mouth says. "I'll let you know if you missed anything big last year when you were away, though. Don't worry about it."

I hate you, his eyes say.

Right on cue, like he knows I'm two seconds away from "accidentally" knocking Darin down the stairs, Ratio stands at the base of the bleachers and raises his hands. "Opening warm-up. Tune as you go."

Tuning in the gym is a joke. The acoustics suck, the chatter of the other students only gets louder to be heard over our instruments, and it's almost impossible to hear your section, much less the entire band.

Mr. Brant doesn't have this problem. He could hear a mistuned instrument through several brick walls, no matter how shitty the acoustics.

"Flutes, what is that?" he yells from beside Ratio. "Someone is sharp enough to cut this building in half."

Lauren gestures at one of the freshmen, motioning for her to adjust how her flute fits together to improve the pitch.

Below me, Anna mirrors her friend in an attempt to get

Terrance to push his mouthpiece farther onto the cork. "It's too *flat*, Terrance," she says under her breath. "Not sharp. You're making it worse by moving it outward."

I hear similar murmurs around me, section leaders and up-perclassmen frantically, exasperatedly guiding the Gilligans into musical symmetry, shepherding them toward a concert F that sounds like one note instead of three wrong ones.

It's not perfect—the trombones at my back are still flat as hell—but there's no time for perfection, because the cheer-leading coach waves her hand at Mr. Brant and we're off to the races, playing the school song as the football players file in and the cheerleaders' pom-poms trace their familiar patterns in the air.

I should be concentrating on the pageantry. Part of me missed this in Bloom, where they only held pep rallies if the team made it to the state championship, which they never did. But when the cheerleaders perform their stupid skit, com-plete with the same costumes that get recycled every week, every year, and a football coach comes out in cowboy boots and jeans to shout over the feedback of his microphone about love of the game and passion, the hollow feeling settles back into my chest.

It doesn't feel right. And I can't figure out why.

I wonder what's different. The gym is the same, our Friday polos are unchanged, but something inside me has shifted. Is it possible that the wildfire can reach even here? A place where my parents rarely appeared together, if at all?

Below me, Anna is half watching the cheerleaders and dance team perform together, half leaning forward to pull faces at Lauren while she dances, but she schools her fea-tures after a glare from Mr. Brant.

The suffocating feeling eases as I watch Anna smile, the wildfire retreating by inches. *I can rewrite this year,* I think.

full flight — 71

This year was always going to be different, no matter what happened in Bloom, or with my parents, because of Anna and her laugh and the way her hair is always curiously winding itself around whatever object is closest.

Fortunately, the pep rally and my sense of unease are over almost as soon as they have begun, and Mr. Brant urges us toward the band hall to load up gear for the game.

"Change into travel clothes," Ratio yells through cupped hands at the bottom of the bleachers. "Shorts, travel shirt. That's your white tee with the band logo on the breast pocket and *school appropriate* shorts, freshmen. The truck needs to be loaded by three forty-five. Bus doors close at three fifty. Let's move, people."

I pretend to be startled when Anna reaches up to touch my knee again, but I'm not. She's a constant low whir of energy in my consciousness. I couldn't ignore her if I tried.

"Who are you sitting with on the bus?" she asks.

I'm jostled abruptly to the side as Darin rushes around me, the force of it too hard to be an accident.

"Sorry, Wes," he says.

I hate when he calls me that, and he knows it.

"Bus?" I ask stupidly.

Anna smiles. "Band bus? Sitting? You?"

I'm about to answer, when her head turns sharply to my left. I hear it, too: her name, shouted from somewhere in the bleachers on our side of the gym.

"Ugh," she whispers under her breath. "Sorry. One second. This will be quick."

She scrambles over the saxophones, the clarinets, and trots down the steps, fast walking until she stops in front of a section of junior high girls huddled shoulder to shoulder.

I recognize her sister, Jenny, from Tuesday. She leans forward and touches Anna's saxophone, which Anna yanks back with a shake of her head. Her expression is severe, so different than how she's ever looked at me, and I'm surprised at its vehemence.

A short argument ensues, Anna gesturing over her shoulder toward the band, toward me, and Jenny shrinks back between her friends, clearly cowed.

All traces of Anna's irritation are gone when she comes to stand beside me, her face open and smiling.

"Sorry," she said. "Pesky siblings."

"I wouldn't know," I say.

"Count your blessings," she says, and even though she's laughing, I see the annoyance still bubbling beneath the surface. "So . . . seat buddies?"

I wonder if she knows that I have been dreading the seating arrangements all week. The band bus is its own ecosystem, a teeming habitat of individuals hopped up on snacks and candy provided by the band moms. The bus is as ever-changing as it is constant, never the same from week to week, yet somehow universally understood from one school's band to the next.

It's one of the few times the whole band is together in one space and not expected to be working. There's no marching, no music. Just us, the cracked plastic bus seats, and the open road.

Most everyone in Enfield sits with the same person every week, or if not, it's something that's shouted across the band hall as the truck is loaded up.

I used to sit with Ratio, but he and Jonathan sit together now. I'm not pathetic enough to ask them to split up for my sake.

"We don't have to," Anna is saying, and I'm startled to realize she's been talking and I haven't heard a word. "I just thought—"

"No," I rush in. "I mean, yes. Yes, we should sit together."

"Really, it's fine—" she starts, but I quiet her with a shake of my head.

"We're sitting together, Anna," I say. In my desperation, I'm worried my words come out too demanding or irritated, so I add playfully, "I'm not going to ask again."

"You *are* persistent," she says, smiling. "I guess I'll sit with you. Since you asked so nicely."

And then our conversation is over, and Anna is enveloped by the moving stampede of white polos beginning the trek to the band hall.

Maybe that's why the hollow feeling has come back. Being in band is the process of being swallowed, consumed at all hours of the day by some task or, at the least, by band people.

Anna gets it. The minute she steps away, she's taken up into a group consisting of Andy and Lauren and Chrissie and Jade. She's accepted, welcomed, *expected* to be a part of the whole, even in something as small as walking down the long hallway.

She doesn't fight it, her enveloping.

But she does turn back, eyebrows raised, head tilted.

"Coming?" she asks me.

The other four don't stop their conversation, debating the finer points of the cheerleading skit—*Was Emma supposed to be the villain or the heroine?*—but they do look at me expectantly, like I'm holding up the program. Like they're waiting. For me.

"Yeah," I say. "I'm coming."

And though it's awkward as hell, though I walk behind them and don't say a word, I decide this is a better kind of different.

chapter 6

anna

I started writing it all down the night that I lost my favorite stuffed animal. I was too old to care that deeply, but I had to do something. *I couldn't draw. I couldn't make a movie called* Stuffed Story *about a bear that didn't even look like a bear anymore. I couldn't write a piece of music.*

Instead I wrote it down. I wrote down the memories I had with Bear-Bear, our adventures from the cradle to fourth grade. I didn't have journals then, only an unused spiral notebook left over from the previous school year. But that's how it started, the writing. It started with loss. It started with loneliness. It started because I had lost my confidant and I wasn't sure I'd ever find anyone that understood and listened like Bear-Bear.

I'm too busy negotiating texts from Mom to notice when Weston steps onto the band bus.

I'm in trouble for blowing off Jenny at the pep rally, which is ridiculous because she was only doing that annoying thing where she wanted to show me off to her friends. I told her to cut it out when she pawed at my saxophone, but that's it.

> **Mom:** It wouldn't kill you to go the extra mile.
> **Me:** I had band stuff to do. I wasn't being mean.
> **Mom:** She says you looked mad.
> **Me:** I wasn't. I didn't want her messing with my sax and I had to get ready to leave.

My phone pings with the dreaded and yet entirely predictable Momism.

> **Mom:** She's the only sister you're ever going to have.

I don't answer. Years of experience have taught me there's no satisfactory retort to *that*. Best to leave it alone and hope they've forgotten about it by the game tonight.

I forget about it the moment Weston Ryan's fingers brush my arm.

"Does your offer still stand?" he asks. I wonder why he sounds unsure until I realize I'm sitting in the exact middle of the seat.

"Oh, you need more room than this?" I gesture at the few inches of space to my left. "I thought this would be plenty."

"I'll take whatever you want to give me," he says, as I scoot toward the window. And he says it with such sincerity, such gravity, that I'm certain we're not talking about the bus anymore.

Something inside of me buckles at his tone, his him-ness.

When he sits beside me, everything warms. Have the bus seats always been this small? He feels closer than when we sat on the piano bench, his entire side pressing up against mine.

Our legs are bare from the knees down, and the hair on his legs is brushing against me.

I don't know what to do with this feeling of intimacy by degrees, of someone else turning up the dial of closeness without my knowing when it will jump.

"Would you prefer the window?" I ask. My throat feels heavy.

"I would prefer you to be comfortable."

"I like the window," I say, but under the full force of his eyes, it comes out a whisper.

He smiles the pirate smile, slow and gleaming. "Good."

If he means for the smile to put me at ease, he fails. Instead, it makes me overly aware of my heartbeat. I'm itching to remember every single moment of this because I will have to record it, second by second, in my journal tonight.

When I sit with Lauren or Andy, there's a rhythm, a routine to staking our claims to the bus seat. With Lauren, we squish around on the seat until she can sit at a slight angle and I can sit with my legs folded underneath me like a bird. With Andy, there's always an argument—over who gets the window, whose headphones we're going to share, whose *music* we're going to jointly listen to for the duration of the ride, who's going to be responsible for catching the band mom sandwiches at the end of the night when Mrs. Terrance stands at the front of the bus and chucks them like she's a retired pitcher.

But with Weston, there is no routine. This is dreadfully, awkwardly, sacredly *new*.

We are trying our best to split the seat evenly, but my thighs are bigger, rounder, and they encroach on his territory by inches, not centimeters.

"Sorry," I mutter.

"For what?"

"For taking up more room."

"Should I apologize for taking up less?" he asks.

"What? No? That's stupid."

"So is what you said." Weston grins.

Whatever buckled in my chest is now crumbling to dust at that smile.

"Are you calling me stupid?" I tease.

"Never," he says.

And because I don't know what else to say, I look over at him, sitting so, so close, and say, "Hi."

His smile widens. "Hi," he says, and then, "I'm glad I asked you to sit next to me."

"Me, too." I grin. "So . . . what do you normally do on the bus?"

Weston shrugs. "Listen to music. Read."

"Is that what you did in Bloom?"

His entire body shifts with the question, the seat under us rippling at his movement. "Bloom was . . . different."

"How?" I ask.

"Less orange."

I roll my eyes. "What else?"

We're interrupted by Maddie Daniels tapping on the seat in front of us as she waits in the clogged center aisle. She looks too small to even be able to shoulder a sousaphone, but she's first chair tuba and her arms are leanly muscular. I know from experience that her high fives sting.

"Y'all dating now or something?" she asks us.

Her voice is almost bored, but Weston leans away from her and into me like she's interrogating him. I wrap my arms around his shoulders, my hands coming to rest on his chest. I hope we look like a stereotypical couple's social media post, a cheesy caricature. A joke.

"Even better, we're duet partners," I say, my voice fake and high. I tilt my chin down to rest on Weston's hair, praying he plays along.

Weston does *not* play along.

He straightens quickly, shrugs off my arms with alarming efficiency, and glares at Maddie. "Is it any of your business if we're dating?"

"Weston." I'm whispering, but this time it's to smooth out the wrinkles of anger—and fright?—I hear in his tone. "It's okay."

"It's not, though," he says. It's definitely fear I hear. "Why does she care? It's none of her business."

"She was curious," I say, my face reddening as the people in the seats around us turn to stare. "She was just teasing."

I meet Ratio's gaze, where he's turned around in his seat a few rows ahead, and widen my eyes slightly. *Help*, I beg.

But before Ratio can say anything, aid comes from the seat directly behind me.

"I wouldn't advise dating Anna if I were you, Weston," Andy drawls. "If you get sick, she is *terrible* at being a nurse. She'll bring you poisoned soup to try and finish you off instead of nursing you back to health."

It's so outlandish, so off topic, that none of us can follow. "What?" Weston asks.

Andy kicks back in his seat like he's on a beach chair in the Caribbean, folding his arms behind his head and nearly elbowing Olivia in the face.

"Anna here brought me soup last year during the mono outbreak and it had *soap* in it."

"It did not!" I say, rising up in the seat. "Liar!"

"Cream of Dawn, I think it was." Andy grins.

"For the last time, it's not *my fault* if you washed your hands and dripped soap in the food I brought you."

"Joke's on you, James, because I never wash my hands."

"*Gross!*" Olivia protests.

Andy is laughing, but we've been friends long enough that I can read his expression when our eyes meet over the seat. He raises his eyebrows. *You're welcome for deflecting attention away from your prickly Phantom of the Weirdo*, they say. Even though I try to avoid looking her way, I can see Lauren's face a few seats behind us, her eyes narrowed and mouth twisted in distaste.

Maddie finds her seat, the conversation swells back to its usual drone, and Weston won't look at me, his concentration devoted to pulling at a loose thread on his travel shirt.

"Care to share with the class?" I ask.

"Not really," he says.

With anyone else, prodding and goading would inevitably get a response, even if it was dragged out of them. But Weston is different, so I sit quietly, patiently, sensing that if I hold still long enough, he'll come to me.

The bus has been moving for five minutes, and I'm about to give up hope, when Weston says, "Sorry."

"Me, too," I say, angling so my shoulder digs into the side of the bus. "Was it the hugging thing?"

He sighs. "No. It was the *everyone thinks they're entitled to know everything about me* thing."

"It's Enfield," I say gently. "Everyone knows everything already. And if they don't, they will soon."

Weston is quiet.

"I don't want to label . . . whatever this is," he says, his voice barely loud enough to hear, even though we're so close. "If you label something, that means it can be lost."

I want to tell him that it's silly, that the act of naming something doesn't make it more likely to be misplaced—but I think of his parents. And try as I may, I can't imagine what it would be like to have your parents not be together anymore. I can't begin to guess at the scars it would leave.

Instead of telling him he's wrong, instead of dwelling on the idea of *us* being a label or not, or that he's thought about it, I ask him a question that has been burning in my head since Tuesday. "Have you ever dated anyone?"

He won't look at me, but he answers.

"Yes," he says. "You?"

"No," I say. "Never. Unless you count David Schneider. We dated for three days and then he passed me a note in math class that said something to the effect of 'You're too much like a sister to me.'"

"Doesn't count," Weston agrees. "Why haven't you?"

He's not avoiding my eyes anymore, and I get it now, the way people in books and movies wax poetic about eye color for hours. Because there's nothing on earth the same shade of blue as Weston Ryan's eyes as he stares at me and waits to hear why I haven't dated anyone. Not the sky, not ice, not water. It would be like trying to describe the sound of the wind in the trees as a flute. Close, but not at all accurate. An injustice.

I'll still try, later tonight. I'm going to fall asleep trying to write descriptions that ring true.

"Nobody wanted to?" I answer, but it comes out a question.

Weston snorts. "Impossible."

"Possible and true," I say, keeping my voice forcibly light. "They invented the friend zone just for me. It's not so bad there. I put in a rug. Some nice squishy chairs. The works."

Andy leans forward and thumps the back of our seat hard, bursting the little bubble of silence and false privacy that has swelled around us.

"Music roulette, James," he announces. "Care to spin the wheel?"

"I'm not playing," I say. "Ask Lauren."

"She already turned me down. You're our only hope of starting the first bus-wide sing-along of the season."

"Just play 'Bohemian Rhapsody' if that's what you want."

"*So cliché*," Andy moans, but he does, holding his tiny, crappy portable speaker aloft like it's a Super Bowl trophy. "This better work," he tells me.

I roll my eyes at Weston and murmur, "Always does."

It takes approximately three seconds for the entire bus to join in.

The thing about being a band kid is that either by intense study or osmosis, you pick up a lot about music. It never sounds the same after you've played it for yourself. Songs you've heard your entire life suddenly burst into full color—the intricacies of bass lines, of countermelodies, the way two totally different sets of notes can come together to make something brand new.

"Bohemian Rhapsody" in the surround sound of the Enfield marching band is a *loud* but weirdly accurate thing to behold, complete with sung guitar and piano parts, high sopranos belting "Galileo"s in tune, and head banging you could set a metronome by.

Beside me, Weston sits a little too straight, his eyes hopping around the bus like he can't keep up.

I nudge his side.

"Come on." I laugh. "Nobody can resist this song."

His smile is small. "You go ahead," he says. "I'll be your moral support."

Weston's eyes stop roaming around the bus and focus solely on me. I sing a little louder, a little sillier, trying to entice him to join.

"It's *fun*," I shout.

He rolls his eyes, but very reluctantly, with a look of long-suffering tolerance, he begins to play a small air piano in his lap.

My triumphant applause draws the bus's attention.

"*Weston's on keys!*" Terrance yells from beside us.

I wait for Weston to clam up, to drop his hands and shrink into our bus seat. But he doesn't. He plays wider, more aggressively, leaning forward and smiling a dimmer version of the pirate smile at me, probably conscious that half the bus is watching him in awe.

"I've never seen him smile like that before," Olivia leans forward to whisper in my ear. "He's . . . kind of cute?"

I wonder if he's just been waiting for someone to ask him to join in.

I wonder why nobody has.

When the song is over and Andy cues up another Queen song, Weston's face is lit up, his pale skin glowing a soft red from exertion and laughter.

"See?" I say over the stomping, the clapping, the upperclassmen shouting, "You are rushing the beat. Slow down!" to the Gilligans. "It's fun."

"It was," Weston agrees, and he sounds surprised, before his eyebrows narrow. "But we weren't done with our conversation."

I don't play dumb, though I want to. Part of me wonders, hopes, this line of questioning will lead to him asking me out.

And what if it does? What if *he* does? I run the scenario in my head, plugging in Mom's talk and the way Lauren and Andy told me I was crazy at the lunch table for even considering working with him on our duet.

Would I say yes?

The bus hits a pothole, and we jostle against each other. Hard.

"There's nothing else to tell," I say, rubbing my shoulder. "Really."

"Impossible," he says again, and I wonder if this is why he is ostracized, because he doesn't wear his heart on his sleeve but in his eyes. He is looking at me in a way that clouds my thoughts, and I ask myself how long it is I have *known* him known him. Four days? Is that all? *Impossible.*

"It's partly Enfield's fault, maybe?" I shrug. "Mostly mine. But still, it's hard to want to date someone when you know *literally* every little thing about them."

There is a forced intimacy when your numbers are so small, one that erodes the need to date somebody, because what else is there to know?

But I look at Weston, a wrench in the system, a squeaky, unmoving cog in the machine that is Enfield, and I wonder what it's like for him.

I wonder a lot of things about him, and maybe it's the way the sun is sinking in the sky outside our window, or maybe it's because it feels more private to be huddled together amid the sing-screaming of Queen, but I want to know.

"Your family . . . Are you . . . You don't have to talk about it if you don't want to."

His smile is warm, his pale cheeks still pink from his piano solo. "You can ask me anything."

"Is it just you and your parents?"

Something flickers behind his eyes at "parents," but he hides it by gently taking my hand and flipping it over so he can draw in my palm.

"There are a few acres off the beaten path in Bloom. My aunt and uncle live here," he says, tapping the pad of my thumb. "A two-minute walk up to here," he taps my middle finger, "is where Nanny and Papa live."

"So close," I say.

"And," Weston adds, dragging his finger to the center of my palm, "Dad lives here. You can see the other houses from his front door."

"Wow. It's like a tiny Ryan commune."

He laughs, moving his hand back to his lap. "We call it the

farm, but yeah. Even before the divorce, Dad's big workshop was out there, so I spent a ton of weekends there. And my cousins were usually around, so we hung out."

"And now?"

The easiness seeps out of him and he bristles.

"There's not a custody agreement. I go where I want. Sometimes I stay at Dad's, sometimes at Mom's."

I desperately want him to come back, to relax into his seat, but I also want to know more. My brain goes staticky, stops, and no words come out.

Weston sighs.

"Go on. I said you could ask me anything."

"It's okay," I say.

"It's all over your face," he says. "Just ask."

"Where does your mom live?"

"The house I grew up in," he says, and his voice is not as carefree as it was, but he turns my hand over again. I thrill at the touch. "If this is Enfield," he says, gesturing at my entire palm, "our house is way out here, practically in the next town over." He brushes a finger over the tip of my pinky.

"Your family must not like having neighbors," I say, watching his finger move against mine.

"There are houses within walking distance near the farm," Weston says, "but it's separated by trees and stuff, so you can almost pretend there's nobody else around."

Feeling brave, I turn Weston's palm over.

"Here's the post office," I say, poking the soft part between his thumb and index finger before dragging my nail an indeterminate amount to the right. "And here's my house. It's on a cul-de-sac. When we were younger, after they finally built more houses in our subdivision, all the neighborhood kids would come over after school and we would play together until it got too dark. It was the *best*."

"Do you like being constantly surrounded by people?" he asks.

I pause. "No? I mean, my family is always around, and if I'm not at home I'm at school. But sometimes I need a minute to myself, you know?"

I'm trying to decide how honest to be, how much to show after only *four days*, and Weston must see this on my face, because he curls his fingers inward to cradle my hand.

"I get tired," I say, looking down at our loosely joined hands. "Like, I love my family and I love my friends, but sometimes I just want to be by myself but not alone?"

Everything is coming out a question and my thoughts are scattered, but it suddenly feels desperately important that I gather them into a semblance of order.

"Sometimes it feels like everybody wants something from me, even if they don't say it. I guess that's part of the reason I like band, because you're alone and doing your own music but with a group of people who are also doing music, so you're not actually alone," I say. And when that doesn't make enough sense I add, "If I'm alone, I can be kind of . . . sad, I guess, but sometimes I wish there was someone that could be there with me and not expect anything, you know?"

Weston is doing that intense staring thing, so I meet his eyes before immediately looking out the window. "Sorry," I tell the glass. "That was too much. And it didn't make sense."

"It made perfect sense," Weston says, his voice shaking as the bus bounces over the gravel entry to the football field's parking lot.

At the front of the bus, Ratio is clapping his hands and telling everyone to get ready to put on uniforms as the sing-along skids to a halt and duffle bags and bulky plastic shako boxes are pulled from beneath the seats.

It is alarming how alarmed I am that my conversation with Weston is over, how much I wish it wasn't.

Our uniforms are crisp, suffocating things that we don on the bus, pulling overall-style pant straps over our shoulders, which are then concealed by the world's heaviest jacket.

"I know I'll be happy about this in December," I tell Weston, desperate to keep talking to him, "but right now I'm already looking forward to taking this off."

"Same," he says.

If I thought we were close before, it's only because we weren't changing. Legs and elbows casually collide as tennis shoes are removed and pant pleats are adjusted. My hand connects with Weston, and I overcorrect and hit Olivia behind us.

It's a dance we will all have perfected by the end of the year, but right now it's awkward and full of collisions and "Ow" and "Could you not" in various levels of indignation.

It's not like we're actually changing. That's why we have to wear the travel clothes: because Mr. Brant—and the whole of Enfield—would faint if he thought there was any level of impropriety.

But still . . . I feel weirdly charged watching Weston stick his hand through the arm holes of the jacket, watch a little too closely when he zips and buttons it closed at the front and fastens the braids that sit on our shoulders with care.

"Your collar is crooked," I tell him.

And then, like we've done this a thousand times before, he tilts his head. "Fix it for me?"

His neck is warm from the sun and from the exertion of wrestling into his uniform. He goes still, barely seeming to breathe while I spend more time than strictly necessary fiddling with the strip of white, my knuckles brushing the tiny hairs on his neck.

"There," I say, patting him gently on the collar. "All set."

"Want me to help you with your braids?"

My heart is in my throat, and I wonder if it will fade, this dangerous feeling of curiosity laced with something I don't have a name for. I wonder if I'll get the chance to keep chasing it, if there is a limit to the weird things I can brain-dump on Weston before he decides I'm too much trouble.

"Sure," I say.

It's my turn to go still. Weston's breath is on my cheek as he unfastens the shoulder straps of the jacket and slips the intertwined uniform braids beneath. Am I imagining that his hand lingers? I hope not.

"There," he says, and when I'm facing him, adds, "Sit next to me in the stands?"

"Like you have a choice."

"I do," he says. "You do, too."

We don't have a choice on seating arrangements at games, but it's like he's offering something else. Like *he's* worried that *I'm* the one who might want to get away from *him*.

"If you can find me, I'll sit next to you," I joke. "I'll be the one in orange."

His voice is low when he says, "I'll find you. Call-and-answer, remember?"

"Lesson one," I murmur.

When we get off the bus, Weston puts his hand on the small of my back as we descend the steps, and even though it's gone the minute my foot touches the concrete, I can still feel his handprint burning through my jacket.

We only have a handful of tunes to play in the stands, so we spend a lot of time during the first quarter alternating watching the Bearcats obliterate the competition and messing around with whoever is nearby when Mr. Brant's back is turned.

I'm supposed to be setting a good example for Terrance and Samantha. I'm supposed to be preparing them to be section leaders after I graduate.

But *this* is the fun part of band, the easy part, the part where we're squished together in too-small bleachers with equipment and the percussionists' drums and the music stands for the flutes crowded around us.

"Be ready to play when Mr. Brant holds up the song title," I tell them during the first quarter. "And *don't* get caught eating in uniform," I say through a mouthful of Skittles. "You *will* get busted."

Samantha laughs while the lines around Terrance's mouth deepen into his usual worried facial expression.

"How will we know when it's time to do the show?"

I try to remind myself that I was a freshman once, but it's hard when Terrance asks questions like such a Gilligan.

"We'll know when literally *everyone* leaves the stands, right?" Samantha asks me, barely concealing her irritation. "It's not like we're going to get left behind."

"Exactly," I say. "I promise you'll know when it's time."

"What if I forget how to march onto the field? What if I forget my spot in the opener?"

"Do the best you can," I answer, already dreading the talking-to we'll get from Mr. Brant if Terrance goes the wrong way on the field, like he's done the past few rehearsals.

Weston is directly behind me, his knees gently resting against my back when we're seated. I wonder what he would do if I reclined against them. I wonder if he would shrug me off. But I think of his hand on my back when we got off the bus and I blush.

"You shouldn't be eating," Weston says.

I don't turn around, too busy swallowing the last of the Skittles I smuggled in my shako hat box. Since we don't wear the shakos until we're on the field, it's the perfect hiding place for contraband.

"Don't know what you're talking about," I tell Weston.

"It's bad for your *instrument*," he insists. "Sugar will make your pads stick."

"Green or red?"

"What?" he asks.

I still don't turn. "Green or red?"

Tabitha, another mellophone, stretches a palm toward me, cutting across Darin and Weston. "Red," she whispers.

I plop some candy into her hand.

"I'm not going to make *my* keys sticky with sugar, thank you," Weston tells me, before turning to shake his head disapprovingly at Tabitha. "And *you* definitely shouldn't be. You have enough problems hitting high notes without your instrument rebelling."

Tabitha ignores him, trying to chew her candy without moving her jaw and getting caught.

"Just as well," I say. "I've only got green left."

"Lesson two," Weston says. "Duets are *impossible* to play if your instrument is fucked up from too much sugar."

I spin around. "Don't say that."

"It's the truth." He laughs. "Whether I say it or not, your sax is toast if you don't wash out your mouth before playing."

"Not that," I say. "The *f-word*."

Weston groans. "Not you, too."

"Too?"

"You're as bad as Ratio," he says. "He calls cursing a lack of imagination and knowledge of the human language."

"I agree with Ratio," I say.

"So do I," Ratio says, appearing beside us with a grin, his drum major cape fluttering heroically behind him. "I also agree with Weston that you should put those Skittles away before Mr. B. catches you, Miss James."

"Can do," I say, slipping the empty bag into my shako box.

"Only because she *already ate them*," Weston says.

"*Rat*," I accuse with mock outrage.

"Don't let them bully you, Anna," Jonathan yells from his euphonium section above. "They're just mad because they were stupid enough to get caught drinking soda in uniform when we were freshmen."

It's Friday night. I'm at a Bearcat football game. The stadium lights are as bright as the cheerleaders' smiles, the stands are packed with sweating Enfielders, my uniform rubs against me in its familiar, starched way, and I have been here a thousand times before.

But with Weston and Ratio and Jonathan bantering behind me and the memory of Weston's hand on my back, his hand in my palm, everything feels new, and my insides are bright enough to scorch shadows.

chapter 7

weston

We're on the bus for all of ten minutes before Anna begins to droop against the window, her eyes fluttering closed.

"That wasn't too bad for the first performance of the season," she says with a yawn. "At least for my section."

"Not bad," I agree. "Which means that next week we will really start working on the production number in morning rehearsals."

I expect her to suddenly start talking too fast about our duet and practice schedules and concerns, but she only murmurs an affirmation, her eyes still shut. Her breath is even and slow before we pull out of the parking lot.

I should leave her there against the window, but the second time we hit a pothole in the road, her head thumps against the glass, and I reach around and gently pull her onto my shoulder.

"Softer than glass," I whisper. "We don't want you concussed when I'm trying to teach you the duet."

She mumbles something, but it isn't intelligible.

My insides burn when Anna nestles against my shoulder, her arms curling around mine. She's like a sleepy koala, a creature made of postgame band mom–provided sandwiches—she ate hers, *and* mine when I offered it—and laughter that has come to rest against my side, and I don't know whether to marvel or panic.

What did it feel like the second the Kauaʻi ʻōʻō heard its call played back from a recorder? Even if it knew deep down it wasn't another bird, maybe the jolt of momentary hope was worth the pain that came after. Maybe, even if it doesn't last forever, even if it's never more than this, it's enough to have Anna's head resting on my shoulder.

When I was little and Dad would take me sailing on his old boat he'd inherited from Papa, he'd say, "Don't drop anchor where you can't sail." But one glance at Anna's down-turned head, one sleepy squeeze of her arms around mine, and I feel the weight in me drop.

I don't care if I bash my ship to smithereens.

I don't care if my ship stays here forever.

Usually I look forward to weekends, a full forty-eight hours where I can pretend school doesn't exist.

But no school means no Anna, and it's killing me.

When Ratio and Jonathan don't answer my Saturday morning request for *King's Reign* in the group chat, I peel myself out of my bed at Dad's to go find him.

He's out on the back porch, smoking a cigarette.

"I thought you said you were done smoking," I say, pulling up a lawn chair to sit beside him.

Dad gestures to a side table full of tobacco and rolling supplies.

"Rolling my own," he says. "Much harder than buying them at the convenience store."

"But you're still smoking."

He doesn't say anything but gestures with his cigarette at the little row of trees in the mobile home's backyard.

"Got a new birdhouse this week. See? Some of those little brown sparrows you like already made a nest in there."

I don't remember ever saying that the sparrows are my favorite, but they are. I watch the birds flutter in and out of their wooden houses, busily building nests and eating bugs.

"Your mother wants you to call her," Dad says, his eyes trained on the birds. "She texted. Said she tried calling you yesterday, and you didn't answer?"

I didn't answer because I know what she's going to say. She wants to meet for lunch, and she wants to meet for lunch so she can tell me to come pack the rest of my childhood up in boxes, to finish sifting through the artifacts of a history with no future.

"I'll call her," I say, and Dad grunts and nods.

She's always "your mother," now. It's never Dianne or Doll or any of the pet names that echoed through my childhood.

When Dad runs out of hand-rolled cigarettes and irritably goes inside to track down his pack of nicotine gum, I stay on the porch and call Mom.

"Weston," she answers. "I called you yesterday."

Her voice is clipped, a little muffled. She's in the car. Judging from her tone, she probably just got off a conference call. She does that a lot on weekends, especially since the divorce—an endless stream of errands that she can't do during her week of travel, broken up by bouts of tense calls with "the team."

"Sorry," I say. "Football season, remember? I was at the game."

"Right," she says. "But a text letting me know you were okay wouldn't have taken long."

I shift in the patio chair, pressing my toe against a wooden knot as hard as I can. "Got it," I say.

"Let's meet for lunch at the deli," she says. It's not a request. "I could kill for a decent salad."

"Fine," I say.

"Oops, that's Todd on the other line. Gotta run. See you at one?"

"Sure," I say.

"Love you," she says.

"I love you, too."

Dad never reemerges with his gum. He probably got distracted looking for it, or quit the hunt altogether to watch TV.

But I like sitting on the porch, watching the birds flit from tree to house, house to sky.

One of the sparrows reminds me of Anna, hopping on the ground, looking for loose seed fallen from the feeders. It has more pep than the others, seems more persistent.

I wonder if Anna likes birds. I wonder if Kaua'i 'ō'ōs liked birdseed.

Dad pokes his head out to let me know he's going to visit with Nanny and asks if I want to come. I think of drawing the farm's triangle on Anna's palm, of the three little houses in a field, three tracks worn among them from years and years of Ryans walking back and forth.

My mind is abuzz, the wildfire simmering and threatening to expand at a moment's notice, so I say, "No, thanks," and Dad half-waves in good-bye.

I kill time until lunch by playing my horn, running through scales until I get bored and switch to working on the production music. When I get to our duet, my brain snags on the memory of Anna's head tucked between my neck and shoulder.

Maybe I should text her. Just to set up our next duet meeting. We never made plans after the game, and I . . . I don't have her number.

I pretend my phone doesn't exist for maybe five minutes before I fold and text Ratio: I need Anna's number. Do you have it?

He never responded to my *King's Quest* message, but as soon as my text pops up as delivered, my phone rings, a photo of Ratio playing a plastic Christmas decoration like it's a real horn covering my screen.

"You *do* like her," he says when I answer. "I *knew* it. And even better, you won't stop cussing for *me*, but I'll bet all the money in your swear jar that you will for *her*."

"Shut up," I say, knowing he's right and hating him a little for it. "Do you have her number or not?"

"Little Weston, all grown up. I'm so proud."

My hand tightens on the phone. "Sorry for asking," I say, and I go to hang up, then hear Ratio's unintelligible mumble. "What?" I ask, raising my phone back to my ear.

"I have her number. I'll send it to you."

"It's for duet practice," I say, but even the sparrow I've been watching seems to look at me disbelievingly.

"Yeah, and is her using you as her personal pillow on the way home last night part of the urgency?"

"Necessity," I argue.

"Sure," Ratio says. A pause. "You know I'm happy for you, right?"

I reach to tug on my hair, but it's still too damnably short, so I settle for rubbing my eyes.

I can be honest with Ratio, I remind myself.

"It's . . . it's a lot."

He doesn't ask me to elaborate; doesn't have to. "I know."

"What if I mess it up?"

Ratio sighs. "You can't think about that. Really. It'll be over before it begins if you're too busy panicking to enjoy it, you know?"

I nod. Ratio doesn't see it, but he knows. Ratio, I think, might always know.

"Whatever it is, it hasn't even started," I say, tracing my horn bell's edge with my index finger, the cold metal leaving a slight indentation as I run it around the rim. "But I'm already . . . I don't know. Afraid it will end?"

There's a heavy *thud* in the background, and Ratio grunts.

"Sorry," he says. "Helping Dad clean out the garage. Stop worrying so much, Weston. Just ask the girl out, and if it works, it works. If it doesn't, it wasn't meant to be. You'll probably roll your eyes, but it's true. You can't be so afraid of an ending that you don't bother with the beginning."

I *do* roll my eyes.

"If I wanted *that* kind of advice, I'd go to the Chinese food place in Bloom to get dry fried rice and a shitty fortune cookie."

Ratio huffs out a laugh, his voice strained. "Gotta stop cursing, remember? I've gotta run. I need to finish this half of the garage before youth group tonight. You're coming, right? To hand out the flyers for the kids' program?"

This time, I resist rolling my eyes. Ratio would somehow know and chastise me, *and* I would probably lose points with God or whatever if I let him see how little I care about distributing door hangers. I'm an infrequent attendee of the youth group at best, a drifter that comes in and hears the same ten commandments and barely manages to hold back my endless questions at worst. But it makes Ratio and Jonathan happy to have me there, and it's not like there is anything else to do during the regular Wednesday night and occasional Saturday evening meetings, because literally every single person in Enfield is a pious twice-a-week Goody Two–shoes.

"Maybe," I tell Ratio. Really, I want to leave my evening clear to get up the courage to call Anna, to see if her voice speeds up when she talks to me on the phone, like it does in real life. She speaks like that when she gets excited, I've noticed, fast and pointed, like she's worried there's not enough time to say all the things that need saying.

"You'll come," Ratio says with annoying certainty. "See you tonight."

"We'll see," I say, but he's already hung up.

My heart does a strange flip-flop in my chest when my phone lights up with his message bearing Anna's number.

It's only a text message, but I am extra careful when I set my phone in my car's cup holder. I hate that I'm driving to meet Mom for lunch while Dad is at Nanny's, only a fifteen-minute walk away.

There was a time when we would *all* be at Nanny's on Saturday, hands overlapping near plates of food, loud voices and cigarette smoke filling the living room and kitchen, Aunt Susan and Uncle Peter letting themselves in the side door with boxes of Dr Pepper and Diet Pepsi.

As I turn into the parking lot of Enfield's tiny deli, the Kaua'i 'ō'ō puffs its feathers, wondering how long I'll be able to hold off before I call Anna. I wonder, too.

When I walk in, Mom has already gone to the salad bar and has grabbed our usual booth by the window. My bowl of soup is just barely steaming in front of her.

"You're late," she says in greeting, but her voice isn't nearly as thin as it was earlier.

"Sorry," I say. "Bad traffic."

She shoots me a dry look—traffic is a foreign concept in Enfield—but she's not going to ask and I'm not going to offer.

And what would I say if she did: *Sorry, I was busy staring at my phone and thinking about calling a girl. A Happening. A melody.*

"I got an email from your calculus teacher this week," Mom says, lifting an eyebrow. "It's a little early for that, don't you think?"

I take a bite of soup to avoid answering, and Mom sighs.

"Weston, I'm not sure what to tell you that hasn't already been said. If you want to go to college for music, you need to at least pass high school." Mom has put her fork down and is staring at me intently, and it occurs to me how rare it is to be the recipient of somebody's full attention. What a rebellious thing, to stare, when the world is always half-looking at phones or tablets or something other than *you*.

I think of Anna, how bright her eyes are, how they watch me like I'm someone to be figured out instead of ignored, how much I missed them on the bus ride home when she slept on my arm, but how happy I was that she chose me as her perch.

"Music programs only care about how you play," I say. "My grades are fine."

Mom pushes her bangs out of her eyes, her red hair bright under the low lights above our table.

"Fix it," she tells me. "You are gravely mistaken if you think colleges are going to ignore barely passing grades. It's competitive out there. They want to know that you're willing to do the work."

I think it's going to be an argument, but it's not. Mom has a list of things she wants to discuss, apparently, one she pulls up on her phone by jabbing at her screen.

"The boxes," she says. "You didn't go through them."

"I haven't been to the house much," I say, which is true. I don't tell her I'm actively avoiding it.

"Weston, you need to get this done. I have realtors scheduled to come next month."

Which is the closest she's come to telling me she's selling the house.

Her eyes scan over her phone. "Ah," she says. "I texted your father. He's agreed to go to your away games so I can come to your home games. He'll go to any games I'm traveling during, too. That way one of us is always there."

She adds the last part like it's an arrangement for my benefit instead of a way to ensure they won't run into each other.

I can't blame them for not wanting to show up together. They've been in Enfield forever. Anywhere they go, they'll be watched by the prying eyes of not-so-close friends and acquaintances eager to piece together their own narratives as to why Mom and Dad aren't married anymore. Enfield is made of people who wield southern charm like a weapon, bludgeoning you with niceties until they get some scrap for the gossip mill.

I understand, but part of me splinters at how casually we're discussing this over soup.

"This week's our first home game," I say. "Will you be there?"

This coming Friday will also be the day of reckoning for Anna and the duet. I wonder if she'll still want to sit next to me if Mr. Brant gives her part away. I wonder if she'll still want to sit next to me if he *doesn't*.

"I'll be there," Mom says. After a pause, she adds, "It'll be nice to see you play in orange and white again, Weston."

There's a lump in my throat when she moves her chair back to head for the restroom. It doesn't help when she leans forward and kisses the top of my head before walking away.

When she's out of sight, I pull my phone from my jacket pocket and spin it on the table, tormenting myself with the possibility of calling Anna. Or worse, not calling her.

The spinning distracts me when Mom comes back to the table with her phone pressed against her ear.

"Yes, Todd. *Yes*, Todd. I'll have it in your inbox by Monday. Uh-huh. Before I get on the plane."

There's a long pause, and Mom digs out a pen from her bag and draws a squiggle on the unused napkin in front of her. She slides it over to me, and I consider it while she negotiates meeting times with Todd, her partner on her current project.

It's an old game, one she started while working from home when I was little. She draws a few random lines, and I have to turn them into something recognizable.

Beneath the jagged lines, I draw a stick figure, hunching under her lightning squiggles and getting pelted with raindrops. I push the napkin back, and I can't tell if she's concentrating on the call or on my drawing.

"I'll ask Patrice," she says into the phone.

She picks up the pen, but I can't see what she's drawing because the napkin is hidden by her salad plate.

"Uh-huh."

She pushes the napkin halfway across the table and I pull it toward me. My stick figure isn't alone anymore; another stick figure stands beside him, holding an umbrella over their heads.

If Mom were different, I would look up and we would make brief but meaningful eye contact. We would share a moment, one that nobody else in the deli would understand, but we would know it meant that, even though things are different, we're still each other's shelter in the storm, still us.

But she's my mom, and I'm me, and she's looking out the window as she rubs her temple and talks into the phone. I take the pen and draw more lightning, extending it to hit the umbrella and travel in squiggly shocks up the arms of the new stick figure.

Mom finds this funny, though, and she laughs out loud when she sees it, quickly covering her mouth. "Sorry, Todd. No, of course I'm not laughing at you."

Mom and I smile at each other, and I take the pen and draw an arrow to the stick figure getting shocked and label it "Todd."

When I get in the car, after Mom's Prius zips out of the parking lot, I take as much air into my lungs as I can and tap the Call button.

chapter 8

❧

anna

When he was working multiple jobs, I didn't see Dad much. He became the fun parent, the fly-by-night one showing up with tired smiles and silly jokes before disappearing back into the land of adulthood.

He would sneak into my room late at night, a stuffed animal under his arm, kiss me on the forehead, and whisper, "I love you, Bagels. Here's a new friend. Don't tell Mom."

My bed grew full to the brim with them. Each one becoming my new favorite, until the next.

Later, I asked Mom if she knew about all the times Dad snuck in to bring me toys.

"Of course," she said. "I was with you day in, day out. You don't think I noticed when you started carrying around a toy I had never seen before?"

"But why did Dad tell me not to tell you?"

"Because secrets bring people closer together, Anna," she said. *"For better or worse."*

We're at the grocery store when my phone buzzes.

It's an unknown number from a local area code. A ridiculous part of me is hoping it's Weston, so I wander away from where Mom, Dad, and Jenny are arguing over how many loaves of bread we need.

"Hello?" I answer.

The service must be terrible. There's only rumbly static.

"Hello?" I say again.

"Anna?"

I remind myself it's been less than a week of knowing this boy, that it's ridiculous to have my heart rate skyrocket the second I recognize his voice, but it's useless. I would know that voice anywhere, and there's no stopping my brain from playing the snippets of us on the bus while desperately hoping that his voice on the line means there will be more recollections, there will be more time.

"Weston." I smile. "I thought it was you."

"How could you think it was me? I didn't even have your number until an hour ago."

"I don't know," I say, running a finger over boxes of tea. "I just did."

Weston is smiling. I can hear it in his voice when he says, "I'll have to take your word for it."

Farther up the aisle, the family cart is turning the corner. Dad waves to get my attention and points at the next aisle over.

I'll catch up, I mouth.

Dad shoots me a thumbs-up and follows Mom, who is squabbling with Jenny about God knows what.

"Anna?"

My stomach flutters at hearing him say my name.

"Sorry, sorry. At the grocery store with my parents." I pause. "Thanks for not letting me beat my brains out against the window last night."

His laugh is low, relaxed. "My pleasure."

"So . . ." I lead.

"Oh, yeah," Weston's voice is adorably flustered. "I called you. Right."

A lady shoves past and gives me an irritated look as she reaches for the box of tea I've been poking backward on the shelf. I don't care. A million angry shoppers could come for me and it wouldn't stop my creeping smile as Weston—calm, collected Weston—stumbles over his words.

"You called me to . . . ?" I prompt.

"I called to see if you wanted . . . Okay, it's stupid, but Ratio is making me come to youth group and put notes on people's doors about the kid program and . . . Do you want to?"

I've borrowed his rogue's smile, can feel it pushing up my cheeks when I say, "Do I want to *what*?"

He groans. "You don't want to. Just say it."

"I didn't say that," I argue. "I only want to understand what it is you're asking."

"I'm *asking*," and his voice is muffled like he's talking through his hand, "if you want to go to youth group. With me. Tonight."

There were never magazines in our house growing up. Mom has always said they rot your brain, giving you a warped sense of what the human body is supposed to look like.

But there were magazines at Lauren's house. Sprawled across her bed or piled messily on her desk: *Seventeen*, *Teen Vogue*, *CosmoGirl*, glossy jewels that offered advice on everything from finding your face shape to how to let your crush know you like them without being *too* obvious.

I rack my brain for what I'm supposed to say, mentally

flipping through pages of models with perfect skin and pursed lips and coming up empty.

"You promised," Weston says, and his voice is unreadable, "the truth."

"Yes," I say on an inhale.

"Yes, you want to go or yes, you'll tell the truth?"

"Yes," I say, "I want to go. With you."

Dad's head pops around my aisle, and when he spots me, he waves at me to follow. I beg him with my eyes for one more minute, and he gestures even more emphatically down the endless rows.

Got it, I mouth.

"You don't have to, you know," Weston is saying, his voice faster, more insistent. "I'll still help you with the duet. I'll still sit next to you on the bus so you can sleep without getting a brain injury."

And maybe it's because I'm tired from counting my bedroom stars late into the night, from trying to make my pen describe Weston's eyes just right, but words that would not be *Cosmo* approved, that are too much and too sincere, are out of my mouth before I can stop them.

"Weston, I'd go anywhere with you," I say, and I flinch.

This is why I get friend-zoned. These are the types of words that should *stay* inked in a journal. Never spoken out loud. Especially to a boy who hasn't technically agreed to be anything more than a duet partner.

The shadows begin to press in on me until Weston huffs out a gentle, awed laugh. The sound of it strokes my ear and makes me shiver, chases the negativity far away from where I stand by the boxes of tea.

Weston is not afraid of my too-muchness. "Meet me there? At the Collins' church?"

I'm relieved he didn't ask to pick me up, relieved I don't have to tell him that he can't because of my parents.

"See you there," I say, and after a second of us breathing quietly into the phone, he hangs up.

I don't know what the opposite of a shadow is—a beam of light, maybe?—but it follows me to the dairy aisle, where Dad is helping Jenny choose yogurt flavors.

"Who was that, Anna?" Mom asks.

"Band stuff," I say. "Also, is it okay if I go help out with the Collins' youth group tonight? They're hanging flyers to advertise their new children's church thing."

Mom doesn't bat an eye at this. In a town with nothing to do, most of the high school population spends their weekend hopping from church group to church group, activity to activity. It's all church to our parents, holy and sanctified, with no chance of there being drugs or sex or alcohol. It's safe.

"Sure," Mom says. "Just be home by nine. You have to get up early for church in the morning."

"Got it," I say.

I tell myself it's not a lie. Mom never asked who else would be there. She *certainly* didn't ask if Weston would be there.

But deep down, my people-pleasing heart twists and shadows form. If she knew I was going because Weston asked, that the boy I promised not to date would be there, the answer would be different.

Not a lie, I remind myself when I get home and spend far too much time trying to choose an outfit that is casual but cute, but not in a totally obvious way. *Not a lie*.

When I pull up to the tiny church, there's a huddle of seven kids by an open church van. Ratio seems to be the leader, even though Jonathan's dad is the pastor. Jonathan is content to stand aside, leaning over to whisper something to Weston that makes Weston laugh and shove him on the shoulder, which makes Ratio's eyebrows lower.

"Enough horsing around," Ratio says, handing out bundles of door hangers held together by colorful rubber bands. "Anna, you're with Weston, of course," he says as I walk up.

Weston swivels quickly, smiling when he sees me. Ratio plows on. "As your drum major, I feel it incumbent to remind you that your duet needs to be *greatly* improved by the end of the week or you will face the wrath of Mr. Brant and myself. Perhaps this would be a good time to figure out a practice schedule."

"Lay off," Weston tells him. "We've already started. We'll have it ready."

With the team divided and the allotted door hangers distributed, we pile into the van and drive to a neighborhood only minutes from the church. The white van is a smaller version of the band bus, a ruckus of name-calling and Christian rock music blaring from the speakers spiking my energy.

It's almost startling, the contrast between the van and the silence of the sidewalk as Weston and I wave good-bye to the other pairs and head off down our own street.

It only takes a moment for it to settle over us, the blanket of aloneness.

There was the band bus, closeness forced on us by the cracked plastic seat, and the practice room, with its door that might open any second, but then there is this: elbows bumping as we walk too close, and the realization that we can say or do anything we want. There's no one around to hear, no one to watch except the empty Saturday evening houses and the occasional lawn mower.

It's like a superpower. It's a freedom I didn't know I wanted. But now that it's here, I'm breathing it deep into my lungs, soaking up Weston's profile as the sun starts to sink in the sky.

"What?" he asks.

"What, what?"

He smiles the pirate smile. "You're too quiet and you're staring. What are you thinking?"

"I'm thinking we should probably talk about the duet practice schedule like Ratio said."

The rogue's grin is replaced by a grimace. "Fair. But what else?"

My pause is short. "I'm also thinking we could say anything to each other."

"Can't we always?"

"You know what I mean."

He nods. "I do."

"So . . ." I lead.

"So what?" He grins.

"What are *you* thinking?" I ask.

Weston kicks at a rock on the pavement, his eyes following its path as it skitters down the sidewalk.

"My parents are on my case about my grades."

I try my level best to take this information in stride, but my reply comes out astonished anyway. "It's only the second week of school."

"*I know.*"

We walk up another driveway, apply another door hanger, and are back at the street before I ask, "So . . . what's the problem? With your grades, I mean."

I'm learning Weston's smiles are slow, but his frowns are quick.

"Since last year my grades have kind of been shitty." He breaks off, his eyes widening. "Sorry! I know you don't like cursing. Um . . ." He pauses, regroups, searches the pavement for an alternate word. "My grades have been *complete crap*. I actually couldn't perform at a couple football games last year because I was failing in Bloom."

I don't know what it's like to make failing grades. My lowest report card grade ever was a B in math and I was devastated, my years-long streak broken by a single test grade.

If I had to guess, I'd say Weston is less concerned with his grades and more concerned with his parents. It seems obvious. If his grades were okay up until a year ago, something big had to have changed that.

I'm too much of a coward to ask him outright about the divorce, so instead I say, "I can help you study if you want. I know you're a year ahead, but I can help you make flash cards and stuff."

"Thanks," he says, and it sounds sincere. "But . . . sometimes I don't get it. Like, why I have to spend all this time doing math and science and history when all I want to do is play music. Colleges don't care about grades when it comes to music programs."

I don't want to tell him that I've heard the exact opposite. Music programs are highly competitive. It's not enough to be a good player, or even a *great* player; they're looking for academic prowess, too.

I think of my wobbly future, the dark open place that should mean I can do anything but instead leaves me paralyzed with fear. Who is Anna James when she is not at Enfield? When she doesn't live at home with parents who perform spontaneous sock puppet shows while putting away laundry? Who has to do something other than wake up, go to band rehearsal, go to school, and do what she's told?

"At least you know what you want to do," I tell Weston, pushing back the shadows. "At least you have a passion."

"And you don't?" Weston asks, wrestling the thick paper hanger onto the door of a house that desperately needs its porch swept.

"I don't know," I say. "I like listening to music. I like reading. I like drawing. But I'm not very good at any of it." I pause.

"And none of those things make money anyways, so I don't know what I'm going to do."

Weston scoffs. "Who needs money?"

My eyebrows shoot up. "Spoken like somebody who has plenty," I say.

"But money isn't everything. Wouldn't you rather be happy?"

I think about when I was very little and Dad worked two, three, sometimes four jobs at once so Mom could stay home with me and Jenny. I think about overheard phone calls, Mom calling Grandma, crying, my grandparents showing up the next day with bags of groceries, and toys for Jenny and me. All of it confusingly interspersed with memories of vacations across the United States, in Mexico, in our own backyard.

Lots of people have a clean story of how their family had money and then didn't or suddenly went from nothing to everything. I wonder if one big change is easier to adjust to than a million little ones.

But right now, there is room in my world for new shoes just because you like the color, eating out on the occasional weeknight, and—most important—band fees and instrument rentals.

And just like that, I feel guilty.

"I know people have had it a lot worse," I say. "Like, a lot worse. I never worried if I would have food or shelter or anything I needed. There was never a Christmas that wasn't filled with presents for me and Jenny. We never *actually* went without."

"But?" Weston asks.

I sigh. "But I remember when my parents would go without so that Jenny and I didn't have to, and that's not a choice I want to make someday. I want *everything*."

A cat watches scornfully from its window as we walk up to the next door. Weston's eyebrows are scrunched in thought when he slips the hanger over the elegant, polished handle.

We're back on the sidewalk before he says, "But isn't part of having everything also being happy with your job? Your life?"

"But I don't know what it is I want to do," I say. Another lie by omission. My brain is shoving the image of my journal into my eyes, flipping the pages through my stories and thoughts and quotes I've recorded to prevent them from drifting away.

"Can I ask you something?" Weston asks.

"Of course."

"If you're not sure what you want to do . . . why do you try so hard? Why bother?"

If he were anyone else, I would give him a canned answer like *I want to keep my options open*, or maybe *Because I want to be the best I can be*. If he were anyone else, he wouldn't be *asking* the question in the first place, because my friend group is a flock of overachieving Enfielders who treat every single test and homework assignment like a footrace, a competition to be the biggest fish in our puddle-sized pond.

"I don't know," I finally say. "It's what I've always done, and adults really like it when you try?"

His face is completely blank, thinking. I get how people could look at him and assume he's not listening, but he *is*— more than anyone else, probably.

"What if you spent all your energy on something that made *you* happy?" he asks. "Instead of trying to make other people happy, what if you did something just for you?"

I think of my journal again. How sometimes, when it's dark and I'm tired of counting stars and the shadows are tucked away, I'll scrawl stories in the margins. How the world's too-muchness sometimes seems like a beautiful thing instead of a scary one, and I have to find a way to pin it down on paper or else it might slip away forever.

I think of how I could never tell my friends this, how part of knowing them so completely is also knowing I could never make them understand that sometimes I feel this responsibility to be an observer while at the same time feeling like I have nothing to add, nothing new to observe.

But maybe I could tell Weston.

"I love to write." It comes out so quietly, he stops me with a hand to my arm and leans forward.

"What?"

"I have a journal," I say, looking up at him with burning cheeks. "And I love to write in it. I don't, like, *Write* with a capital *W* or anything, but . . . I do it."

This feels more intimate than waking up with my head on his shoulder on the bus, but I can't look away as a different kind of slow smile lights up Weston's mouth, his eyes, his whole being, even if I'm afraid I'll combust with embarrassment.

"You're a writer," he says with a laugh. "*Of course* you are. What else *could* you be?"

"What's that supposed to mean?"

"I just mean . . ." He trails off and rubs at his short hair. "I don't know. That you are . . ." He pauses, gesturing at me and gently kicking my shoe. "You. And I can't imagine you doing *anything* else."

I snort. "Not even playing the duet correctly?"

Weston's eyes are blazing. "No, I mean with your *life*."

"How could you possibly know that?" I ask. "You've never read anything I've written because there's *nothing to read*. It's journal stuff mostly, like, about my life. It's not like it's good."

"It's yours," he says. "It has to be good."

If Weston sees me in half the light I see him, with his heartbreaking sincerity and enthusiasm and ability to suss out my emotions miles before I can sort them myself, then I am maybe, possibly, beginning to understand why he was so disbelieving on the bus when I told him I hadn't dated anyone.

I pity the world that looks at Weston Ryan and stops at his

jacket. I pity the world that has to rotate around a star without somebody so painfully *alive* and vibrant.

These are things I can tell my journal, but for now I turn the conversation back onto him. "You're the one who said such pretty things about our duet and the call-and-answer and all that," I say, hoping my voice doesn't betray my inner thoughts. "Why don't *you* be the free-spirited writer or hippie-dippie musician and *I'll* be the practical one that gets good grades and good jobs and whatever?"

I stumble over the last bit, the accidental implication that we're *together*, two halves of a whole that require one person to be the sensible, rooted one and the other to be the artist, the dreamer.

But Weston is quick to remind me that he is not afraid of my too-muchness.

"We can be both," he says. "Or we can take turns."

"Whose turn is it right now?" I ask, as we walk up another driveway, hang another colorful piece of cardboard that promises children games and the opportunity to memorize Bible verses.

Weston waits until we are back on the sidewalk to answer, both of us standing still as the Texas sky roars above us with its orange and pink splendor.

"Music is just math, you know," he says. "It's structured and exact, but there's so much about it we don't know. Music is sensibility pretending to be art." Weston pauses. "So I guess I could be the sensible one for a while, if you'd like."

I'm looking up at the sky, tempted to take a picture with my phone but knowing it won't do the colors or this moment justice. I can feel Weston's eyes on me.

"It's beautiful," I say, nodding my chin to the clouds. "Like, really beautiful." When I realize Weston is opening his mouth to respond, I panic, lunging forward to cover his mouth with my hand. "Do *not*," I say, "ruin this by saying something *completely cheesy* like, 'Yeah, it is,' while looking directly at me. Do not be that person."

His eyes are shining as he slowly removes my hand, lacing his fingers through mine and holding tight.

"Can I say something different but equally cheesy?" he asks.

My heart skips. We are dancing on the edge of a canyon, inching closer with every casual touch, every turn of the intimacy dial, and something in me—which sounds an awful lot like Lauren or Mom or Andy—warns that I should run in the opposite direction.

If I tell Weston yes, if I let him tell me pretty things, let his long fingers stay curved around mine, I'm allowing something. I'm taking a risk. I've been careful, considerate, patient for all sixteen years of my life. I've done what I've been told, what I've been asked, or what I think will make other people happy.

But maybe I'll take Weston's advice. I'll go into the canyon, because I might die if I don't find out what hides there.

"You can tell me anything," I say.

Weston's smile is the fastest I've ever seen as he leans forward to whisper in my ear, "I hope if you write about us tonight it feels like the beginning of a very long story."

I like this canyon.

Later, after I've showered and braided my hair so it will be wavy for church in the morning, I wrestle the journal from beneath my bed.

I think about what Weston said, how music is math. I wonder if people are actually just math, too.

I wonder if I can reverse the equation that is me. If by collecting my memories on paper, I can break myself into enough parts to equal a whole.

You're a writer. Of course *you are.*

I write the first thing that comes to mind, Weston's lips against my ear, and I keep writing.

I'll be tired at church tomorrow, probably get in trouble from Mom and Dad for the telltale dark circles under my eyes, but I don't care.

When I am old, with gray hair and aching joints, I want to remember the way the pavement cracks felt beneath my shoes when I walked next to the tall boy, the one with blond hair that grows alarmingly fast, blue eyes that really see *me*, and a smile that was wicked fast when I said I was a writer. I want to remember how I shivered when he whispered in my ear.

I want to remember climbing back into the church van, hands empty of door hangers and mouths full of old Vacation Bible School songs sung at the top of our lungs. Unlike on the band bus, Weston joined in immediately, his low voice balancing out our high-pitched shouts, our hands not clasped, but touching in the backseat.

Even when I'm old, something I can hardly imagine, I want to remember what it felt like to come home and look my mother in the eye and know that I was deceiving her— knowingly, forcefully—when she asked who had been there.

"Ratio and Jonathan and some sophomores," I told her. "That's it."

I want to remember that, when I lied, the big Texas sky didn't fall down, the canyon didn't crumble beneath my feet. I want to remember that Anna James, always careful, always doing what she's told, totally forgot to set up a time to work on the duet.

I want to remember that my first thought was I'd lie forever if it meant seeing Weston.

chapter 9

❧

weston

The relief that comes with Monday and seeing Anna is short-lived. After the warm-up mile, we are on the grid, using wooden blocks labeled with our initials to mark our spots in the production number, marching without instruments as we count out loud at the top of our lungs.

There's barely enough time between reps to catch Anna's eye, to have her smile at me and to smile back while Ratio watches smugly from his podium. There's certainly not enough time to decide how much trouble I'd be in if Mr. Brant caught me shooting Ratio the finger, so I don't.

But I walk beside her to second period, and it's not enough time, not at all, but it will have to do.

"Weston," she greets me, when I gently bump her shoulder with mine.

I want to touch her, to have her hands in mine and to press the tips of her fingers with mine to feel their heat. I want to tell her that I spent most of yesterday alternating between playing *King's Reign* and staring at my phone, wondering if it would be too much to call her again, to text her to say hi, or if I had creeped her out by confessing that I was allowing the beginning of whatever we are, that I don't want it to end.

Instead, I try to pour all of this into her name. "Hello, Anna."

"Hi," she says, and if she hears any of what I was trying to say, she doesn't show it. "So . . . we never talked about practicing the duet."

"I know. We should have started yesterday."

"I know." She sighs, her shoulders hunching. "So, today then? After school?"

"After school," I echo in agreement.

We're at the row of upperclassmen lockers now, and it's not *nearly* enough time to find a clever way to ask if she thought about me at all between Saturday and today.

But maybe Anna really does know me, because she bats off Lauren's tugging at her backpack, and Ryland's insistence that she owes him a stick of gum and to pay up, to stand with me for a minute longer in the crowded hallway and say, "Saturday was fun."

Lauren shoots her an incredulous look before glaring at me, but Anna's tone—tentative and sweet—is distraction enough that I'm able to ignore it.

I laugh, lowering my voice so that Lauren can't hear. "If you think *that* was fun, you should come to group on Wednesday nights."

Anna's ears turn pink. "Will you be there? On Wednesday?"

I shouldn't tease her, but I can't resist. "Will *you* be?"

"I don't know if I can make it. I might have duet practice with this musical tyrant that keeps popping up on bus seats and weekends."

"*Tyrant?*" I say in mock outrage. "I heard you've only had the one rehearsal with him, and he didn't even make you touch your saxophone."

The warning bell rings, and Anna's ears are redder than I've ever seen them. "He knows way more than I do, which is annoying," she says. Then she adds softly, "But he's cute. So I'll forgive him."

She's gone—tugged away by the persistent Lauren—before I can figure out what my face is doing, how my insides are re-arranging themselves to make room for Anna James calling me cute.

I can just see her, face hidden by her open locker, one red ear poking out beneath her damp, tied-back hair. I would almost consider letting Darin have first chair for a week if I could hear what she is thinking.

All through my classes, I am stuck in my head, replaying her words. Eventually I start to wonder if it actually happened, if she actually thinks of me as attractive or it's something my brain invented to make me feel okay about thinking about her so much.

Maybe I misheard her.

Ratio throws a pen at me in math when he sees I'm not taking notes. I throw it back, and when I look up at the white-board, I'm too far behind to make any sense of the problem.

So instead I keep thinking about Anna.

I slip out of my teacher assistant period as early as I can without drawing notice from Mr. Brant, the day having become a blur that only comes back into clear focus when I round the corner to the cafeteria and see Anna at her lunch table.

She is hunched over with Kristin, her dark hair butting up against Kristin's blonde as they peer down at Kristin's home-work.

I can just barely make out their words.

"It's either an allegory or symbolism," Anna says, pointing at another page. "See? You could make an argument for both."

"But we're only supposed to pick *one*," Kristin whines.

Andy leans over and swipes the paper, glancing at it for two seconds before announcing, "Oh, it's totally an allegory. Allegories can be symbolic, but not all symbols are allegories."

Lauren doesn't even look up from the last of her salad. "I'm surprised you stopped making out with juniors long enough to learn anything in ninth grade."

When they start bickering, Anna straightens and turns her head sharply from side to side, rubbing her neck with closed eyes.

When she opens them, she's staring right at me. Her cheeks redden, her lips quirk into a smile, and I feel my anchor scrape the bottom of the seafloor, coming to a complete halt.

"Cute, huh?" I murmur to her, as she comes to stand beside me after the bell rings.

She thumps me with her empty lunch box.

"Did you forget the tyrant part?"

"I don't forget anything you say," I tell her. "And Anna?"

There's no music in the world that could be as beautiful as her eyes. Whoever says brown eyes are boring hasn't looked into hers.

"Yeah?"

I reach down and touch her fingers, a brush disguised as an accident. It's not the right time to tell her I find her inexhaustibly interesting to look at. Beautiful, yes, but more than that, someone that I could look at forever and discover something new each time. And it's *definitely* not the right time to let her know that I would think about her too much, no matter what she looked like.

But I don't want to leave her with nothing. A selfish part

of me wants to cloud her thoughts as thoroughly as she has clouded mine.

"What I told you on Saturday," I say. "Did you write about it?"

She looks down. "Yes."

"And?"

Her eyes are smiling when she looks back up at me. "I like beginnings," she says.

I don't have class seventh or eighth period, but I hang around at the band hall to wait for Anna. It's empty when I step through the doors, the wide expanse of carpet uncluttered by backpacks or instruments.

"Weston." Mr. Brant's voice slices through the silence. "I thought that was you."

"Sir," I say in greeting. "I'm waiting for Anna so we can work on the duet."

He nods once, his eyes following me as I set my backpack on the row of shelves next to the door.

"I got an email from Mrs. Chase after your assistant period," he says. "She says you didn't turn in your English homework after she gave you a chance to make it up."

"Forgot again," I say. "I'll do it."

"It's too late, Mr. Ryan. She was emailing me to let me know it would be a zero. It's only the second week of school. I shouldn't be getting emails from your other teachers already."

This *fucking* town.

"I'll take care of it," I tell Mr. Brant, trying to keep the irritation from my voice. "It won't happen again."

"It better not," he says. "It's a state year, Weston. If I get more emails like this, I'm going to have to give your part to Darin. We can't afford uncertainty, especially when *you* are the one who is supposed to be helping Anna."

I freeze.

"I can do it," I say, and he must hear the adamance in my voice, because Mr. Brant stares at me for a long time, nods once, and walks back into his office.

I'm at the piano when she comes in, my hands sprawled and angry against the keyboard. I'm pulling up the sea, summoning a tidal wave of music to wash away Mr. Brant's concern, my grades, my parents, everything.

But Anna is the calm after a storm, her song becoming heavy in my fingers when I think of her talk of beginnings, of *us*.

I have to play it, the lifting melody that starts in the depths of the keys and then soars to the sky. It's only a beginning, a possibility, but I can't get it out of my head, especially when she's so close I can smell her shampoo.

These opening lines have sung me to sleep for the past week. Every time I'm near her, every time she smiles at me or her eyes light up over her curved cheeks, another tiny piece of music falls onto the staff.

Anna sets her case down and ignores the chair in the corner completely, coming to sit directly next to me on the bench.

"I can't tell if you were angry when I came in or if you're just a really good pianist," she says, when her song trails off into silence.

"Can't I be both?" I ask.

She looks up at me. "You *are* angry, then."

"No," I say. "I'm not."

I know what she's going to say before she says it.

"The truth," she says. "Remember?"

I lean back on the bench and stare at the ceiling so I don't have to look at her when I speak.

"Mr. Brant asked about my grades before you came in."

From the corner of my eye, I see her mulling this over.

"Why?" she asks. "I mean, if you hate being asked about your grades, you can change them, right?" She pauses, and adds, "I *know* you can. And I offered to help, remember?"

And I don't know if anyone has ever asked me that before, the *why* of it, and I try to process around the swell of pride in my chest that she thinks I'm smart, that she's not questioning my intelligence.

Just your ambition, my brain sneers.

"I guess . . . I don't know. I can do the work," I say. "I understand the assignments. But it's like, between the end of class and the next day, my brain goes somewhere else, and I can never get everything done."

"'Somewhere else' being a place where homework doesn't exist, right?"

She asks like she cares, like she's trying to understand.

"Yeah, exactly."

Anna nods decisively. "Okay, new plan: We'll work on our homework together, and *then* we'll do duet practice."

"But we need the time for the duet," I say. "We only have the week."

"It does me no good to learn the duet if you aren't there to play the other half," Anna says.

I make myself smile even though my insides churn as I say, "I'm replaceable, you know. Darin has had my half memorized since Mr. Brant handed out the sheet music."

"I don't *want* Darin to be my partner," she says with a small smile. "I want *you*, remember?"

Another piece of her melody clicks in place, another bar of music that makes my fingers itch to play it on the keys, to see if it sounds the same in real life as it does in the perfect concert hall that is my head.

"Then we better get started," I say.

And we do. We settle into the real work of it. She doesn't need to just be able to *play* it by Friday, or even play it well, she needs to be able to not play it wrong. Her muscle memory needs to be completely programmed so that if she forgets, if the pressure and expectations get to her, she can play it without thinking.

And we only have four days to do it.

"What about evenings?" I ask her, when we break to stretch our fingers. "Can you practice then?"

Anna scoots to the back of her chair, her saxophone resting on her knee. "*Maybe.*"

I raise an eyebrow, hoping this will be enough to get her to talk without my asking what we both know I want to ask.

She sighs. "My parents are . . . protective."

I nod. "Most are to some degree."

"No, like, *obsessive*," she says, leaning forward. "Like if I'm not home at five on the dot today, Mom will call. Or text. Or send out a search party. Whichever pops into her head first."

I rest my foot on the rubber stopper of her chair. "And they don't like me."

She waits until I meet her eyes. "I don't care what they think."

I wonder if she knows the corner of her mouth twitches when she's lying.

"You do care," I say, and I don't realize until this exact moment that somewhere between last week and today, I've been quietly building not only a melody for Anna, of Anna, but an entire world where her presence is more than a possibility.

Somehow, I went from trying to push her away, to giving up, to beginning to thread her into every thought, every consideration.

"They'll come around once they get to know you," she says softly. "And until then . . ." Her voice trails off, her forehead adorably scrunched, before she looks straight at me, eyes clear. "I can do evenings. I'll have to, or we won't have enough time."

I open my mouth to answer, but I guess my face isn't as unreadable as I've always thought, because Anna cuts me off.

"Hey," she says. She rests her hand gently on my arm, and by some instinct I move to cover it with mine. She smiles at that. "I'm in charge of me. Not them."

Her mouth doesn't twitch.

I don't argue with her, even though I know this conversation isn't over. Instead, we sink back into the rhythm of playing a measure at a time and then stringing it all together.

It's slow, tedious work. This is the part of music that kills people, the cost of it. It's not as easy as sitting down and reading notes on a page, especially when it's not *only* you.

Duets and ensembles and people all pouring themselves into one work, one movement . . . the timing has to be perfect. And even if I feel like she is taking up half my brain or more, Anna and I do *not* share a brain, which is all the more evident when she plays through an accidental, plays a B flat as a B natural, and our combined notes sound less like music and more like a kid banging on pots and pans.

She stops immediately, flinching.

"Um, okay, that was bad," she says, angling her saxophone so she can look at her reed as if it's to blame.

"I need a break anyways," I say. "And we need to figure out if we're going to work more tonight."

"We are," Anna says with certainty, and her mouth barely twitches. "But let me call my parents really quick."

I step out of the practice room to give her privacy. I don't want to hear her lie.

Still, I'm lighting up at the idea of taking her home—we obviously won't be able to practice at her house—wondering if I should take her to Mom's, where we would be completely alone, or if I should take her to Dad's, where we would constantly be interrupted by his telling a story I've heard again and again. There is nothing in the world Dad loves more than a new person to listen to his stories, about pretty much anything.

But even so, taking her to Bloom is more appealing than to Mom's, where the wildfire simmers and might gulp Anna up entirely as soon as we walk through the door.

I don't want to risk it, don't know how I would feel to have Anna in the middle of my childhood living room, near the piano I've played since I was seven.

As I pace in front of the closed door, I decide she could either make everything more bearable or be taken by the flames.

It's not a risk I'm willing to take.

chapter 10

༻ঔ৶

anna

Once, when I forgot to get a progress report for school signed, I forged Mom's signature. I'd seen the even loops of her letters on permission slips and checks for field trips since I could remember.

It was too easy. So was the lie that came later when she asked, "Anna, isn't it time for progress reports?"

"Yes," I said, "but our homeroom teacher forgot to print them, so she said this time you could just look online and email her if you had any questions."

Mom shrugged. "All As?"

It was a question that wasn't a question, but I nodded anyway.

It was a fib. A white lie. And it bothered me how much I wasn't bothered.

It's the safer bet, calling Dad instead of Mom.

"Hey, Bagels. What's up?"

"Hi, Dad. I've got this *massive* science project due at the end of the week," I say. "A couple of us are getting together to work on it this evening. Is it okay if I'm home late?"

"You know that's a question for your mother," he says, "but I don't see why not. What about dinner?"

"We're chipping in and ordering pizza," I say, making my words purposefully slow. "Anyway, we're about to head out and I was going to carpool, so can you tell Mom for me? She didn't answer when I called her cell."

My mouth tightens as I wait to see if he'll accept the lie, feeling more guilt when he does so readily.

"Sure, sure. But be home by seven, okay? You've got rehearsal tomorrow night. It'll be a long day."

"Thanks, Dad."

"Text us when you get there," he says. I'm about to hang up, when he asks, "Whose house are you going to? Lauren's?"

I don't know why I balk at this lie, but I do. "I think so."

"Just text," Dad reminds me. "Love you."

"Love you, too."

The notes still aren't coming. They get stuck in my throat, under my tongue, before spewing out of my saxophone all at once like a geyser.

It's made worse by Weston's unnervingly attentive gaze.

"Drop your jaw," he tells me. "You're clenching up, and it's making your notes wheeze."

"I know, I know," I say.

"And you're cutting that quarter rest into an eighth. It's clashing with my last note."

I lean back in my chair and groan. "Yep."

Weston has been all business, taking the lead and running through our lines measure by measure. He is infuriatingly knowledgeable about the saxophone mechanics, telling me when my jaw is clenching or my mouth has edged too far off the mouthpiece.

"Physics," he explains, when I ask how he could possibly know so much about an instrument he doesn't play. "You aren't giving the air enough room to move, and so it misbehaves."

Any illicit giddiness I felt lying to Dad and Mom about being at Lauren's has dissipated with the hundredth repetition of the same measure and Weston's annoyingly accurate diagnosis of why my playing sucks.

My lips are killing me, more evidence that my embouchure is wrong and I'm clenching too tightly, and I pinch them between my fingers.

"You need a break," Weston says.

It's not a question, but I answer anyway. "Yeah, I do."

He's trying to keep his smile hidden, trying not to let me see that he's amused. "You're grumpy."

"*You're* grumpy!" I snap, and Weston's smile grows.

He stands, setting his horn back in the open case. "Come on," he says.

"Come where?" I ask.

"You need a break," he repeats. "A long one."

"Agreed, but where are we going?"

"You'll see."

I turn the neck of my saxophone upward so the reed won't chip and balance it on top of my case before following Weston out the door, down the stairs, to the side of the trailer.

"A four-wheeler?" I can't keep the surprise from my voice when Weston rests his hand on the seat and grins at me. "You think it's going to be easier for me to learn the duet with two broken arms?"

Weston laughs. "You won't break anything."

"You don't know that," I say, eyeing the four-wheeled death

contraption. "Do you know how many people have come to school with casts on their arms and legs and *necks* because of these things?"

It's large and bulky, the seat looming high enough above my waist that I'm worried my stubby leg won't be able to sling over it. Even if it wasn't moving when I fell off of it, I would probably still get hurt.

Weston's hand brushing against my wrist takes longer to register than it should.

"I won't let anything hurt you," he insists. "I promise."

I'd probably find that a lot more reassuring if my central nervous system wasn't on high alert.

He climbs up onto the seat with practiced ease, his jacket bunching around his waist and his hands coming to rest on his knees.

He holds out a hand, and somewhere in my fear, curiosity raises her head, eager to know what it feels like to wrap my arms around him, to watch the world speed by with nothing between me and the hard ground except Weston's promise.

"You won't go too fast?" I ask.

There is a new smile on his face. It's not the seductive rogue smile or the shy one. It's a beacon, one I'm drawn to like a moth to a flame. But there's no danger in it, only pure unadulterated glee.

Weston raises a blond eyebrow. "Not unless you ask me to." He grins.

As I sling myself up beside him—knocking my knee against the seat in the process—I tell myself that I am brave, that surely I must have a better chance of dying by a lightning strike or in a tragic trombone slide accident than on a four-wheeler.

It takes me a few moments to figure out where to put my hands. His chest? His waist? Maybe a gentle choke hold around his neck to discourage top speed?

I settle for tucking my hands in the pockets of his jacket and then clamping onto his waist for dear life.

"Ready?" he asks, and he doesn't wait for my answer before he turns the key and the engine roars to life, the power of it rumbling our seat.

He starts off slow, the huge wheels eating up the gravel walkway like glass. There is no discernible difference between the rocks and the grass, and I find myself leaning slightly to the side to watch the wheels at work.

"Cool, huh?" he calls over the engine.

At first, he only putters just above a walking pace, taking us from his dad's mobile home, through a grassy field, past his grandparents' house, between his dad's workshop and storage shed—here my grip tightens thanks to the proximity of splintering wood that jabs out at us from either side—and back to the front of his dad's trailer. Down a little dip in the wheel-hewn road, I can see his aunt and uncle's house. It looks just like the map he drew on my palm, a perfect little triangle of Ryans.

Weston kills the engine.

"Okay," he says, twisting to face me. Our faces are close enough that I can smell the sticky lemon scent of his Chap-Stick. "It's your turn."

"I beg your pardon?"

He doesn't wait to argue, turning off the ignition, stepping off the seat, and scooching me forward so he can resettle behind me.

"The thing about the duet, especially since it's a give-and-take, is you've got to be able to pull your weight, drive your part of the music," he says, his breath tickling my ear in a tantalizing way I try to ignore.

"Do *not* pretend this has anything to do with your duet lessons," I threaten darkly.

Weston's arms wrap around my waist, and for once I'm not

at all self-conscious about my size. He is warm and smells like leather heated in the high afternoon sun, and now that my hands are wrapped around the handlebars and his arms are wrapped around me, I'm suddenly eager to drive.

"Squeeze the bars *gently*," he tells me. "Otherwise you'll catapult us over the top and we'll both have broken arms."

"And legs," I add cheerfully.

"Or necks." He laughs. "And this is the brake, so make sure you keep your hand off that one until you need it."

Weston leans forward, pushing me lightly against the handlebars as he turns the key in the ignition. I take a deep breath, pray that Mom and Dad aren't going to find out about my lie because they have to pick me up from the hospital, and gently nudge us forward.

It takes approximately two minutes for my fear to fall away, and another minute of Weston's surprised laughter for me to gun it, the beast of a machine roaring with happiness as we jet across the expanse of knee-high grass.

I feel stupidly alive, like the shadows can never catch me and the future is too far away to be a concern, like I will always be here with a smile on my face and Weston holding on to me with one arm while he brushes my ponytail away from his face with the other.

Eventually, large loops in the grass grow boring, even as the speedometer creeps up to twenty, thirty, then forty miles per hour, the massive engine willing to go as fast as I will let it. Weston shouts near my ear, his finger pointing out to the dirt road beyond us. "We can go," he yells. "We just have to be careful and watch for loose gravel."

I roll to a stop in the middle of the field, leaving the engine on as I twist to say, "If we're heading to the road, can you drive?"

He unwraps his arms from me and nudges me to the back of the seat in answer, swinging himself in front of me and waiting until I'm settled against him before heading for the road.

It's like nothing I've ever felt before, speeding through these old country roads with nothing between me and the air. I tighten my left arm so I can hold my right hand high in the air like on a roller coaster, the wind pushing against my palm as I laugh.

There are different kinds of freedom. There's the kind that looks a lot like adulthood, where you don't have to ask permission or beg forgiveness when making choices that don't cause harm. And then there's this: the wind whipping my hair into tangles I'll have to unsnarl with my fingers when I drive home. There's the knowledge that I will lie to my parents' faces about where I've been and what I've done. And there's the decision to not feel guilty about it, to accept this as the price to pay for watching the world speed by as Weston Ryan drives us down tree-covered roads and over shallow creek beds.

We don't end up practicing again. My phone alarm is beeping as we pull the four-wheeler into his dad's workshop.

"I have to go," I say. "To make it home in time."

"I know," Weston says.

But there's no urgency as we walk toward my car. We don't move quickly. It feels like we are stretching the limits of our little world, one we've woven with whispers of touch, knees bumping and hands on waists.

When I get into my car, Weston braces his arm on my open door, his hair gleaming in the dying light.

"Will you write tonight?" he asks me.

I nod. "Yeah, I will."

"What will you write about?"

The catlike smile that spreads across my face belongs to somebody else. "Guess," I say coyly.

"I don't have to guess," he says, "because I know you."

"I bet you all the money in my wallet you're wrong."

Weston's smile softens, quiets into a searching look. "Beginnings?" he asks hopefully. "Are you going to write about beginnings?"

"You know, eventually beginnings turn into middles," I say. "I can't write about the start of something forever."

I'm leaning in, doing exactly what the magazines warn against. I'm pushing, trying to get Weston to admit what I suspect is true but want to hear all the same: that not only is this a beginning, but there's no end in sight. That he feels these too-big feelings, too, and I'm not alone in stupidly imagining a world where this—where *we*—could go on forever.

He flashes me his mischievous smile. "Maybe when we get past the opening measures of the duet we can talk about middles," he says.

My heart sinks, but I keep my voice casual when I say, "Fair enough." I turn my keys in the ignition and my car's rumble is so much quieter than the four-wheeler. "I should go."

Weston nods and, in a movement so quick I could have blinked and missed it, leans forward and lowers his head.

Like he is going to kiss me.

Like it is normal, expected, *habit*.

At the last second, he stops, his eyes wide.

"Sorry," he says. "I . . . I don't know what I was doing."

If I were braver, if I was the girl who didn't balk at four-wheelers and difficult duet notes, I would rise up and kiss him myself.

But I'm me. I'm the same Anna who has thought something was going *somewhere* only to be told "You're a really great friend" or "I love getting to know you as a person."

I settle for smiling and saying, "Maybe you'll figure it out and you can tell me. So I can write about it, you know."

I can't read Weston's expression.

"See you tomorrow," he says.

All the way home, I wonder if he was going to kiss me, if I would have liked it, if his lips would be warm or cool. If they would taste like lemon.

When I walk through the door, Mom and Dad are watching TV in the living room, one of those stupid reality singing shows that is more about the celebrity judges than about the people trying to be discovered. Two of the judges are arguing loudly about nothing to do with singing.

"How's the science project?" Mom asks.

I wrestle my keys onto the wooden holder by the door that proudly declares, "As for me and my house, we will hang up our keys."

"Good," I say. "I'll probably have to work on it after school every day this week. It's a biggie."

"Seems early in the school year for such a big project," Dad says.

I hadn't thought of that. But he doesn't sound suspicious, so I recover quickly. "It's really just Andy being his usual perfectionist self. He wants to start out the year with a high A."

The crowd on the TV cheers. Mom and Dad say nothing, blessedly done with this conversation.

"I'm going to shower," I tell them.

I'm afraid if my parents get close to me, they'll smell the Bloom wind still trapped in my hair, see the country road dust beneath my fingernails.

I'm afraid they'll smell the leather of Weston's jacket where it was warm against me.

Even after the shower, I'm convinced the smell of leather lingers. I know it's in my head, but I hold on to it all the same, willing it to stay beside me until morning.

chapter 11

weston

Tuesday morning dawns with the realization that I *almost kissed Anna James*.

It was a reflex, something my body did automatically after watching her tuck her short legs into the car, slip her keys into the ignition, and turn her face to me expectantly, like she was waiting for me to *do* something.

My addled brain, still high off the feel of her arms around my waist, her hair tickling my cheek, acted on impulse.

I *leaned*.

The fucking scary part is that she didn't lean away. Not even a little. Not so much as a flinch.

I run the moment over in my head, rewinding and slowing it down, so I can pause on the exact millisecond that she realized what I was doing and the way her breath kind of caught in her throat and her eyes widened.

Not in fear. Not in disgust.

Want.

My phone clock says there's no time to dwell, though. I'm running behind, a cardinal sin in band.

"Early is on time," Mr. Brant always says, "and on time is *late.*"

Inevitably, a freshman will think they're being funny and original by asking, "Then what is late?"

And the entire band will shoot them death glares as we *all* do ten push-ups as a group punishment for sassing.

But nobody will be made to run the extra laps I'm going to earn for every minute I'm late.

That'll be just me.

I end up four minutes late for warm-up stretches. I'll owe an extra mile for my tardiness, which I'll have to run off on my own time, but not today.

I stand in the back and Ratio shoots me a glare from where he leads the stretching at the front with the other band officers.

Anna keeps looking over her shoulder at me. She's standing between Lauren and Terrance, her short arms and leg extended as far as they go, trying her very best to get the stretches *exactly* right.

When she catches my eye, she smiles.

In my year away at Bloom, I'd forgotten how intense fall can be in Enfield.

Not only are you adjusting to new teachers and classes, and not only is all your free time devoted to learning a marching routine and memorizing music, but somehow you have to find extra hours lying around to practice for the talent exhibition dinner the band puts on every October.

It's an annual event to raise money for the band's eternally waning budget, the extra funds brought in going toward uniform cleaning expenses, replacement music stands, and school-owned instrument repairs.

On top of everything else, I've been suckered into practicing a six-hands piano piece to play at the dinner with Ratio and Andy.

It's not as completely random as it sounds. The three of us share a piano teacher—or did, until I stopped taking lessons when I moved. I could have still gone, but it was yet another thing to feed into the wildfire, another thing I didn't want the divorce to touch.

It did anyway, but still.

Ratio had been *pissed* that I quit, and it was made all the worse because I didn't tell him; our teacher did.

But I didn't let him talk me back into lessons. And it's not like I stopped *playing*. I played more than ever, music suddenly an outlet like it had never been before, a way to momentarily douse the fire.

"This shouldn't be too difficult for us, Andy," Ratio says, once we're crammed onto the bench in a practice room after school. "We might have to wait for Weston to catch up, though. He's out of practice."

"I practice way more than you do," I say, but neither responds. They are already leaning forward to dissect the music and decide who gets to play which part.

The bench creaks under our combined weight.

Once we agree on the order—me at the low half, Andy in the middle, Ratio up top—we begin to slowly make our way through the music, pausing to mark places that will need to be worked up or where our hand placement will have to be more carefully choreographed.

But we're experienced players, *great* players, and even though we are sight-reading, the music flows as easily as water from a tap.

"I hate this crescendo," Andy says, when we finish playing all the way through, pointing at the marking on page three.

"Can we just *not*? Weston clearly doesn't need to play those quarter notes at a forte, right?"

"Agreed," I say, reaching across Andy to point at a different page. "And maybe Ratio can bring this bit out more? I couldn't even hear it."

"Yeah, but if you do that, soften the eighth note accent," Andy agrees.

It's a level of music interaction that I missed in Bloom, this common language of understanding what's on the page versus what we actually want to hear. The three of us know the right words to convey what we mean.

And as much as I love—*love?*—working with Anna . . . she's new. She's voracious, a quick study, but she's got so much to learn.

This is a different level.

Like he's picked her name from my thoughts, Andy finishes arguing with Ratio about hand placement and turns to me.

"So . . . you and Anna, huh?"

Ratio leans an elbow on the top of the piano, propping his head on his fist. "Yeah, Weston. Do tell."

If it was only Ratio, this would be fairly normal, but the addition of Andy—a guy I've said maybe ten words to before today—is bizarre.

"We are *so* not having this discussion," I tell them.

Andy and Ratio share a look, and Andy slowly lowers the keyboard cover.

"Ratio, can't you, like, command him to talk about it?" Andy asks. "I want to know if there's a *real* reason that Anna has been ditching us at lunch to go to the band hall."

"I think that falls outside of my reach as drum major, unfortunately."

"You *think*?" I ask.

Andy is unbothered at our closeness, guilelessly using our proximity to his advantage by flicking my shoulder repeatedly.

"What *are* you doing?" I ask.

"Thumping," he says casually. "It drives Anna nuts when I do this." I must look confused, because Andy smiles and adds, "I figure if she likes you, y'all must have a lot in common, right?" *Thump.* "So, this probably irritates you, too."

"This would irritate *anyone*," I say.

Ratio and Andy don't say anything, and I can practically hear them waiting for me to take the bait, to ask if Anna has talked to Andy about me.

"She *likes* you likes you, you know," Andy says, to break the silence.

My heart races, and I wonder if they can hear it in the quiet of the room. "Does she?"

Andy's flick is replaced with a punch. "Duh, dude. *Ask her out.*"

Ratio makes an irritated gesture, which jars Andy into my side. "That's what I told him, but he won't listen."

"Well, who *will* he listen to, then?" Andy asks.

We turn our heads to the door like meerkats when we hear a soft knock.

It cracks open to reveal Anna, her eyes wide and smiling.

"Is this a party?" she asks.

Andy and Ratio turn to grin at me, their smiles thin and devious.

"*No*," I tell Anna, while glaring at them, "it's not. We were practicing for the talent show."

"Weston here was just saying how much he's enjoyed working on the duet with you," Andy tells her, his voice innocent.

Anna's smile grows as her ears turn the faintest of pinks. "Did he tell you that we agreed to practice a little before rehearsal tonight? Can I borrow him?"

"You are *more* than welcome to have him," Ratio says.

Andy pushes me sideways off the bench. "Keep him," he says. "He thinks his repeating quarter notes are the melody."

I grab my bag and stand at Anna's side, both of us crammed into the open door.

"Come on, Anna," I say. "Let's go somewhere a little less crowded."

"I can't speak for Ratio," she laughs, "but any room with Andy in it is too crowded."

"Is that why you told me you tried to poison him with the soap?"

Andy laughs, and Anna elbows me in the ribs harder than I think she realizes. "You weren't supposed to tell him that," she stage whispers.

Ratio and Andy are still laughing when we close the door on them.

I wonder if maybe the last Kauaʻi ʻōʻō wasn't as lonely as I think. Maybe he found other birds to pass the time with, friends to ease the loneliness.

They weren't his. They weren't other Kauaʻi ʻōʻōs.

But they would do.

chapter 12

∾

anna

It was early September when Jake Pender, a football player who thought himself a gift from God to the good people of Enfield, began to bully Kevin Perry at his locker after school.

Jake was careful. He smiled. But we knew. We knew.

And we didn't do anything about it.

But one day, I was tired from marching rehearsal, sick of the late September heat that permeated everything, and it made me bold.

"Shove off, Jake," I said, coming to stand between them. "You know, your mom's always asking me how you are at school. We work together sometimes in the little kids' church. Maybe I should take the time to chat?"

He stepped back slowly, eyes narrowing. "Maybe. 'Bye, Anna. Have a good day, Kevin."

After he was far enough away, I turned to Kevin. "Hey, I'm sorry. He's a jerk. You okay?"

Kevin shrugged. "Happens all the time," he said. "Used to it."

I'd expected a thank you. Or a grateful smile. But I was the jerk for thinking he owed me anything in the first place when I had done nothing to stop it before.

Weston and I rehearse Wednesday afternoon until the last possible second, only leaving the band hall when Mr. Brant turns off the lights and threatens to lock us inside.

"You're doing better," Weston tells me, as we walk to our cars.

"Enough to do well on Friday?"

"We almost have it," Weston says, and there's not an ounce of doubt in his voice. "Really."

I like how he says "we." I like how he has lumped his fate in with mine.

We, I think, might be my new favorite word.

"When will we practice again?" I ask, if only to hear myself say the word out loud.

Our steps slow as we come to my car, and I try to dig through the side pocket of my backpack with one hand to retrieve my keys. Cutting my struggle short, Weston pulls them out and opens the back door to help put away my case, my bag.

"We should practice tonight," he says. "It's only today and tomorrow left before the playoff."

I watch him as he carefully arranges my saxophone on the floorboard, my backpack in the seat. His hair is growing in the slightest bit, and his skin is darker from two weeks straight in the sun, but no one would dare call him tan. I think this is the most color he'll ever have.

I've noticed his facial hair has flecks of red in it when the sun catches it just right. I wonder if he's a genetically suppressed redhead, if somewhere in an alternate universe there is a redheaded Weston with the same pale skin and blue eyes.

If alternate-universe Weston *also* has arms that are leanly muscular, with tendons that stretch taut as he kindly wrestles things into my car.

"Tonight," I agree.

Wednesday dinners are almost always tacos, but when I come through the garage door and hang my keys, I smell Dad's homemade pasta sauce and garlic bread.

"You're *late*, Anna," Dad says, as I drop my backpack on the couch. I hope they don't ask where my saxophone is. It's in the car, waiting for our escape to Weston.

"Sorry. Was working on that project. I texted that I would be late."

They are already sitting at the kitchen table, their forks suspended over half-eaten plates of pasta, as I slide into my seat.

"You've been late all week," Mom says. Her voice is stern, but not angry.

Not yet.

"Sorry, sorry," I repeat. "It's this project." Apparently, I'm great at outright lying now, even though two weeks ago the thought would have been abhorrent, because I purposefully echo what I said last time. "You can blame Andy. He swears he's going to rise to second in class rank this year."

"What's your ranking?" Dad asks, and blessedly everyone is back to eating spaghetti, the thin line of tension dissolved.

"Twelfth, last time I checked," I say through a mouthful of garlic bread. "But we're all so close in GPAs that our rankings switch around each time there's a major test."

Jenny stabs at her spaghetti. School doesn't come naturally to her like it does me, which is probably why she says, "Mom, Anna has to come to my dance dress rehearsal tomorrow, right?"

"I can't," I say before Mom can respond. "I have that playoff for my duet on Friday, and Lauren promised to help me run through it. Also, we've got the final touches for the project to do at Andy's."

It feels dangerous, mentioning the duet when I've purposefully not brought it up around my parents. I don't want them to have a reason to even think of Weston Ryan, to suspect how I might be spending my time.

"*Anna*," Mom begins, and I put my fork down at her tone. "In this family we support each other. It's important to your sister that you come to her dress rehearsal."

"But I'll go to the *real* performance on Saturday," I argue. "Why do I have to see it twice?"

"I watch you play at the football games every Friday, and it's the same thing every week," Jenny says. "Right, Mom?"

I stop the words on my tongue, but they clang loudly in my brain: *Nobody asked you to come.*

Which isn't strictly true, or fair.

It's not like Mom and Dad can leave her alone when they come to the game. She's twelve, but a "young twelve," as Mom calls it.

When our parents try—and I suspect fail—to silently communicate on their side of the table, Jenny and I carry on an entire argument with our eyes.

I don't care that I'm probably mean for giving her the dirtiest look I can; she knows what she's doing.

"Jenny, honey," Mom starts with a placating tone, and right on cue, Jenny's eyes start to water.

"But what about my *rehearsal*," she begs. "You can sit *closer*. You can see *more* of the routine."

Her performance is good, I'll give her that. If I can play the duet half as well on Friday, I'll be in good shape.

"I'll be able to see you plenty on Saturday," I say, softening my tone so Mom can't recognize it as the jab I want it to be.

Jenny knows, though, her face crumpling at the edges in one last attempt to convince Mom to make me come to her rehearsal.

This is why I can't stand her, ninety-nine percent of the time.

After dinner, I tell Mom and Dad that I'm going to youth group for their Wednesday night meetup.

"It'll be nice to have a break from the project and stuff," I say. "I had a good time with them last weekend."

Mom stops loading the dishwasher to look at me. "If you have time to go to youth group tonight, you have time to go to your sister's dance recital tomorrow."

Rehearsal, I think, but I bite the side of the mouth to stop the word from coming out, making myself smile instead.

"They're having a special speaker tonight," I lie. "A missionary. I planned around having time to go."

Dad moves past us to dump a handful of table crumbs into the sink, setting the soggy sponge back in its cow-shaped holder.

"Let her go, babe," he says. "She'll go to Jenny's deal on Saturday."

Mom isn't thrilled, but she's not mad, either. I give her a kiss on the cheek when I leave.

"Thanks for letting me go tonight," I say.

She pats my hand where it rests on her shoulder. "You know we love you, Anna. I just want you to remember your little sister, too."

"Who could forget?" I ask dryly.

Mom swats my hand.

"Go to church and pray for a better attitude," she says.

"Is *that* what we're going to waste our miracle on?" Dad asks, laughing.

I stick my tongue out at them and close the door behind me.

"Siblings are annoying," I tell Weston in greeting when I get to his dad's house. "Jenny tried to sabotage us meeting tomorrow."

"How?"

"Oh, she has a freakin' dress rehearsal for her dance thing, and she wanted me to come."

Weston pulls a plastic chair from the kitchen to the living room and gestures at me to sit. "She doesn't actually want you to come?"

"Yes. No. I don't know. I don't *care*. I'll see the real thing on Saturday."

He drags another chair beside mine, mellophone in hand. "I always play better when I know people are watching. Maybe she's nervous."

"She's *not* nervous," I say. "She's annoying. And she knows it."

Weston doesn't say anything. He just sets our music on a crappy music stand prone to toppling, raises his brows at me, and begins a silent countdown. And we begin.

It's all kinds of distracting when he stops playing to point out a missed accent or a place where I'm rushing the beat and his knee brushes against mine.

I've *almost* got my half of the duet, I'm sure of it. The more we play, the nitpickier Weston becomes, stopping for the barest hint of playing into a rest, the slightest mistake.

It's mind-numbing, lip-numbing. I need a break.

"Let's go four-wheeling," I say.

I can tell it takes all of Weston's self-control to say, "We play for Mr. Brant the day after tomorrow."

I groan, sliding farther down in my chair. "Tyrant."

Weston's mouth quirks. "You'll thank me when you don't have your part given to Ryland."

"I can't believe it's already been two weeks of my *junior year*," I say. "Like . . . it's only one more year after this, and then I'm out in the real world."

"Tell me about it," he says. "Try being a senior and having literally every person in your grade call everything 'the last first day' or 'the last first football game' or 'the last *second* football game.' Everything is pageantry and remembering something before it's over."

"Aren't these supposed to be the best days of our lives, though?" I say. "Aren't we supposed to cherish them or whatever?"

Weston sets his mellophone down beside him and rubs his fingers. "But that's stupid," he says, "because if it's true, what's the point of living past this? Why does anybody bother?"

I get the sense that we're done working on the duet for a moment, so I unclip my saxophone and pop my neck.

"That's a terrible habit," he tells me, the intensity ebbing.

"My neck hurts," I say. "Almost always does. Terrance and Samantha say *their* necks are fine, but mine is constantly sore. I guess I wasn't meant to be a saxophone after all."

Weston stands up, and I'm about to join him, when he puts a hand on my shoulder. "Stay," he says. "I'm going to help your neck feel better."

"Good luck," I say. "If the football team's physical therapist can't do anything about it, you certainly aren't—"

My words die when he lifts my hair and cups my neck between thumb and forefinger, gently kneading.

"Tell me if I hurt you," he says.

But his words are distant. I am in a vortex of thoughts and tingling feelings that swirl from my neck through the rest of my body as his fingers caress me in a firm but careful grip.

A *boy*, an attractive boy who lets me sleep on his arm, is *rubbing my neck*.

All my life at church—including the group I'm supposed to be at tonight—they have told us "youth" all the things we're supposed to *save*. It's not enough to be sexually pure. It's not enough to love God and read your Bible. To be truly holy, they say, to be *desirable* as a future spouse, you have to keep your emotions pure, too.

It never seemed like a problem I needed to worry about, really, so I never thought about it. I had crushes. I liked boys from afar. But I never once thought that the storm brewing inside me could feel so dangerous. So *real*.

Part of me feels guilty, dirty, for even thinking about all the things we've been told not to while Weston is standing so close.

I make a sound, an embarrassing whimper, when his other hand comes up to put pressure on my shoulder, too.

"Better?" he asks, laughing. I tilt my head back to see that Weston Ryan is smiling at me.

And it occurs to me that he's heard the same things about purity and love and *waiting* all of his life. Of course he has; he's from Enfield.

I wonder if what he said about not being good for me or being dangerous or whatever has anything to do with the way he is looking at me now: grinning, but with that burn lurking in his eyes, the corner of his mouth.

"Much better," I whisper.

"Good," he says. "Ready to practice?"

I'm not, but we do.

That night, my journal propped open on my pillow and my phone flashlight beside it, I stare at a blank page, trying to figure out how I can remotely explain what it felt like to be at the mercy of Weston Ryan's strong piano fingers.

Instead, what comes out is anger and a venom that surprises me. My pen flies across the page, trying to make sense of a world where Weston and his slow smile and kind hands are dangerous or wrong or something to be avoided.

I write about Lauren, how she *still* won't acknowledge Weston's existence at rehearsals, even when he's right beside me. How she still gives him *looks* when she thinks I can't see. I write about Andy, who, after their talent show practice with Ratio, admitted that Weston might not be so bad.

Why did Weston not get the benefit of the doubt that Andy gives everyone else? What is so different about him that he's not considered worth friendship until he proves himself?

And why can't he see what I see in him?

chapter 13

weston

When I wake Thursday morning, I can't shake this weird half dream of losing my jacket, of Ratio gently taking it from my shoulders and saying, "It's for your own good, you know."

It's not the first time I've had a jacket stress dream. God knows I've gotten enough shit for it over the years.

I know it isn't so much my jacket as it is the fact that I *want* to wear it, which I have never understood. James Dean wore a leather jacket. Lots of the guys on TV wear them. And even though it started off as a joke when I tried one on during my birthday shopping trip with Mom in seventh grade, I really, really love it. It makes me feel like if the zombie apocalypse happened or an old man with a magic staff called me to adventure, I'd be ready to go at a moment's notice. Or at least I'd have plenty of pockets. Who doesn't want more pockets? The interior lining alone has *four*.

The dream remnants make rolling over in bed feel like a

chore. My sheets here at Mom's, heavier than my others, beg me to stay.

I can't imagine going to school right now; my headspace is somehow completely compromised by my quickly fading dream. But I also can't imagine not seeing Anna for an entire day.

It feels like a good day to break the barrier and text her.

Have you ever skipped school before?

Three little dots appear and are quickly replaced with, Of course not. And a second later, Funnily enough, I feel very sick today. Probably best to play it safe. Don't want to infect the band. Want to be in good shape for the duet playoff tomorrow.

I call her. She answers on the second ring.

"We could practice the duet," I say. "So, it wouldn't really be skipping."

"It would still be skipping," she says, and I can hear her smile, her car door opening, and the scraping of her case as she slides it into the backseat. "But I'm all for justifying it to ourselves. How will we get away with it without Mr. Brant knowing?"

I roll my eyes. "Text Lauren and Andy that you're home sick with food poisoning. They'll tell Mr. Brant. I'll call Ratio and let him know my throat is killing me and I have a fever. He'll tell me to stay home, and tell Mr. Brant."

Anna snorts. "You make it sound so easy. Where should I go, though?"

"My mom's house," I say. "I'll text you the address."

"Okay," she says.

Anna and I do not practice. At least, not right away.

When her car crunches onto the gravel drive, I watch from my upstairs window as she parks, steps from her little black Toyota, and stares up awestruck at the house.

It's almost comical, how her mouth pops open as she looks from the wraparound porch to the turret, how her eyes roam the Victorian that Dad built just for Mom, with lots of windows for optimal natural lighting and gazing out at the endless trees that circle the house.

Anna must be mentally calculating, trying to fit this into the equation of my life after seeing Dad's mobile home, my old green van. From where she stands, she can't see the red sports car I wrecked two weeks after Mom and Dad bought it for my sixteenth birthday, which still sits behind Dad's old work shed.

She's staring, frozen in place, when I come through the side door to stand on the porch above her.

"You live in a fairy house," she says wonderingly. "You didn't tell me."

"What should I have said?" I ask, folding my arms and leaning against the white railing.

"'Hi, my name's Weston. I live in a fairy house in the middle of a forest. Do you want to see it?'"

"Would have been that easy, huh?"

Anna looks at me, her eyes quietly bold as she takes me in more thoroughly than the house.

"Easier," she whispers, the tips of her ears turning pink.

I laugh. "Want to see something cool?"

Anna's eyes smile before her mouth does.

"Is this the part where the years of abstinence sex education come into play?" she jokes. "Is the 'something cool' your bedroom in your empty, parentless house?"

She's still smiling, but her voice hitches, so I don't tease when I say, "Of course not. I . . ." The white painted wood beneath my hands feels sticky in my palm. "I would never pressure you to do that, you know," I tell her. "I mean . . . you *do* know that, right?"

Anna looks as glad as I am that we are separated by a porch and the stretch of landscaping between us.

"I know that, Weston," she says, interlocking her fingers and twisting them. She doesn't look at me. And then, under her breath, she mumbles something that sounds an awful lot like, "You wouldn't have to pressure me."

And for once, the wildfire that blazes around me has nothing to do with the divorce or this house or anything remotely painful.

It has *everything* to do with Anna's red ears, her shy eyes, the way she unwinds her fingers to rub her neck, the way her voice dips low when she has just enough bravery to ask a question but not enough to look me in the eye when she does.

There are a million things I want to ask her in this moment, but I'm afraid I misheard her, that this is a cosmic joke and the punch line is me.

Your parents felt this way about each other, too, my brain whispers.

It's enough to sober me, to chase the questions far away and rebuild some of the barriers I've helped tear down. I pretend not to have heard her.

"Do you want a tour of the house?" I ask.

If she is bothered by my clear evasion of *that* conversation, she doesn't show it, running back to her car to fetch her saxophone case before bounding up the steps to my side.

"Yes, please."

We come in through the side door, because nobody ever bothers using the heavy wooden one at the front. It spits us right into the living room, with its bright yellow floral couches and soft green walls, my piano the focal point beside the staircase.

Anna makes her way to the piano immediately, her eyes wide.

"It's so much bigger than the one at Andy's house," she says, carefully touching the highest key.

"It's a grand," I say. "His is a baby grand, if memory serves."

"It's beautiful," she murmurs, touching another key but not pressing down. "Why does this one have a crack in it?"

I come to stand beside her, and it's an effort not to replay the entire conversation I sidestepped on the porch, to ask her if *she* would *ever*.

"Ivory," I say, pointing to the keyboard. "Restored, of course. It's over a hundred years old. Mom keeps saying she's going to call the restoration guy to come fix that key, but until then I just use glue."

"It's beautiful," Anna says.

"It is," I agree. I'm careful not to look at her when I say it so she doesn't accuse me of being cheesy.

But it is beautiful. Hours and hours I've practiced on these keys, this bench, pouring myself into the strings, the pedals. I was calling, I realize, waiting to see if anyone might answer. And here she is, Anna James, sparkling and pink-cheeked and *here*.

We make our way up the stairs to my room, with its deep red walls and antique globe wallpaper that borders the vaulted ceiling.

Anna makes a beeline for my desk beneath the double windows, turning the replica of the *King's Reign* hourglass over where it sits beside my laptop.

"What is this?"

"An old-fashioned timer."

Anna rolls her eyes. "I *know* it's an hourglass. But why do you have it? It's so . . . ornate."

"It's a replica. From a video game. *King's Reign.*"

"It's cool," she says.

And it takes everything in me not to explain that it's not

just *cool*; it's a limited-edition collectible made of Chechen wood and carved by master artisans in Germany.

"It was a gift from my parents," I say instead.

"So, you like video games?"

My eyes trail her as she wanders around my bedroom, inspecting the books on my shelves and the framed family photos Mom put up near the window. It feels like having my insides cracked open, and I'm frozen, waiting for her to decide if she likes what she sees.

My stereo, which Ratio calls "asininely large," takes up nearly half the wall beside the flat screen I inherited from my parents when they upgraded their bedroom TV a couple years ago. I suddenly wish I'd thought to dust the top of it, but maybe she's short enough that she can't see. At least I straightened my brown comforter.

"Yeah, I like video games," I remember to answer.

"Why?"

Her question isn't accusatory or judgy. Only curious.

I sigh. "I guess because the story waits for you, you know? If I'm not there, nothing happens."

"So, you like video games and music because they give you power?"

"I like video games and music because I am *essential*," I say. And because she's not the only one who has grown disturbingly astute in this relationship, I add, "*You* like writing because it gives you power."

Anna's mouth pops open as she turns from where she was examining a photo of Mom, Dad, and me on a beach in Mexico, our grins huge beneath sunglasses and hats.

"Are you calling me power-hungry?"

I smile. "I'm saying that maybe we both gravitate toward interests that give us something we need."

She wanders back to the hourglass, turning it over in her

hand. "Do you think relationships are the same?" Anna asks. "That they give us something we need?"

My mind goes to my parents—the *last* thing I want to think of when Anna James is in my bedroom asking me about relationships. But I think of how they used to smile at each other across church foyers and now have an attendance schedule around football games to avoid being in the same space. I think about them, because what happens when your needs change? What happens when the person you love is no longer enough?

You break up. You divorce. You finally say what you mean, and it's all angry.

I don't want that to happen to me and Anna.

"I think relationships are a waste of time," I tell her coolly.

Anna sets the hourglass down with a *thump* and walks toward me with unnervingly slow steps. When we're almost touching, she stands on tiptoe and gently pulls my head down so she can whisper in my ear, "I know you, Weston Ryan." Her lips smile against my ear. "And I know when you're lying."

I can't think of an answer, can't think through the roar of smoke in my ears, but Anna must know that, too.

"Let's go practice," she says, her voice hushed.

So I follow her bobbing hair down the stairs where I knocked out a tooth when I was six, past the kitchen with its yellow walls and table that's held hundreds of after-school snacks, and into the living room, with the piano that stands watch as Anna James and I work our way through the duet that binds us.

Later, after what feels like hours of practice broken up by bouts of Anna forcing me to sit at the table and do homework with her, Anna's face glows with triumph the second time we play through the duet perfectly.

"I'm not a Gilligan!" she crows. "I'm not completely useless!"

Her laughter, normally infectious, makes my stomach contract. Her Christmas tree ring glitters in the light as she moves to set her saxophone in its case.

"Let's go to that tree house you were telling me about earlier," she says, leaning forward to shake my arm. "Let's go celebrate. We *did* it!"

Her face falls when I don't respond, my face stone, but I tell myself not to care.

This is the good-bye part. We'll go to the fort, we'll laugh and have a good time or whatever, and tomorrow, after we play our duet, everything will go back to normal. I'll beg Ratio to sit next to me on the bus. Anna will go back to sitting with Andy or Lauren or someone that isn't me.

I hope they let her sleep on their shoulder.

I hope they check her hat box for smuggled candy.

"Weston?"

My back is turned. I don't want her to see the way my eyes are stinging red.

"Let's go, then," I say, and my voice is hollow.

"What about my—"

"Leave it," I say, rubbing my eyes. "We'll come back for them."

Anna is quiet as she follows me out the front door, down the porch steps, and toward the trees.

"*Weston*," she says when the platform is in sight, the setting sun blinding us. "What's wrong?"

I won't answer. *Can't* answer. I can't tell her how I'm afraid that after tomorrow she'll have no reason to stay. I can't tell her that for all my talk about relationships being toxic and temporary, the thought of not seeing her every day, of never getting to touch her neck or her hair again, is *killing* me.

"I know you," she whispers, and it almost hurts to have her touch my back in a hesitant but familiar way. "I *know* you."

My swallow gets stuck in my throat.

"Tell me something you know," I say. "The truth."

Anna gently turns me so I'm facing her, my legs pressing back against the trunk of a large oak.

"I know you're not telling me something," she says. "And I know it probably has to do with . . . me?"

She says it like a question, but her eyes are steady as she looks up at me.

"Now, tell me something you know," she says. And with a quirk of her lips that isn't so much a smile as a grimace, she adds, "The truth."

There are too many thoughts flitting through my head, so I pick the one that springs most readily to my lips.

"I know that after tomorrow things will be different," I say.

Her face doesn't change. "In what way?"

It's too much to hold eye contact with her. To look into those fathomless brown eyes resting beneath wisps of hair tangling in her lashes, under curious eyebrows, framed by ears missing all their pink.

I try to turn back, to get out from beneath her gaze, but Anna stops me with a firm hand.

"Weston, what will be different tomorrow?"

She sounds alarmed, so I don't resist when she pulls me back to look at her. Does she not know?

"After the playoff, we will go back to . . . whatever we were before," I say. "There won't be anything holding us together."

Anna's eyebrows drop faster than gravity. She raises her hands. Lowers them. Brings them up to tug her ponytail into place. Drops them to her sides, curling them into fists before loosening them.

"Oh," she says. "Sitting next to me on the bus last week and holding me while I slept? Showing me your house, your *life*? That was nothing?"

Her voice is hard, but I can't figure out why she's so angry at me for telling the truth.

"After everything I told you about the friend zone and how much I hate, hate, *hate* it there. It's just . . . done? You're done, right? That's what you're saying?"

If this conversation was a carousel, it would be one where wires have gotten crossed and it is now going too fast to hold on. Demonic carousel horses rising and falling at a speed faster than light.

"Well, let me tell you what *I* know, Weston," she charges on. "Let me tell you what I've figured out about *you* over the last two weeks. I've learned that you are brilliant. Like, stupid brilliant. But you don't treat me like *I'm* stupid for not being as brilliant. Because you're kind. You don't think you are, because I guess somebody somewhere made you think you were too different to be anything but a freak, but you're not a freak. You're . . ."

Anna pauses to inhale. I open my mouth, but she steps impossibly closer and presses a finger to my lips.

"No," she says. "I'm not finished."

I pull her finger away. "Let me tell you something *I* know," I say. "We'll take turns."

Her phone alarm goes off, but Anna reaches into her pocket and turns it off without looking. "What do you know?" she asks.

She sounds like she did after last week's Tuesday night rehearsal, when I told her I was no good for her.

She sounds tired.

She sounds lonely.

She sounds like *me*.

And the tiny part of me that I've been batting away, the one that believes in the possibility of *actually* getting to keep Anna James in my life, is starting to glow. The Kaua'i 'ō'ō flutters on a fence nearby, watching. Waiting.

"I know that your parents don't like me," I say, but there is no fire in my words. "I know that you say you don't care about it, but you do."

"That was two things," Anna says. "It's my turn."

She said at least three things to start, but I let her continue.

"I know that you are using all the excuses in the world to try and say we can't be . . . that you and me aren't . . ."

I raise my eyebrows. "The truth," I remind her.

"Together," she finishes. I thrill at the word on her lips, even as my stomach plummets.

Her chin lifts slightly, like she's daring me to argue, but her eyes are hoping I won't.

"I know it's not that simple," I tell her. "I know that *you* know I'm a wreck. I'm not like Andy or Lauren or Ratio or any of them. I know this because they've *told* me so. For years."

"*That's not a bad thing*," Anna interjects. "Different isn't *bad*."

"But different is always hard," I tell her. "I know that much."

Anna's phone rings. She looks at the screen with a sigh and raises it to her ear.

"Hi, Mom. I was about to call. I'm running a little late. We were putting the finishing touches on and then Andy ran up to the grocery store to grab more glue." She pauses and laughs, but it sounds forced. "Yeah, typical. I'll be home soon. How did Jenny's rehearsal go? Oh, good. Tell her congrats for me. Yep. Love, love, love you, too. 'Bye."

We're quiet as she struggles to put her phone away in the dim light.

"I know that kills you," I say softly. "Lying to them."

"It doesn't, though," she argues, her head snapping up. "Did I give you any indication that skipping school today was this huge deal?"

"It *does* bother you," I say. "And that's okay."

Anna looks away. "Whose turn is it?"

My shoulders loosen, and I lean against the tree again. "I don't know."

The silence between us is not silent. Locusts scattered in the trees sing out their twilight symphony. There are no duets here, just a chorus of voices clamoring to be the loudest, the brightest.

"Can it be my turn?" she asks.

"Sure."

She is painfully close.

"I know it's that everyone thinks *I* am the good influence on *you* and not the other way around."

"But aren't you?"

"Aren't *you*?"

"I know that you're good," I tell her, leaning forward to tower over her, to try to make her understand. "I know that you have good friends and good grades and are too good for someone who isn't even sure how to be good to himself anymore."

Her eyes widen, but I press on. "I know that the only reason I asked you to skip school today was because even though I know I can't be with you, that I *shouldn't* be with you, I wanted you near me."

The sun is not so much setting as already set, but her eyes still glow beneath me, her head upturned.

"I know we could be good for each other," she says. "I know that I want to be near you, too."

The wolves inside me are circling, their growls mixing with Anna's melody as it swims through my head.

It would be nothing at all to lean forward and kiss her. I wonder if she would make the same sound she made when I rubbed her neck yesterday.

We hover like that, our lips only centimeters apart, and Anna says, "I have to go home." She sounds regretful.

"Okay," I say. We aren't kissing, but my lips definitely brush hers when I add, "We have to play our duet in the morning."

"I know."

Her eyes are closed, her lips begging for me to close the distance between us properly.

I'm *this close* to giving in.

But I want to wait. The pieces of me that remember suitcases by the door and the empty feeling that comes when the floor falls out from beneath your feet wants to see what we look like when the duet is complete . . . when she doesn't have any practical reason to stay.

I don't kiss her, but I clasp her hand in mine. I press it hard against my lips, and her pink cheeks turn up in a small smile.

"Tomorrow," I say. A promise.

"Tomorrow," she echoes.

After she grabs her case, I walk her to her car.

"I almost forgot," she says, reaching into her backpack where it sits on the passenger seat. "I was going to give you this after rehearsal, but then we didn't go, so . . ."

She presses a glow-in-the-dark star into my hand, its eerie green plastic winking up in the landscape lighting.

"It's for good luck," she says. "For tomorrow. It's . . . it's a wishing star. Or a thinking star. Or just a hunk of plastic you can throw away after I'm gone."

"Thank you," I say, wishing I had something to give her.

She must read this in my face, she must *really* know me, because she smiles and says, "You don't have to give me anything.

You already gave me a four-wheeler ride *and* a neck massage *and*, you know, hours of musical assistance."

"Not bad coming from a tyrant." I smile.

It's nearly midnight when she texts me a blurry unfocused photo of her ceiling, a constellation of glow-in-the-dark stars, captioned "Same sky."

I fall asleep with the star she gave me nestled in my palm.

chapter 14

❧

anna

"What does a kiss taste like?"

We were twelve years old and sitting in a circle at summer camp, pigtails and buns and stringy shower hair reflected in the glow of our phones as we lounged in cabin 13.

The authority on the subject was a girl named Vanessa who had, she gleefully recounted, kissed her girlfriend on the lips *before summer break.*

Vanessa sighed like she had seen it all. "Well," she said, "it tastes like whatever the person ate last, so for me it was watermelon Popsicles and Sprite."

"What did it taste like for her?*" I asked.*

Vanessa smiled, barely able to contain her laughter. "Hot dogs!"

I wondered how long it would be before I found out what my first kiss would taste like.

I arrive early and the band hall is eerily empty.

Weston isn't here yet, so I take my favorite reed out and stick it in my mouth to moisten while I rub my saxophone with my polishing cloth until it gleams.

"I'm not going to be judging you on the shininess of your instrument," Mr. Brant says, and I jump at his voice.

I didn't hear him come out of his office.

He smiles when I meet his eyes. "Door wasn't closed," he says in explanation. "I'm glad to see you are feeling better, Miss James."

"Thank you, sir," I say around the reed. "It was just a stomach bug."

"Why don't you come into my office, Anna? Set up your stands and chairs if you want them."

"We have the music memorized, sir," I say, sliding the ligature over the reed and tightening it to hold it in place.

Mr. Brant's smile is small, nearly hidden beneath his full beard. "All the same, come in while we wait for Mr. Ryan. Ms. Moe is just in the back here, beginning to sort through music for the Christmas program."

His office is the size of a classroom, the walls lined with built-in bookshelves full of scores and CDs and records. There's a jar with rows of names etched into the bright blue glass, a gift from the graduating class of 2003. It's filled with lemon drops, which nobody ever dares to take because they'll be lectured on the dangers of sugar and instruments.

Trophies that couldn't fit on the band hall shelves or front office display cases are crammed next to stacks of paper, buried beneath sticky notes, the accolades far too numerous to all get special attention.

But they serve their purpose here, reminding me that the Bearcat band does *not* lose, ever.

I'm not going to be the one to break the chain.

Mr. Brant sits in his office chair like a king. He looks at me

with that all-knowing band director gaze, as if he can divine
how many hours I've spent practicing this duet just by staring
at my saxophone.

"I'm glad you're early," he says, gesturing at one of the cushy
armchairs along the wall. "Take a seat, please."

I do, wishing the blinds of his office were open so I could
see when Weston comes in, but they are almost always shut.
I suppose even the long-suffering Mr. Brant needs a place to
get away.

"Ratio tells me you're going to start helping Weston with
his homework," he says. "Is this true?"

I shift uncomfortably in my seat. "I'm encouraging him to
do it," I say, "but I'm not sure how much help I'll be with the
actual *doing* of the homework."

"But he's responding? He's completing the assignments?"

I narrow my eyes. "Sir?"

Mr. Brant mumbles something to himself. "Okay, here's
what we're going to do: You're going to keep helping Weston
with homework until the end of marching season . . ."

There is a long pause.

"And?" I prompt.

"*And* then there will be no issues when it comes to the
marching competitions."

Mr. Brant's and my relationship is an odd one. I see him
more than I see my parents during marching season. I—along
with most everyone else in band—have accidentally called
him "Dad" at least once, and if something was wrong, I know
I could talk to him and he would listen and do his best to help.

He's a good teacher, a good man, who for some reason has
decided it's worth being away from his wife and kids for a
significant portion of his days to teach a bunch of sweaty high
schoolers how to play music and march in time on a field.

But I've never been one of his favorites. How could I be?

I'm the newest, the idiot that joined her freshman year without knowing anything about anything, the one who is constantly trying to catch up.

I'm not used to this level of frankness, and it disarms me enough that I say, "I was going to help Weston even if you didn't tell me to, sir."

Mr. Brant leans back in his chair, steeples his fingers, and squints at me. "Ah."

"What?" I ask.

"Ratio failed to mention this part," Mr. Brant said.

"Which part?" I ask.

Mr. Brant ignores me and raises his eyes to the door.

"Mr. Ryan, welcome. We were just talking about you. I trust you, too, are feeling better today?"

"Yes, sir." Weston's voice is still-not-awake deep, raspy around the edges. When he comes to stand beside me, I can smell his shampoo.

We don't look at each other. *Can't* look at each other. There is one task at hand, *one*, and trying to see if he has thought about our almost-kiss as much as I have is *not* that task.

"Ms. James appears to be returning your favor of teaching her the duet by assisting you with your studies. I was thanking her on your behalf, and the band's. Let's finish your senior year strong, shall we?"

"Agreed," Weston says.

Mr. Brant swivels toward his computer to give us a moment to tune. I adjust to Weston, moving my mouthpiece and dropping my tense jaw until my tone is round and fits snugly alongside his. Even with all the practice, my insides are boiling with nerves, my face flushed.

"You've got this," Weston whispers, and I know if we were alone, he would reach forward to touch my hand.

I'm too anxious to do anything but nod.

When we play the duet, Mr. Brant insists we play with our marching step-offs, marching our part in the show without actually moving forward, to show we know which parts of the music match up with our moving directives and can mark time appropriately while playing.

I hadn't prepared for this, and I'm afraid it will throw me off, but before we inhale to play the duet, Weston looks at me and winks.

It'll be okay.

Weston and I don't break eye contact as we inhale together.

In one week, we've managed to take our duet from a gaggle of notes to a seamless stream of music, the melody haunting and eerie. The saxophone holds up the horn's line, and the horn, in turn, forms a base as the saxophone carries the melody.

It's going well. I nail my dynamic markings, don't forget to decrescendo at the appropriate time, and I don't miss any accidentals.

But I'm *too* focused, too in my head. I miss a step-off, and it throws me off enough that I play right through my rest, my notes clashing with Weston's like they did at the beginning of the week, before the four-wheelers and the *way he looked at me* when we said good night and . . .

When I look at him, Weston's eyes are wild with panic.

I've lost my place.

There's no coming back from this.

I stop, my entire body flashing from overheated to ice cold, and drop my saxophone from my mouth to hang limply from its strap.

I *will not* cry. Not here.

Weston isn't watching me anymore as he finishes his part, his horn singing the last notes on its own.

Only four more measures, *four*, and we would have made it. It would have been solid enough to pass, surely.

In the silence, Mr. Brant says nothing. Weston and I say nothing. Weston is looking at me again, but I don't look back.

Beyond the closed door, the muffled Friday morning sounds of people stumbling in for uniform check and laughing are starting to fill the band hall. I hate them. Hate that they can laugh while I wait for the guillotine of Mr. Brant's *no* to slice through the silence.

"She has it, sir," Weston says, and it's hard to tell who is more surprised that he is the first to speak, me or Mr. Brant. "She's worked hard. She's earned this."

Mr. Brant exhales. "Be that as it may, Weston, I've got to think of the whole band. Do you have any idea how quickly the regional qualifying contest will be here? And area contest after that?"

I will my mouth to open, to promise that this is something I can handle, but it doesn't.

"Thirty-six days until regionals, sir," Weston answers quickly. "And area is the following weekend."

There's a long stare.

"Give us another playoff," Weston says. "Give us another week."

My mouth won't open. It's jammed shut as I think of all the things I want to say, all the ways my parents will be disappointed. They won't say it, but when I tell them, Dad will suddenly find something to clean and Mom will remember that she needed to talk to Jenny.

I think of Weston, our strange, tenuous knowing, and how that, too, might crumble if someone else is partnered with him, if our relationship boils down to me helping him with homework as an edict from Mr. Brant.

He'll feel like a charity case. He'll feel like he failed me if I'm not the other half.

"Mr. Brant," I say, "can we try it one more time?"

Mr. Brant nods once, and Weston and I quickly settle back into our playing stances. I suck spit out of my mouthpiece; Weston silently pushes his keys down to make sure nothing is sticking.

When he looks at me, we breathe together, and we play.

This time, it's perfect.

This time, it's all the way through, both of us ending on the last crystal-clear note.

"Nerves," Mr. Brant says when we finish. "You still have work to do. We'll see how it goes next week. We'll be working solely on the production number, so you'll be playing it on the field. A lot."

"But . . . we passed?" I ask.

It's not that Mr. Brant never smiles. It just has to be an awfully big smile to see it through his beard.

"You passed," he says, and I've never been happier to see his grin emerge.

My whoop is loud in the office, and Mr. Brant flinches but doesn't stop smiling.

Weston's eyes are alight as he watches me.

"Thank you, sir," he says. "Will there be another playoff?"

"I don't think that will be necessary," Mr. Brant says. "If you can keep your grades up, and Anna continues to show such marked improvement, I think we can safely say a month is more than adequate to reach perfection, yes? I have full confidence you will be ready by regionals."

Because band is band, and the wheel of productivity never stops, there is little time to celebrate before the usual Friday morning begins. When we exit the office, Weston and I are separated as we go to sit with our officer groups for uniform check. Ratio calls out each and every piece of our uniforms while our officers inspect us to ensure we have everything present.

It's a Friday tradition, one with a large amount of eye rolling and loaning of spare black socks and the occasional travel shirt, but it gives me the chance to smile across the room at Weston and for Andy to see and to pretend to gag on his finger.

It's a home game tonight, so there's time to lounge in the band hall between the end of the pep rally and the start of the pregame frenzy.

I could almost forget that the rest of the band is busy, too—as busy as Weston and I are with the duet—memorizing music for the production number, the closer, and running the problematic parts from the opener again and again until their leg muscles bunch up from marching or their lungs give out from playing.

When I walk into the band hall after the dismissal bell rings, there are at least ten people lying flat on the floor, two of whom are lightly snoring.

"What *happened*?" I ask Andy.

He is leaning against a wall, staring off into space.

"Um, *marching season* happened? Where have you been?"

Lauren comes up behind me, perky and beaming. Fridays are like vacation days for her. No swim practice, no cross-country training, only the Friday night performance with the band and the dance team.

"She passed her duet with Mr. Brant this morning," she tells Andy over my shoulder, "so she's all hyped up."

"Am not," I argue. I don't add that *pass* is a strong word. "You'd know that, Andy, if you had bothered to come to lunch today."

"I had a test to make up," he says, coming to stand with us. "Actually, do you want to run through that math homework really quick? I don't want to do it over the weekend."

This is how Weston finds us when he comes out of the far practice room, math textbooks sprawled open, handwritten notes scattered around us, and Lauren, Andy, and me on our stomachs, arguing heatedly about domains and ranges of function.

He stands over us, his eyes jumping to our homework problems as Andy and Lauren get *this close* to stabbing their mechanical pencils into each other's eyes.

"You realize that you can just program your graphing calculators to tell you if you have the right answer," Weston says.

Lauren huffs. "No, you can't."

Weston squats beside her, and I wonder if he notices how hard she has to try to not flinch as he leans over her to pick up her calculator.

It takes him less than a minute to tap a sequence of buttons that, based on Lauren's gasp when he shows her the screen, does exactly what he promised.

"*Show me*," she says.

"Me, too," Andy says, scooting forward. "Piano bros before piccolos, dude."

Weston looks a little wary, having Lauren pressed against one side and Andy on the other. His face is comically baffled when he looks at me, my friends over him, arguing about who gets their calculator programmed first.

"Give him some room, y'all," I say.

My chest lightens, seeing Weston with Lauren and Andy, even if Lauren looks dubious about his presence. She warms up, though, when he takes her calculator first.

"Ladies first," he tells Andy.

"That's sexist," Andy argues. "Equality means you should flip a coin or something."

Weston's mouth quirks, and he raises his eyes to me. "I'll let Anna decide."

"Oh, for sure Lauren," I say. "If you think soap soup is bad, I'd hate to see what she would do to me if I didn't pick her first."

"And don't you forget it," Lauren threatens. She sticks her tongue out at Andy, who rolls his eyes and turns to Weston.

"Girls. Are you sure you want to get involved with one?"

"*Now* who's sexist?" Lauren says indignantly.

Weston is still looking at me, one side of his lips quirked as Andy and Lauren rage around him.

I wonder where we stand. I wonder if, here, on the other side of our "passed" duet and a day of skipped school and glow-in-the-dark stars, we can find a way forward.

A way to be Anna and Weston just because we *want* to be.

Hi, I mouth at him.

Hi, he mouths back.

Weston programs Lauren's calculator, then Andy's, but when he reaches for mine, I say, "You can do mine tomorrow when I come over for shared homework time," I say.

The pirate smile is knee-weakening. Even though I'm sitting down. Even though he is in his Friday band polo.

"*Can* I now?" Weston grins.

He hovers near me the rest of the day, through the game day festivities of playing the school song, the fight song, the national anthem on the field before kickoff. He's a warm, constant presence when we play in the stands, when we perform our opener at halftime, when the Bearcats soundly crush their opponents 33 to 14.

The only time he leaves my side is when his mom comes to the bleachers devoted to the band, standing near Mr. Brant and waiting for Weston to come down and say hello.

"Mom," he murmurs. "One second."

I've seen her before, but it's different now that Weston is *my* Weston.

The thought catches me off guard, the ownership, but I bat it away, focusing on Mrs. Ryan with her slim pants and well-tailored top. She looks like she belongs on one of those investment shows alongside bald men in suits and women in patent leather shoes who vie for entrepreneurs' favors. I can't reconcile the short red hair, the no-nonsense jewelry, with the Victorian house and the son who towers over her.

I'm worried that Weston will be in a mood when he returns, but he seems more at ease.

I ask him about it after the game, after we've all rolled the pit crew equipment back to the band hall, hung our sweaty uniforms on hangers to go to the dry cleaner's for the week.

We're back at my car, the parking lot emptied of all the Enfielders that had come to watch the game. It's hard to remember what it's like to be in one place, to stand still and not always be *going* and *doing* and *banding*.

I wonder what it would be like to be with Weston Ryan and not have somewhere to go, somewhere we've just come from.

"So that was your mom," I say.

He's in his leather jacket. Even though the nights are cooling as September plods on, they don't require sleeves, and certainly not a heavy jacket.

"Yeah," he says. "She barely made the game. Her plane was delayed."

I don't know what to say, so I say nothing.

"Look," he says, pointing up at the smattering of stars. "Same sky."

He tilts his head back to look, the stars visible despite the Friday night lights still blaring beyond the parking lot.

"So you *did* get my text message," I say, watching him and the way the stadium lights pierce the night to rest on his up-turned face. "You didn't reply."

"I fell asleep," he says, dropping his gaze from the sky to my eyes.

He's still looking at me when he wrestles inside his jacket. His hand disappears into a hidden pocket and comes back out clutching the star I gave him.

"You carried it with you?" I ask, delighted. "What else do you have in there?"

His pirate smile is back, lazy and indulgent, as I lunge forward to give myself easier access to the lining. My hands prod along the edges for bulges or slips in the fabric, my nail lightly catching on a loose thread.

Suddenly, I remember myself, and look up.

Weston is as close as he was last night in the driveway. He's amused, and maybe a little wary.

"Sorry," I whisper.

"I know I don't mind," he tells me. His voice is quiet. "I know if I could fit you into one of these pockets, I'd carry you everywhere with me."

My heart thumps much too quickly in my chest; it beats loud in my ears.

"I wouldn't mind going everywhere with you," I say. And because I have to be sure, I ask, "You're not sick of me? You don't . . . you don't just feel sorry for me because I told you that stuff about the friend zone and—"

Weston cuts me off with a kiss. It's my first kiss, and even though I have nothing to compare it to, I *know* it's a good one. A great one. The kind that ends a movie and kicks off a happily ever after.

I always worried I wouldn't know what to do, that if the time came and somebody bothered to try, I would have unresponsive fish lips or be overeager and a failure.

Weston makes a noise low in the back of his throat, and I know, I *know*, that I shouldn't have worried.

He tastes like lemons and chocolate is my last coherent thought before my brain is shrunk to the size of a single-celled organism whose only job is to never stop kissing.

We're breathing heavily when we separate. My hand is fisted in the lining of his jacket, his hands splayed along my neck, my chin.

"What about not being good for me?" I ask, when I catch my breath. "What about my parents? What about—"

He's kissing me again, kissing me like he can't breathe or he's starving or we're the last two people on earth or all those cheesy things you read in books.

It's devastating. It's complete.

I *know* there's no going back.

Mom and Dad are awake, side by side on the couch, when I get home. Mom's hair is wrapped in a towel from the shower and Dad moves it to the side when it falls against his shoulder.

"Hey, Anna," he says. "Great performance, huh?"

"Yeah," I say, and for the span of a heartbeat, my addled brain wonders if he means the kiss. "It went super well. Next week we'll add in the production number, and then the show will be two-thirds of the way finished."

"Mrs. Anderson tells me you passed your duet today," Mom says knowingly, as if I were keeping that hidden for a big reveal.

"I did," I say. "Yeah, it went well."

Dad's eyes crinkle in the light of the TV. "*So* proud of you, Bagels," he says. "We knew you could do it."

"Thanks, Dad."

"Don't forget, we're leaving for Jenny's dance recital tomorrow morning at ten," Mom says. "She has to be there early to warm up."

"Sounds good," I say. "Good night."

I rush through showering, mixing up the shampoo and conditioner and not caring.

I want to be alone in my room, looking at the stars on my ceiling. I want to text Weston Ryan and see if he got home safely, see if he's thinking about me, too. I want to record everything in my journal—the way Weston's breath caught when I kissed him back, the way he cradled my head with gentle urgency, *everything*.

I don't have to wonder if he's thinking of me. When I get out of the shower, there's a text waiting for me, an image.

A single, solitary star pressed to the ceiling, barely glowing and blurry in the dark.

I'm glad I'm under the same sky as you.

chapter 15

∽

weston

The prospect of a Saturday, of no school, no band, but *all* Anna, is intoxicating. I can't contain my energy, waiting for her to come over. Even *King's Reign* with Ratio fails to sufficiently distract my internal clock from counting down the seconds until she gets here.

Anna doesn't tell me what lie she told to get away from her parents so late in the day on a weekend, and I don't ask.

"How was the recital?" I ask, when we walk to the four-wheeler.

"Boring," she says. "But Jenny didn't mess up or anything, so I guess it was fine. The little kids were cute. One of them toppled over and got mad and sat in the corner of the stage for the rest of her group's performance."

"Not a total loss, then?"

She shrugs, and I'm starting to think I imagined last night, or maybe she regrets that I kissed her, or—

"I'd rather have been with *you*," she says, and her eyes are not at all shy when they meet mine.

"Well, you're here now." I grin, swinging myself up into the seat.

Her smile is breathtaking. "Same sky?" she asks, looking up and immediately thinking better of it, with the Texas sun and its searing glare.

"I'll take your word for it." I laugh.

When her arms wrap around me, I turn my head to kiss her, to make sure it's still real.

"I'll kiss you again if I can drive." She smiles as we part.

"You can drive," I say, dropping my voice low. "You can have everything. No kisses required."

Her smile is soft when she leans forward and kisses my forehead. "I *like* kissing," she says. "Now, move over. You drive too slowly."

The fear that being together will break us—that *I'll* break her—isn't gone, but it has a hard time keeping up with Anna's driving, and an even harder time being heard over her delighted laugh.

A tentative future I didn't think was possible starts to materialize, one where Anna is there and smiling and wearing Christmas socks and begs me to play carols year-round at the piano and I pretend to hate it but don't.

I love it.

We quickly fall into a routine of Anna slipping from under her parents' thumb to meet me, then spending the occasional night at home so they don't suspect. On those days, the night is endless, each second without her a painful tick that can only be muffled by working on her song at the piano.

And kissing. Kissing is new and wonderful and an *addicting* part of our routine. How are we supposed to do anything else?

I wonder. How does anybody get *anything* done if they have someone who kisses like they're enjoying it as much as you are?

But Anna makes us be productive, stops our kissing long enough to get me on an irritatingly thorough homework plan. She has it written out on a sheet of paper, and try as I might, I can't make out the squiggles and arrows that, she says, will get me on track to raise my grades to Bs or higher by regionals. The only thing I can make out is a huge, pink-penned star next to the science test in two weeks, the one I have to ace to raise my grade high enough to compete in regionals.

"My teachers think I've had demons exorcised," I tell her one Wednesday evening. We're at Dad's when we're supposed to be at youth group. "Mrs. Chase says my English grade has improved *so much*. She's threatening to give me extra reading *so I don't get bored*."

"You love it." Anna smiles.

"No, I *tolerate* homework. I *love* you," I say, turning my math packet over.

Anna freezes beside me.

"Did you . . . did you just tell me you love me during *homework hour?*"

"Yes, because I do," I say, and I realize with a shock that I'm not worried her surprise means she doesn't love me back. "You love me, too."

I grin at her astonished face, lean across the table to pop her mouth closed.

Everything happens so quickly with Anna. She is still a Happening, maybe more than ever. One moment, we're on the four-wheeler after I beg to take a study break, Anna growing dangerously bold as she takes curves in the road like she was born with an engine under her feet; the next, we're on the floor of Nanny and Papa's guest room, a million and one pictures of me splayed on the bed.

"And here he is next to Papa in his old red Chevy," Nanny tells Anna, as she makes the appropriate *ooh*s and *ah*s and *aw*s.

Nanny is eating it up.

"Look how *blond* he is," Anna says, pointing at one of the photos. "I thought his hair was light *now*, but this is, like, platinum."

"Little angel baby," Nanny says fondly, pulling another photo toward them on the bedspread.

Papa is in his chair, napping, in the other room, so I don't have anyone else to talk to while Nanny and Anna are devoted to the walk down memory lane. Figuring I might as well help—so we can get this over with and I can have Anna back to myself—I go into the tiny closet to make sure all the photo boxes have been taken out.

I can't stop my laugh.

"What have you found, Weston?" Nanny asks.

Her voice sounds muffled as I cram myself between some heavy coats and cardboard boxes to extricate a plastic tub of toys.

"You kept all this?" I ask Nanny.

"What is it?" Anna helps clear a space on the bed, eagerly worming her way under my arm to look in the opened tub. "*Oh*, is that a helicopter?"

"*With* working propellers," I tell her. "Or at least, they did when I was little."

The photos forgotten, Nanny moves to our side of the bed, smiling. "You and your cousins used to play with these for *hours*," she says, taking out a handful of the small metal army men. "But you didn't like when they were 'mad at each other,' so you would make them play games together instead of going to war."

"Sounds about right." Anna laughs.

She begins to take out the soldiers, lining them up along the floral bedspread.

"Want to play?" I tease.

I am more surprised than I should be when Anna grins. "Um, yes, please."

It's just as much for Nanny's benefit, I realize, when Anna wages a "war of kindness" on Rufus the cat, who is too old to care that he is being used as a helicopter landing pad, his tail the perfect place for an army canteen. Nanny pretends to leave us alone, but her shuffling walk when she comes to stand in the doorway to watch us play is much too loud to go undetected.

"Thanks for this," I murmur to Anna, when Nanny has shuffled away again.

"For what?" Anna asks. "For my team smoking yours in the three-legged race? You're welcome."

I touch her Christmas sock with my foot, and she smiles her thinking smile at me. It's no less radiant, just smaller, her eyes crinkled but distant.

"What is it?" I ask.

"You make yourself sound so alone," Anna says. "I just . . . it wasn't what I was expecting."

"Yeah?"

"You have this whole history, these memories and toys and . . . I don't know why I thought maybe you had sprung up out of nowhere on your own, but I did. I feel stupid."

Rufus gets up to stretch and sends plastic army men sprawling on the hardwood floor.

"It's not stupid if I didn't tell you," I say.

"But why *didn't* you tell me?" she asks.

"Because it's different than it was," I say, not wanting to say the word *divorce* because it feels like a harbinger of doom to say it in the presence of someone I love. "It's been different for a year, and I'm still not sure what's the same."

I keep my voice low, not wanting Nanny or Papa to hear, and Anna leans in.

Her hair smells like fruity shampoo and hay and country roads and *her*. It drives me a little crazy, makes my head go blank, and then I'm kissing her ear, lightly tracing my tongue around the outside of it.

"*Weston*," she admonishes, but she is laughing. "Your *grandparents* are here!"

"They're old, not stupid," I say. "They know a girl as pretty as this playing with an army set on the ground means I'm defenseless."

I kiss down to her neck, and she makes one of those little gasps in the back of her throat that I love.

I'd keep going, except that Nanny *does* come back, having found another bin of photos in the basement that she wants to show Anna.

"Later," Anna whispers. She pats my chest and lightly drags her hand across it when she follows Nanny to the kitchen table.

I desperately wish later could be now.

Band still rages on around us. Each morning, Anna and I are separated by yards and lines of music, our duet no longer a concern, even when Anna occasionally misses a note in the hundreds of times we run the show.

"Contest is coming," Mr. Brant reminds us multiple times a day. "Practice until you can't get it wrong," he says.

It's the part of the season where we have learned the steps, the music, our forms, and yet it still feels like there is so much to do before regionals. The long-ignored dynamics, how loud or soft a section plays, have to be sorted out so the judges way up in the box hear the right blend of melody. The pull-and-touches, how you begin to march if you are at a standstill, have to be crisp and dramatic without leading to pedaling.

Gilligans have to be put through their paces, day after day, the people around them just as weary of saying "Again" again as they are of doing it.

There's comfort in the monotony, the schedule. Mr. Brant is always talking about upholding tradition and pride in everything we do, which is fine, but there's something wonderful about knowing *exactly* what you're supposed to be doing and carrying it out.

It's made even better when you don't feel alone, when there's a warm, Christmas sock–wearing girl with a quick smile and a quicker laugh walking with you to class, sitting beside you on the band bus or in the bleachers, forcing you to chant along with the cheerleaders and the rest of the band. It's stupid, but it makes her smile *so wide*, and you can't tell her no.

You can't tell her no when she sits on the floor and leans against your bent knees as you play the piano with the ivory keys, her chin resting on your thigh and making it harder than it should be to concentrate on "Sea Pieces." You play the raging storm louder than the dynamic markings demand, not trying to pour anger and misery into the keys—for once—but instead channeling the longing that burns in you at her touch, at the way her hair is draped across your lap.

The notes come out too low and loud because of it, but she doesn't seem to notice as she traces patterns over the denim of your jeans.

You're happy.

Not much has changed—your parents are still divorced, you still have teachers hounding you, you still wonder if maybe there is something fundamentally wrong with you—but also *everything* has changed, because she's here.

And somehow the rest doesn't matter so much.

chapter 16

anna

I've wandered too far from my parents and Jenny and can see nothing but sand, ocean, and the distant glow of our hotel at night in Mexico.

When an old man comes out of the shadows, I'm old enough to know he could be dangerous but young enough to believe nothing bad could ever happen to me.

"Your family," he says. "They are looking for you." He points down the beach, and I don't protest when he adds, "I will walk you."

I slow my steps to match his in our slow trudge.

"Do you live here?" I ask.

"I live everywhere," the man replies. "But tonight, I live here."

Something about the way he says it makes my heart swell, like he is not of this world. I can't wait to write it down, to record how the stars shined and the waves lapped at our feet.

But the magic is ruined when my parents get ahold of me,

when the "How could you?" and the "Where have you been?" crash against my ears.

Later, instead of wonder, I write about how a good memory can be tainted by what comes after, how nothing is untouchable.

My Weston scribbles notes on the inside of my band folder for me to find later. My Weston promises to play on the piano whatever song I can name, *by ear*, if I would just please, for the love of God, let him stop studying for his calculus test. My Weston begrudgingly learns to accept Andy's near-constant teasing but tells Ratio to kindly ef off when he does the same to me. My Weston actually apologizes when he says the f-word, and promises he's trying to break the habit.

My Weston laughs hysterically when I try to prove that I'm not allergic to swear words by saying the f-word out loud and it comes out rhyming with *deck*, not *duck*.

Even if I have to dodge my parents with lies and half-truths, even if it bothers me the longer it goes on, I can't stay away from him.

I tell him as much, one night, when we've parked the four-wheeler in a field to look at the stars, when October is knocking on September's door and the nights are growing colder.

"You *never* bring a jacket," Weston says, when I shiver against him, shrugging his off and helping me into it.

I take a deep breath, inhaling the scent of leather and lemon and *Weston* that has no name.

"I'm beginning to think you're doing it on purpose," he says wryly.

"Oh, I am," I say. "I'm thinking of burning anything I have with sleeves so you will always have to give your jacket to me."

"People will start thinking you're weird," he says, leaning forward to brush a kiss on my neck, right above the black collar. "Trust me, I know."

It's like he can't wait another second to touch me. Weston is like that, I've learned. He touches. But it's not a possessive thing. It's more like he wants to prove that I'm still there. To Weston, I am something to marvel at.

"I'll be weird if I can be weird with you," I tell him.

"We might be the only ones," he says, situating himself so we can tilt back to look at the sky. "Won't it make you lonely?"

We're not the only ones. Everyone is weird in their own way, and I hope he's starting to see that, to realize he's not as alone as he thinks.

But I know what he wants to hear, what he *needs* to hear.

And even though I know he's wrong about being alone, about being the only one, what I say is still the truth: "I could never be lonely with you."

And I'm not, I find. The shadows hardly ever come for me now, their oily fingers remaining distant storm clouds that never cross the horizon. When it's late and I'm tired, the ocean in my head doesn't dredge up every wrong thing I've ever done. Instead, it is filled with Weston. Only Weston. My Weston.

"Tell me something you know," he whispers in my ear.

"I know the world is poison for some of us," I tell him. "And we're just trying to find antidotes to save ourselves."

It sounds ridiculous, but I don't worry about anything being too strange or abstract for Weston.

"I think you're wrong," he says. "I think we're looking for antidotes because we want to *live* longer."

"But why bother if the world is poison?" I ask, not because I disagree but because I want to hear his answer.

Weston is quiet for a long time. I think this is a big part of why I like him, and maybe why other people are a little afraid of him. Quiet in Enfield is rare. Quiet in Enfield leaves room for rumors to fill up the space your void of words leaves behind. To them, quiet isn't a sign of thinking but of not contributing to the tumbling mass of words that is always swirling, always controlling everyone in town.

But Weston doesn't care what people think of him.

Or maybe he does and has found an antidote.

"I think the world hurts us in a lot of different ways," he says, his words a breath along my ear. "But I also think the antidotes can be enough to make you forget there was poison in the first place."

His voice is heartbreakingly sad, the kind of sad that makes me twist in his arms and pull his head down to mine, our lips clumsily bumping into each other before settling into an upside-down but still delightful kiss.

"We can be each other's antidotes," I say.

It's all going well—like, *absurdly* well—until the day I arrive at lunch and Lauren and Andy are at the table alone, no sign of Kristin. At first I think she must have gone home sick after band, but she's sitting next to Jessica a few tables away.

"She *ditched* us?" I ask. "Freshmen; so ungrateful."

I'm too busy unpacking my lunch box so I can eat as quickly as possible, so I can go to the band hall, so I can see Weston for the last ten minutes of lunch, that it takes me a moment to register their expressions.

"Wow, did someone die?" I ask. "What's going on?"

Andy opens his mouth first, but Lauren elbows him sharply in the side.

"We're *worried* about you," she says.

Every part of me bristles. I set my sandwich on top of my napkin. "Because of Weston? I thought y'all were over that?"

"We are—" Andy begins, but Lauren jabs him again to cut him off.

"We are *concerned* that you haven't told your parents that you two are a *thing*."

"If by 'thing' you mean 'dating,'" I say, my heart thrilling at the word, "then yes. But I don't see why you should care."

"Because we're your friends," Lauren says.

"But we've been dating for two weeks. Why the sudden concern?"

"Because Lauren told her mom," Andy says in a rush, before Lauren can stop him. She shoves him, and Andy's athletic build totters on his seat at the force of her swimmer's arms.

"*Andy!* I told you that *I* would tell her."

"She needs to know what's going on," Andy says, waving a hand at me. "It's not like we're ratting on her. She needs to know so she can tell her parents before *your mom* gets to them."

Lauren turns to me, folding her hands in front of her. "Look, I'm sorry. It slipped."

Her tone is indifferent, frank. I hate it.

"How does that just *slip*?" I ask.

Lauren rolls her eyes. "You know Mom. She was talking about how they're planting the new Memorial Memorial Memorial Tree, and she said something about hoping Weston didn't destroy this tree, and I . . ." She trails off.

"You told her that he wouldn't do that? That you've gotten to know him a little bit better and she is *wrong*?"

"Not exactly," she says, and finally has the grace to look ashamed. "But I *did* say he couldn't be all bad if he was dating you."

"Okay, but *you know my mom*," I say. "She's going to kill me for dating him and not telling her and Dad. *I'm screwed.* Why would you do this to me?"

"It was an accident!" Lauren says, so loudly that Kristin's

head snaps to our table with a concerned look. "It's not like I would do it on purpose."

"But you didn't *not* do it on purpose," I say. Years of frustration are seeping through the cracks in my head, the shadows questioning whether Lauren was *ever* a friend.

Which is ridiculous. *Of course* we're friends. She's just busy, and this isn't one of those spend-every-waking-hour-together kind of friendships.

But it occurs to me, in the midst of my heated anger, that if Weston has felt even one percent of what I'm feeling right now, he must be so, so lonely.

I hate that for him. I hate what this feeling could do to a person over time.

"I never agreed to lie for you," Lauren continues. "You never *asked* me to lie for you."

"Friends shouldn't have to ask." Calming my voice takes effort I don't have, but I do it. "But it's fine. Really. I was going to have to tell them soon anyway. They would have figured it out."

Lauren deflates a little at this, sinking into her seat and stabbing her fork in her pasta salad.

We spend the rest of lunch in silence, and I can't bring myself to go to the band hall like normal, so when the bell rings, Weston is leaning against the staircase, a small, worried smile on his face.

"Are you okay?" he asks.

I drop my head onto his chest. "Fine," I mumble.

"Promise?" he says.

"Just tired."

"I know you're lying, Anna," he says, his voice dry.

"You don't."

"I do. You didn't come to the band hall . . . and your mouth twitches when you lie."

"You can't see my mouth," I say into his shirt.

"*I know you.*"

His hand comes up to gently touch the back of my head, and I shiver.

That's what I'm worried about. I'm worried he already knows, that we've both known, that the day of reckoning is much too near, the day I'll have to fess up to my parents, when I'll have to explain to my mom that I have fallen for the boy I promised not to love, the one she and everyone else refuses to give any consideration because of some stupid jacket and some stupid Memorial Memorial Tree rumor that people are *still* whispering about.

But we're in the middle of school, and I can't deal with any of it right now.

"Class," I mutter to Weston. "See you later?"

His eyes are worried when we part, but he kisses my forehead.

"Your face is red," he whispers.

Above us, the bell rings.

In math class, I don't look at Lauren.

I stay at home instead of sneaking out to Weston's.

Mom and Dad are so excited when I tell them I have nowhere to be that they announce an impromptu game night.

"You can pick, Bagels. Apples to Apples? Yahtzee? Monopoly?"

"*Please* not Monopoly," Jenny begs, and it hurts to see how excited they are that I am staying home on a weeknight.

"You can pick, Jen," I tell her.

She picks Apples to Apples, and we take turns reading cards with adjectives and laughing as we try to find a card that best matches it.

I hope they can't hear how hollow my laugh sounds, because even to me it sounds broken.

I try to tell myself that it's stupid to wait, that I should tell them now, when Mom is laughing because Dad is forced to read the green card with the word *sexy* on it and Jenny is covering her ears and humming.

Stupidly, I let myself imagine Weston at the table, in a phantom chair that doesn't exist, because this table was built for four. No more.

Maybe I've gotten very good at lying, but nobody notices my humming brain. Nobody comes to check on me when I lie in bed and let the shadows stretch along the walls and smother the glowing stars, let the waves in my head wash me out to sea.

Tomorrow, I will tell them.

Tomorrow, after one more day with Weston.

You okay? his text asks.

It'll be okay, I text back. See you in the morning.

He sends me a GIF of a Christmas tree twirling happily on its stand along with the words "I wish I could make every day Christmas for you."

Me, too, I text back.

Every day is better because you're here, he says.

It's enough to make the ache in my chest buckle, and I cry into my pillow so no one will hear.

chapter 17

weston

The wildfire burns night and day for Anna. Every time I'm not with her, I feel like I can't breathe, like there's not enough air to fill my lungs.

Yesterday was torture.

She didn't come to the band hall after lunch, and I didn't get to see her after school—she needed to spend the evening at home—and . . .

Fuck.

Something is wrong. Like, really wrong. My head has been full of nothing but cursing for the last twenty-four hours, no matter what I promised Anna about swearing.

Fuck, fuck, fuck.

I'm at her car door before she has a chance to open it the next morning, the gravel of Mom's driveway crunching beneath my shoes.

"Okay, what's wrong?" I ask the moment there's a sliver of space.

"Nothing," she says, but she's been crying, and her eyes are red.

"*Anna.*"

She sighs, walking past me to the front door, then into the living room to run her fingers over the piano keys. Mom's home, but she's blessedly out for the day at book club and errands and whatever it is she does when she's not working.

"I don't want to tell you," Anna says.

It must be really bad.

"Are you sick?" I ask, coming to stand over her as she presses the keys.

"What? No."

"Are you moving?"

"*No.*" She hits the lowest note. She hits it again.

I run my hand through my hair. "*Tell me.* Please? I'm dying here."

She smashes her palm on as many keys as she can touch, which isn't many. Her hands are so small. "I have to tell my parents. About us."

I close my eyes and work very, very hard to not let her see the panic running through me. She has become frighteningly good at reading my every facial expression, and I don't want her to see how this is killing me.

I start to think of the stupid Kaua'i 'ō'ō. Would it rather have had two weeks, maybe a month, with another bird, even if it knew it would have to leave in the end? Even if the Kaua'i 'ō'ō knew that it would, once more, be alone?

The cliché answer is yes, of course, it's better to have loved and lost than to have never loved at all. But is that *actually* true or is it just something that gets repeated over and over in hopes that it can become reality?

I look at Anna's bent head, and the thought of not knowing her, even though this could be the end of everything, is not a reality I'm willing to consider.

"Tell me something you know," I whisper. "The truth."

Her voice is clouded when she answers. "I don't care how much trouble I get in; it's worth it," she says. "If that's what you're asking. Don't think for a second it isn't."

Tears are pressing on the backs of my eyes.

"I only wish we had more time," Anna says. "I was going to have to tell them eventually, but I don't . . . I don't know what they'll *do*."

"How much time would you want," I ask her quietly. "If it was up to you?"

Her eyes are unbearably alive, even when they're filled with tears. I almost want to look away, but I'm glad I don't, because she whispers, "Forever."

"Forever in Enfield High?" I ask, breathless. "Forever-until-graduation forever? Or forever forever?"

Anna's eyes narrow. "You know me," she says. "Which do you think it is?"

I take her to the tree house to find out. It seems impossible, Anna James stretched out beneath the crisp blue sky with her long hair curling around knots in the wood, strands falling through the slats in the same place that Ratio sits when he's here.

We talk about forever, what it looks like, how we can taste it but there's no word to describe the flavor.

I tell her about Bloom, about the weekend a bunch of band kids went to a party and drunk texted me that I was a creep, possibly a Satanist. I tell her about how a girl named Ruth, the one I had a secret crush on, texted me the next morning to apologize, but her apology ended with "I hope you find Jesus, otherwise you're probably going to hell. Seriously." It was punctuated with the praying hands emoji.

Anna refuses to believe anyone could be that cruel until I show her screenshots of the texts that I could never bring myself to delete.

"I'm going to curse," Anna declares, after she's read them through twice. She is standing up on the platform and wiggling around like she's trying to direct all her bad feelings into her throat.

I reach up to grab my phone from her death grip. "Don't break my phone in the process," I beg.

"This is . . ." Anna pauses to inhale. "They are the *worst*, Weston. The literal worst."

"*That's* your idea of cursing?" I laugh.

Anna points a finger at me. "Do not laugh," she threatens. "This is serious. You don't . . . Weston, promise me you don't believe a word of the cr—the shit they said to you."

"There it is," I say proudly. "I knew you had it in you."

"There aren't words bad enough to describe what they did," Anna says darkly, and my heart thrills that she's so furious on my behalf.

"People get drunk, Anna. They text people stupid stuff all the time."

"Not like this," Anna says.

She leans down, and I think it's to take my phone and delete the messages. Instead, she grabs my head between her hands and says, "Do. *Not*. For a minute. Let someone tell you that you are broken because you are different. *Don't you dare.*"

Being the subject of Anna James's undivided passion is terrifying. It's jumping into ice-cold water after sitting in a sauna. It's looking over the edge of the tallest building in the world and a tiny part of your brain is contemplating what it would be like to fall from such a height.

She is a Happening, a violent storm that has been trapped

in skin, and anyone who looks at her and only sees the mask she puts up is a fool.

I reach up and hold her face, too.

"Don't let anyone tell you that you can't write," I tell her. "Don't let anyone *ever* tell you that you can't have exactly the life you dream of."

Tomorrow, everything will be different. We'll have to face a world full of opinions about what kind of people Anna should date, what I should be allowed to do.

But we have today, which is more than I ever hoped to have.

When we kiss, it's impossible to know who started it first.

The Kaua'i 'ō'ō hops from branch to branch and silently watches as we leave the tree house, hand in hand.

chapter 18

◌ஓ

anna

We were on a rocky, secluded beach somewhere in Washington, or maybe Oregon. Jenny and I tripped over the rocks, our sneakers soaking up splashes of freezing water and making us squeal as the waves rolled inland in steady, breathing heaves.

"How does it know to do that?" I asked Dad, when he came to stand beside me.

"What?"

I pointed. "How does the water know to move in and out?"

"Oh, you mean the tide. That's just how the ocean works, Anna."

"But how does this water know how to tide, Dad?"

I was desperately aware that my brain was trying to grasp something big, and he didn't understand what I meant.

I've always loved the idea of an unstoppable force. A volcano that could erupt at any moment. The promise of the tides.

Maybe, in hindsight, this love of the inescapable was preparing me for Weston.

Maybe all of it, the little bits of personal history, my memories, have brought me here, to this moment. To his room. To him.

Because it feels like the tide, being alone with him. It feels inevitable, shirts and socks and underwear falling from our bodies like rainwater joining the tumultuous sea. If he is the raging ocean, I am the wind driving down to meet him, and no force on earth—or out of it—can stop us.

Nothing can hold back this tide.

We've been circling closer to this whirlpool for weeks— lingering, open-mouthed kisses that end in questioning glances, time alone when the electricity between us feels like it might spark and start endless wildfires.

I've known it was coming, just like I know that the tides will always come to caress their beaches over and over again.

"You're sure?" Weston breathes, and I wonder what it costs him to even ask. He is stronger than I am, to even think of holding back this tide.

But I'm glad he asks. I don't want anything to be taken from me. I want to be the wind to his sea, an active participant in a storm neither of us is sure will ever end, once it begins.

"I'm sure," I say.

And despite everything, despite the God of the youth group we are supposed to be at forbidding this tide, despite the years of adults telling us that we'll be dirty and unwanted and ruined, I don't regret it.

Not for a second.

I still don't regret it, even when it's over and we're lying side by side, Weston's fingers trailing over my hair, my cheeks, my ears. I don't regret it when we have to wade back into our puddle of clothes and separate them into his and mine. I don't regret it when we laugh about his still-on socks, my nearly destroyed ponytail.

I don't regret it when we go to the kitchen and silently pass a glass of water between us, drinking thirstily, conscious of the other's every move. I *definitely* don't regret it when Weston leans forward once, twice, three times to kiss my forehead, my eyelids, my lips, and to whisper, "You sure you're okay?"

"Better than okay," I say.

I don't regret any of it, even when I finally remember to check my phone.

Even when the screen is alight with multiple missed calls and texts.

From Dad.

Where are you?

From Mom.

Who are you with?

From Lauren.

They know. I'm sorry.

Weston wanted to come with me, but I'm glad I didn't let him.

I have never seen my parents this mad.

Not when Jenny stole my Popsicle and I shoved her so hard she bruised. Not when I played tag in the church hallway with friends and knocked over an entire table of Communion grape juice and wafers.

They were angry then.

They are *furious* now.

They've had time to organize a plan of attack in disciplining me, to decide exactly how this conversation will unfold, because when I come through the door, they are standing in the living room, side by side, arms folded like they are posing for a cheesy staged photo.

Dad is the first to speak.

"Where have you been?"

The guilty conscience I've bludgeoned repeatedly over the last couple of months must not be quite dead. There's a hint of fear in Dad's voice, and I hate that I'm the one who has put it there.

"*Where do you think?*"

This is the wrong thing to say, but I knew that when I said it.

"Your mother ran into Mrs. Anderson at the grocery store," Dad says, and Mom can't contain her seething silence any longer.

"You are *grounded*," she says. "Do you hear me? You go to school, you go to band, and you come home. No extra rehearsals. No 'projects' or trips to 'Lauren's' or 'Andy's' or anywhere else. Are we clear?"

She has started shouting, and Dad tries to get her to lower her hands from where they have been forming air quotes.

"Babe," he murmurs, but she shakes him off.

"Okay," I say, trying to keep my voice level and failing. "So I try to tell you that Weston is great, that he's someone I can be with and be safe and good, just like when I'm with Andy or Lauren or whoever, and you don't listen. You don't even consider it. You tell me to not spend any time with him. When you don't even know him. *What am I supposed to do?*"

"*What you are told!*" Mom yells. "Because you are the child and we are the parents."

Dad is still trying to deescalate the situation, calmly rubbing Mom's shoulders and shooting me a pleading look, but this makes me angrier. Couldn't he stand up to her *for once*? Tell Mom that she's clearly overreacting?

But he couldn't.

We know who's in charge here.

"Are you serious?" I ask her directly, ignoring Dad. "I'm

sixteen. I make straight As. I'm in *marching band*, the least rebellious extracurricular known to humankind. I go to church
every Sunday. I make my bed every morning. I take out the
trash when it's full without being asked. Are you *seriously* saying I'm grounded for wanting to spend time with my boyfriend?"

The only light in the darkened living room is the table
lamp with its single bulb. The warm yellow glow usually looks
friendly, but today it's interrogation lighting.

"You are grounded for disobeying us, Anna Lynn." Mom's
every word is a bite. "You are grounded for lying."

"*No*, I'm grounded for dating Weston," I say, my voice rising.

Mom's face twists when I say his name.

"If I were dating William James," I blaze, "you would let
me go to Bermuda with him alone for a week or a month or a
year. You would help me pack!"

Dad takes his chance to interject. "Don't raise your voice to
your mother."

"*She raised her voice first!*"

We're breathing hard, and Mom is getting amped up for
round two, when Jenny walks in, her fluorescent pink pajamas
burning my retinas in the darkness of the living room.

"What's going on?" she asks.

"*Nothing*," I say.

Mom shoots me a look, but lowers her voice to tell Jenny,
"Go back to bed, Jen. We're just talking."

When she's gone, Mom turns back to me. Her voice is all
the sharper for being so quiet.

"Your sister misses you," she says. "Your parents miss you.
You have spent every waking hour trying your best not to set
foot in this house, and it ends here."

"Let him come over, then," I beg. I don't know when I

started crying, but tears slip into my mouth. "Let him be a part of us."

I can tell that Dad is hoping we're done with the angry parts, the shouting bits, because his voice is a touch too bright, too eager, when he says, "You still lied, Bagels. But maybe in time he can—"

"No," Mom interrupts. "If you are as good as you say you are, then this boy is the reason you've been lying, and he's not welcome in this house. Now, give us your phone and your laptop. You can have them back when you're at school, but that's all."

My brain is too tired to keep up, so I ask the most mundane of questions in my stupor. "But what about homework?"

"Kitchen table. Supervised," Mom says, the words gritted out like it's all she can do to not start shouting again.

I should cut my losses. It would be smarter to try to reason with her in the morning, when we've had time to sleep off our hurt and fury.

I'm stupid. I'm *so* stupid for not telling them sooner.

But I'm also angry. I'm *furious* that they are like everyone else, that they have to be *convinced* of the worth of someone that the town has decided is not worth investing in.

"You would love him if you'd give him a chance," I tell them. "I know I'm grounded. But you are *wrong*. And you must know that, or you wouldn't be this mad. You *know* me. I wouldn't lie to you for fun or because it's easier. I lied because you judged him before you met him, just like everyone else in this stupid town with its stupid churches that say 'Love your neighbor' and all that shit. Nobody *means* it, not really, or there wouldn't be Westons or Annas that feel this lonely, this left out." My voice cracks.

"You feel lonely?" Dad asks.

"Well, *yeah*," I say, the rage leaving my voice. "Enfield is a place built for overachievers and always doing your best, and if you start to wonder if your best isn't good enough, if you start to freak out at how much you have to do or feel like you're letting people down, it . . . it messes with you."

I'm rambling, all the thoughts I've been afraid to share spilling out in a geyser of fear and guilt.

They look stunned.

"But you do so well," Mom says, her voice edging from angry to parental concern and disbelief.

"Yeah, but what if I wasn't?" I ask. "Who would I be then?"

"You're not making any sense, Anna," Dad says.

"I could flunk out of high school and Weston would still love me," I say, and my voice increases in volume. "I could quit band, quit the academic competitions, quit volunteering at church on Sundays, and Weston wouldn't look at me any differently."

"We will *always* love you, too," Mom says, wavering too close to exasperation. "Enough with the theatrics. You're grounded. You're a good student, a good daughter, but you messed up. It's our jobs as parents to punish you."

For the first time, I try to see my parents as human, really human, standing in the dim light of the living room with their teapot bodies and their tired eyes.

They'll have to wake up for work soon. Dad will wake up earlier to make sure he can start the coffeepot for Mom. She'll make him toast before he leaves. She'll probably burn it. She always does, somehow.

They'll work for hours and come home and make dinner that Jenny and I may or may not eat. They'll do laundry, sweep the corners of the kitchen with a broom that has been used so much it's misshapen, and they'll go to bed and do it all over again the next day.

But I'm human, too. I'll be too tired in the morning to go

to school, too emotionally wrung out, like a sad kitchen dish towel, but I'll go. I'll make it through marching in the sharp glare of the rising sun and shower in the band locker room that smells like chlorine and mildew. I'll go to classes, smile, pretend everything is fine.

I wonder if that's the problem with parents and their kids, if we're doomed to always see each other as something that needs to be fixed or battled against or molded.

At least they're here, I guess.

At least there's a pair of them here, making my blood boil.

"How long am I grounded?" I ask.

"Your father and I will discuss it."

"Okay," I say, and my voice is tired. *I* am tired.

"Go to bed, Bagels," Dad tells me. "We'll talk more tomorrow."

I wish I could send Weston a message. I wish I could do something other than draw endless spirals in my journal because it's too dark to write without the light from my phone.

I count the stars on my ceiling, and when the shadows come, and the waves in my head churn, I quiet them with the memory of Weston, his crisp, tan sheets, the way he held me when it was over, like the holding was even better than what came before, and like I was a strong, dangerous thing that he loved but that made him feel a little scared.

"I've never done that before," he whispered into my hair.

"Me either," I said.

Quiet. So quiet.

"It's like a duet," I said, "isn't it?"

He kissed my hair. "It is."

chapter 19

weston

Anna's eyes are dull when I see her the next morning at rehearsal, and it kills me. It's a heady mix of remembering the
sweetness of last night and the crash and burn of what came
after, of the text messages and her parents and the radio silence when she left.

I've never felt so helpless before, pacing my bedroom,
knowing she was getting raked over the coals for something I
was just as much a part of. More than once I'd reached for my
keys, determined to go defend her, but it was useless. I would
only make it worse.

"How bad was it?" I ask.

She doesn't shrug off my hand when I rub her shoulder, but
she doesn't relax into me, either.

"Bad," she says. "I'm grounded. For life, I think. They didn't
really specify a release date."

Her socks are mismatched: one white Nike anklet, one high black one that she has scrunched down. She's not wearing her Christmas tree ring.

"They took my phone and computer," she says. "That's why I couldn't text you."

"I'm sorry," I say.

I love you. Please don't let this break us. Please don't leave me when I've just found you.

She sits next to me while we wait for the second period bell, her hair wet from showering and dripping all over my jacket.

After school, I walk her to her car, but she isn't bouncing on her toes or smiling or any of the usual Anna things.

"You're quiet," I say.

"I'm sad," she replies. "I'm angry."

Alarm bells ring in my head, and I panic. I try to keep the fear out of my voice when I ask, "Are we done?"

Because that's how it happens. One day everything is fine, or at least *doable*, and the next it's over. Suitcases by the door over. Text messages telling you to find Jesus over.

It's like the stupor Anna has been in falls away, her eyebrows shooting up and her mouth finally showing an expression other than *meh*.

"Weston, no," she says, her hands grabbing my arms. "Are you serious? *Of course* we're not *over*."

I'm quiet for too long, trying to concentrate on my breathing, trying to make it stop whooshing out of my nose in quick gusts.

"*Tell me* you know that," she says. "Please."

"I wish I was someone else," I say instead, once I catch my breath. "I wish I made good grades and acted like a normal person and was someone your parents would want you to date."

"It doesn't matter what they think—" Anna starts, but I cut her off.

"It *matters*," I tell her. "Now I can't even see you outside of school. It matters what they think because they're your keepers."

"If my parents were like yours, this wouldn't even matter," she says.

Unfair. What I'm thinking is completely and totally unfair, but my feelings are jumbled and confused and everything is coming out wrong.

"You wish your parents were divorced," I say flatly. "You want them to be separated so they can't possibly keep tabs on you."

"Weston, that's not what I said."

"It's what you meant."

Anna's face falls, and she runs her hand nervously over the back of her neck.

I'm an asshole. Maybe everyone calls me *freak* because it's a kinder word than *jackass*.

I think she's going to get into her car and leave, but Anna steps forward and wraps her arms around my middle, her head resting on my chest.

"Have I ever told you that I'm sorry they divorced?" she asks quietly. "Because I am."

It's the most natural feeling in the world to hug her back.

"It was a while ago."

"Yes, but that doesn't make it better," she tells me. "That was a crappy thing for me to say. I'm sorry. I didn't mean the divorce. But it seems like your parents trust you not to fall off a cliff or do drugs or have se—"

Her voice falls away, and I look down to see her ears are flaming red.

I can't stop my chuckle, and the sound causes her to drop her arms and jerk her head up.

"Do *not* laugh at me," she says, but her mouth is smiling and her eyes are shy and knowing.

Maybe everything *will* be okay.

Nothing is okay.

Our morning rehearsals now begin with a play-through of the opener and the production number before we start to work on the closer. It goes okay; we've done it enough to not need to check our dot or sheet music. Even though it's the exact opposite of what we're supposed to do, we can do the show on autopilot.

This morning is no different, even though it *is*. It's my one chance throughout the day to see Anna, because even though she *could* come see me during lunch, she's worried her mom would somehow find out, that someone might snitch.

"Just to be safe," she says, the second day of her grounding. "So I don't make it worse."

"How long?" I ask through gritted teeth. "How long do we have to keep this up?"

Her eyes are tired when she looks at me and shrugs.

Fuck Enfield and the people who have nothing better to do than comment on the lives of a high school junior and senior.

Every day I'm forced to endure the torture of a once-familiar routine that feels alien without her at my side. Stretches, mile run, and to the grid to start the show, the sun already beating down on us.

I'm thinking about her when I trip and land on my knee in the middle of rehearsal. It's the third day of her grounding. Three *whole* days of Anna-less lunches and Anna-less evenings.

There is more than one audible gasp when I hit the asphalt.

I have never fallen in a show, not once. Not in rehearsal, not during halftime, certainly not during a competition.

Mr. Brant shouts through his mic for everyone to stop, even though I'm already back on my feet with an intact instrument and a not-so-intact skinned knee.

"Unacceptable, Weston," he says, like I didn't already know. Across the grid, Anna is staring at me with wide eyes, her gaze flicking between my face and my knee.

"Sorry, sir," I say, yelling to be heard over the metronome that is clicking away at full show tempo behind us. "It won't happen again."

"No, it *won't*," Mr. Brant says. "Do you need medical attention, Mr. Ryan? No? Good. Clean that up and then back on the field. Back to set, people! We still have half an hour before showers and we're not going to waste it. You, too, Miss James. I'm sure Mr. Ryan is perfectly capable of applying a bandage without your assistance."

Anna freezes where she has started toward me, nods once, and returns to her spot. I can see how tight her jaw is from clear across the grid. I wish I could coax it loose with my hands. That I could kiss it until she laughs or squirms or both.

But I can't. And now, on top of everything else, I've got a stinging knee that hurts like hell and the sobering realization that the absence of Anna James from my life is just as likely to kill me as anything else.

The Kauaʻi ʻōʻō lands on a closed tuba case beside me while I'm trying to stop the bleeding long enough to apply a bandage. My knee is too slick with blood for anything to stick, and eventually I give up, holding a slowly reddening alcohol swab to my skin as I watch the band move on without me, my spot on the field left perfectly intact in my absence.

The yellow and black bird whistles as I watch Anna traverse over the fifty-yard line, her ponytail catching the light.

Is it worth it? he asks. *The pain of loving someone?*

The pain is in the absence, I think. *Not in the love.*

I didn't know birds could sigh, but the Kaua'i 'ō'ō does.

To love, he says, *is to always know that it can be taken away. The pain is in the having, because you know exactly what you stand to lose.*

chapter 20

≈

anna

I made my first C on a math quiz in fourth grade. It was the lon-gest I had ever been grounded. I came home with the big C circled in red atop my score sheet and presented it to my parents like it was a warrant for my arrest.

"I'm going to my room," I announced. "I'm grounded for two weeks."

"Wait, Bagels," Dad said. "You're not grounded. You tried your best, right?"

"If my best is a C, I'm going to think about why for the next two weeks. Please bring my meals to my door."

Later, when I was older, my parents would tease me about it.

"For such a hilarious little girl, you could be so strict with your-self," Mom would say, laughing. "But Lord help the person that crossed you, because you were just as stubborn when you thought you were wronged as when you had wronged yourself."

Nothing is okay.

I go home, I deal with silent stares of my parents, I lie in my room counting stars, and eventually, I sleep.

But it's manageable, weirdly, even though it's torture to know Weston is in the same building as me from the hours of eight to three and there is absolutely nothing I can do about closing the space between us.

It's manageable because I am living—*living*—for Friday's away game and the long bus ride ahead. I'm counting on the usual hubbub of game day excitement and chaos to blot out anyone's memory of me sitting next to Weston as worth commenting on.

I'm terrified that word will get back to Mom and Dad and I'll somehow be doubly grounded. They didn't *say* I couldn't sit next to Weston or talk to him at school, but they will argue it was understood.

I'm thinking about Friday, about burrowing into Weston's side for the first time in what feels like forever, when the lunch bell rings, and I feel his stare prickling my neck. It's like I called for him with only my thoughts, and he answered.

He's leaning against the stairwell when I turn. I flick my eyes from him to Lauren, trying to gauge the chances of her "accidentally" ratting me out to her mom, who would call mine.

"*Anna*," she says, when she sees my look. "I said I was sorry. It won't happen again. Go talk to lover boy. My lips are sealed."

To her credit, Lauren has apologized at least a million times since the incident, insisting repeatedly that she was tired from swim practice and it slipped out. She was practically crying when I saw her at school the next day, cornering me after rehearsal in the locker room.

"I *like* him," she said. "Like, he is still weird, but not a bad weird, you know? He has to be at least semi-smart if he's dating you."

"He's not-weird all on his own," I told her. "You're still completely missing the point. I don't make him any more valid as a person than he was before we started dating. You just care to see it, now."

"That's not fair," Lauren whispered. "*Everyone* makes snap judgments. *Everyone* knows better, but we still do it."

I was too tired after arguing with my parents and a sleepless night to discuss it further, and Lauren had a point.

"I forgive you," I said, "but right now I just want to dry my hair and go to class and try not to fall asleep."

She is giving me the same look that she did a few days ago. Her eyes are narrowed, her mouth curled, like she's trying to figure out my mood and if she stares long enough she will be able to discern my exact thoughts.

"You're still mad at me," she says.

I sigh, glancing at Weston. He's still leaning against the staircase, everyone swarming to class around him. Andy stops to say hello, drumming his sticks on Weston's arm in greeting, and the corner of my mouth lifts up at Weston's bemused face.

"I'm not mad," I say, turning back to Lauren. "I'm tired."

"I'll cover for you in math," she says. "If you are a couple minutes late."

"Thanks," I say, handing her my lunch box. "Grab my book for me, too?"

Her smile is bright with relief, and it makes me feel a little guilty.

"You've got it!"

Weston's smile is the opposite of Lauren's when I come to stand in front of him. It's brittle, worried.

"Hey," he says.

"Hey back," I say, but my voice catches when he doesn't reach for me. He's doesn't brush my hand or my face. He's just standing there, staring at his shoes.

"So, I've got some news," he says.

"I take it it's not good news?"

Weston shakes his head and drags his eyes up to mine.

"No. It's not."

The warning bell rings, and I force out a laugh. "Well, you're walking, so it can't be that you need knee replacement surgery after yesterday's fall, right?"

He doesn't laugh. Doesn't even crack a smile.

"I'm not coming to the game on Friday, Anna."

"*What?* Why? Did you get in trouble?"

Weston runs his fingers through his hair. "I failed yesterday's reading test. It dropped my grade to a sixty-eight. My teacher emailed Mr. Brant, and I'm out until I can get it back up."

It's not just the lost Friday night floating between us, now. It's the *whole thing*. If I've been grounded for a grand total of four days and his grades are already slipping, what's going to happen in a month when we have regionals? What's going to happen if he can't perform in the show?

It's not rational, the anger that bubbles up in me, but I can no more stop it than I can the tears that leak from my eyes.

"So that's it?" I say. "I'm not there to hold your hand for five minutes, and you tank a test grade?"

"*Anna.*"

"No, don't *Anna* me," I tell him. "We worked so flippin' hard on your homework and the duet and . . . and us. What does it matter, if the first time something happens you chuck it all out the window?"

"You know that's not—"

"But it is! It's exactly what happened. You don't think I'm sad? You don't think I'm angry that we can't spend time together?" I'm trying to bottle the words, but I've lost the stopper. "Because I am," I say. "But I'm still getting stu—shit done. I'm still getting my shit done, Weston."

Weston opens his mouth to speak, but my shadows are stretching up the walls around us and I have to get to class, so I turn away before he can say anything.

He comes after me, his hands grabbing at mine. Distantly, a heavy wooden door shuts as classes begin and the hallways are plunged into an eerie silence.

"You can't leave," Weston whispers. It's a statement, but I hear the question underneath. "You aren't, are you?"

"*Of course* I am," I say, pulling my hand away. "I'm going to class. And so are you, if you don't want *another* failing grade."

It's unfair, my anger. And when I turn away, I can't avoid seeing the way Weston's face falls, how his arm falls limply to his side.

The best part of being a teacher's pet is having the ability to tell a lie and have adults immediately believe it.

When I approach Mrs. Ricardo in the latter half of eighth period, while everyone is busy on the daily worksheets, and tell her I'm caught up on homework and really need to spend time in the band hall working on my duet, per Mr. Brant's instruction, she hardly gives me a second glance.

"You finished your worksheets?"

"Yes, ma'am."

"And your project proposal for next week's test grade?"

"Already in your inbox," I say, forcing a smile. "With annotations and a full bibliography."

"Wonderful," she says, looking at me over her glasses. "Go, then. I expect to hear you play perfectly at Friday's game."

"Yes, Mrs. Ricardo," I say, as if she could distinguish my notes from the band as a whole.

When I get to the band hall, it's mostly empty. A few seniors are loitering around with homework and instruments, but *he's* not here.

My stomach has hurt since lunch, and though I'd love to blame the PB&J sandwich with far too much sugary J, I know it's guilt sitting like a stone at the bottom of my esophagus.

I've replayed our argument—*my* argument, really—at least a dozen times in the last two hours, and each time I come out looking like a complete jerk.

It wasn't fair to take out my anger and sadness and frustration on Weston, which is why I've skipped the last half of class to come find him.

But he's not here.

I consider calling him, texting, but I don't want him to answer if he's driving, so instead I let myself into an empty practice room and sit down at a piano.

You would think that, after spending so much time watching Weston play, I would be at least passingly knowledgeable about the black and white keys before me, but I'm not. Instead, I plink at individual keys with one index finger, accidentally stumbling across a melody that sounds something like "Jingle Bells."

I'm absorbed in working the song out by ear when the door softly opens and shuts behind me, the smell of leather and Weston filling my nose in the enclosed space.

He doesn't move from the door, doesn't say anything, so I keep plinking out "Jingle Bells," begging him to say something first, almost hoping he'll be angry at me, because he deserves to be. I was so *mean*. If I had pulled something similar with Lauren or Andy, I wouldn't hear the end of it until next July.

But Weston is different, thank God. Just like everyone says.

When he comes to sit beside me on the piano bench, he

still doesn't say anything, and I don't stop playing. He watches as I plunk out the same three notes over and over. Jing-gle bells. Jing-gle bells.

I can't find the next note sequence, my finger managing to trip over itself even though it's the only one on the keys.

"Dang it," I whisper. "I suck today."

I turn to look at him, finally, and he's looking at me with a slight smile on his face.

"You're not mad," I say. "*How?*"

"Because you were upset," Weston says simply. "Because I messed up and you thought it was your fault, so you lashed out."

He gently removes my hand from the keys and places it in my lap, shaking out his fingers as he settles into playing position, all without looking away from me. He begins playing a lullaby version of "Jingle Bells" mixed with the sleigh ride song.

"That doesn't mean I had any right to say those things to you," I say. "You know it's okay for *you* to be angry, right?"

"I know," he says. We're quiet for a minute as he plays, the song morphing into a jauntier, less sleepy version of "Deck the Halls." "What was it that made you so angry?" Weston asks.

"That I won't get to sit next to you on the bus on Friday," I say, not needing time to think. "Which is all the more selfish and all the more reason you *should be mad at me.*"

Weston ends his improv with a flourish and turns toward me on the bench. His smile is slow, like his pirate smile, but a little sad at the edges.

"I'm angry I won't get to sit next to you, too."

"What happened? With the test grade, I mean? I thought we'd prepared for that."

Weston grimaces. "I was supposed to read the pages on Monday, but . . ." He stops and gestures between us. "I was distracted."

"Any chance you can make it up and raise the grade before Friday?"

"Nope. Already asked. Mr. Brant is furious with me."

"Seems to be the trend today," I say sadly. "I *am* sorry for how I acted."

We're quiet, the band hall behind us filling up with noise as everyone filters in after school to pick up instruments before heading to their cars.

"I thought you were leaving," Weston says. His voice is so quiet, I have to strain to hear him. "I thought you were *done*."

"Weston, I—"

"I know," he says, raising his hands. "I know. It only took me a second to figure out myself. I . . . I've got to learn how to moderate my emotions, I guess. Just because someone is leaving doesn't mean they're leaving forever."

"Right," I murmur.

"Right," he echoes with a smile. A beat. "How am I going to make up for not sitting with you on Friday?"

"Get your grades up?" I ask playfully.

Weston rolls his eyes. "Obviously I'm doing *that*, but what do you want, Anna?"

I lean against his arm, letting my head rest heavily on his shoulder.

"Play me your favorite Christmas song," I say.

And because he's Weston, because he's different, because he's *my* Weston, he puts his hands on the keys and plays with his entire soul.

When Friday night comes and goes and I'm home in my bed, I write about the bus ride and football game without Weston. I let my pen dribble out my every cheesy thought, unfiltered. I don't worry how it sounds like too much to be so attached to someone after only two *weeks*. I don't worry that I sound cliché or dorky writing about how sitting next to Andy on the bus and enduring his kissy faces and gentle teasing about Weston's absence made me look wistfully out the window.

I tell my journal everything, even the bits that make *me* cringe.

And to keep the shadows at bay, I write about what it felt like to be in the practice room with Weston while he played "Carol of the Bells" and "Rudolph the Red-Nosed Reindeer" and "O Come, O Come, Emmanuel."

I write about what it was like when the door was flung open and one of the freshmen flutes gasped and yelled, "We're playing Christmas music up in here, y'all!" And suddenly there was an impromptu Christmas concert made up of a piano, a flute, a saxophone, and a trombone—in October.

It was a disaster, mostly, but we were all laughing so hard it *felt* like Christmas. And it was good.

chapter 21

❧

weston

It's been two weeks of no Anna outside of school, one week since I was exiled from the football game, and I'm sitting cross-legged on my bed at Mom's, looking at the notes Anna has scribbled in my school-issued planner. It is impossible to make heads or tails of them, mostly because her handwriting is awful. Pity she doesn't want to be a doctor instead of a writer. Aren't medical professionals supposed to have terrible handwriting?

My English grade is up, but it's not high enough to get Mr. Brant off my case or to smooth out the worry line that pops up on Anna's forehead when I mention homework.

I've decided it's as much for her as it is for me, working on my fucking study plan, and I'm hoping that fact will help me stay focused, but this is yet another false hope.

The first time my brain wanders, I jerk it back like a dog on a leash. The second time, I let it roam, not realizing the leash is out of my hands until it's too late.

I wish I could text her, talk to her, hold her.

But I can't, so I'll play *King's Reign* instead. Just a break. Just a little bit. *Then* I'll have nothing else to distract me, and I'll get back to school stuff.

I'm working on a side quest when the door opens, and I about jump out of my skin.

"*Mom?* What are you doing here? It's Thursday."

"Took an earlier flight." She smiles. Not only did I not hear her come to my door, but I also didn't hear her roll her suitcase up the stairs or shower or change into an old brown sweater and sweatpants. "I thought we could order in some dinner. Maybe you could invite this Anna girl I'm hearing about."

I set the remote down without pausing the game. "How did you hear about Anna?"

"I talked to Hank," she says matter-of-factly.

"Why did you talk to Dad?"

Mom rolls her eyes. "We still talk, Weston. We were discussing your game this week."

"It's an away game," I say, already counting down the hours until I can sit next to Anna on the bus. Last week was a home game, so that meant no stolen time at all, in case her parents were watching. "That means Dad's coming, right?"

"Well, that's why I called. I thought maybe we could both attend. Especially since your regional marching contest will be here soon, and we'll both want to be there for that."

My dog in the game whines and nudges my player's foot impatiently. Mom's eyes flash to the screen and then to the homework laid out on my bed.

I'm glad when she looks away from me. I need to parse what I'm feeling inside, the confusing relief, the tumultuous exuberance that comes with realizing my parents, *both of them*, will come to my contests.

It wouldn't be so hard to sort out if Anna were here, but she's not.

A month ago, all I would have wanted was for my parents to be together, and if not that, for them to get along well enough to be in the same vicinity . . . and now all I can think about is Anna, how *she* should be here but isn't. How I *should* be able to invite her over for dinner to meet Mom, but I can't.

"Working hard, I see," Mom says, stepping around where I sit on the floor to look at the worksheets and notes. "I thought you said you were on top of your grades, Weston. This looks like a lot to do, and you're playing video games."

"It's fine," I tell her, even though it's not.

She doesn't believe me.

"You need to put the game away until you get your homework done."

I'm about to argue, to say I'll do it later, that I have a plan, when we hear footsteps coming up the stairs and we turn toward the door. I know the sound of these steps too well to pretend to be surprised when Ratio comes into my room, his arms full of books and pencils and a bag of kettle corn.

"Oh, hello, Mrs. James," he greets Mom cheerfully. "I come bearing gifts and homework help for Weston."

"Hello, Ratio. It's good to see you. Your parents are well?"

"They're doing great," he says. "They're ready for marching season to be over, though. They say I slam the door when I leave in the mornings, even though I swear I'm quiet."

"Thank you for coming to help Weston with schoolwork. I was just telling him he needs to quit the video game and focus."

"Couldn't agree more." Ratio grins, and I wonder how much trouble I'd get in for shoving the golden boy of Enfield out my second-story window. "We're going to go work in the living room, if that's okay," Ratio tells Mom. He raises his hand to his mouth and stage whispers, "Less opportunities for distraction for our little Wes-Wes, here."

I'd murder him in cold blood if my room wasn't carpeted.

Ratio and I haven't even had a chance to set out the homework assignments in the living room when there's a knock at the front door, which *never* happens. We're too far on the edge of town to get sales teams or Girl Scouts selling cookies, and anyone who knows us comes to the side door.

I open it curiously, only to have Andy plow right past me.

"What is this, impromptu piano trio practice?" Andy asks. "What's up, Ratio?"

He seems to have no qualms about letting himself into the living room uninvited.

"What are *you* doing here?" I ask.

Andy grabs two pencils from the coffee table, where Ratio is setting up, and starts to rhythmically beat them on the back of the couch.

"Got some intelligence from Anna that you might need some help with science? Science I've got *covered*." He turns to Ratio. "What are you here to help him with, dude? English? Math?"

"*Science*," Ratio says. "Why did she ask us both to help him?"

"Don't know. I'm just following orders. Word on the street is she's still grounded, so I don't want to be on her bad list, in case she's taking the time to concoct some terrible new soup she wants to try out on me."

"Anna asked you *both* to come?" I ask dumbly, turning to Ratio. "Even you?"

"Yeah, she was worried you wouldn't do your homework if she wasn't here to hound you," Ratio says. "Not sure why

I haven't thought about doing this before, to be honest. The assurance of knowing your grades will be high enough to not prevent you from marching is going to add years to my life. *Years.*"

"Yeah, nobody wants to see freakin' Darin doing a solo," Andy chimes in. "I can't stand that guy." He winces when he remembers who he's sitting next to. "Um, no offense. I know he's in your section and stuff," he says, his gaze darting between us.

"I get it," Ratio says. "Neither of us is particularly fond of him."

"Yeah, he's a dick," I tell Andy.

Ratio does not correct me.

Even though he's a grade below us, Andy is a whiz at science, but more important, he's fantastic at reading Anna's disturbingly awful handwriting.

Ratio is good at everything, but his know-it-all edge is softened by Andy's teasing, and the kettle corn doesn't hurt, either.

We've been studying for three hours when they declare me ready for my science test—the biggest boss to beat—and the rest of my homework adequately completed.

The evening is still young, so we start an overly complicated board game that I've only played twice before because Ratio wins every time.

It's one of those alliance-based games, as much about reading people as it is about the board, but where lying is encouraged.

Ratio never lies.

Ratio always wins.

It's fucking ridiculous.

Which is why it's completely delightful and hilarious when, three moves into the game, Andy completely outmaneuvers

Ratio and claims a coveted territory. Ratio doesn't curse, but judging from how red his face gets when he demands that Andy check the rule book for the validity of the play, he comes pretty close.

Mom orders pizza, and Ratio and Andy insist we pause our game to eat with her at the kitchen table instead of eating and playing. It's strangely normal, the four of us crowded around the pizza box, with paper plates and the fancy napkins Mom usually saves for holidays, because she can't find the disposable ones.

It's not normal, I remind myself. Anna should be here, jostling between Andy and Ratio, our worlds perfectly blended.

I text her that night. I know she won't see it until tomorrow morning, when her parents release her phone for school, so I take my time and don't worry about how long it is.

Thanks for sending Ratio and Andy. Andy beat Ratio at Parasitic Negotiations, so he has bragging rights for the next century. I swear we got homework done, too. They helped me study for science and Andy somehow read your TRULY TERRIBLE LIKE HOW IS IT THAT TERRIBLE handwriting and I'm back on your precious homework track. Maybe I can tutor you in penmanship if you ever get ungrounded.

Last, I send her a picture of the star she gave me, this time on my pillow. I kept it by my window all day so it would be as bright as possible.

Same sky. You know.

chapter 22

anna

We're in Colorado, on vacation. Jenny and I have wandered away from where Mom and Dad sit at the picnic tables atop a small mountain. Jenny is taking pictures of elk cows grazing in a nearby field, when a huge bull elk steps into the clearing, his eyes trained on Jenny.

"Jenny. Come. Here." My voice shakes. The elk is so close.

"You're not the boss of me."

I didn't know there was this much terror in the world. I imagine the bull charging at impossibly annoying, always-too-young Jenny.

"Jenny," I say, my voice soft. "Please look to the right."

She turns, angling her camera. She gasps and begins to back away, her sneakers digging into the dirt with each step.

The huge elk takes another step toward us, blocking the cows.

I wish I could talk to animals. I wish I could tell him that I, too, want to protect what is mine. Because Jenny is mine, and I hate *that it feels like a revelation. She's the only little sister I'm ever going to have.*

Two weeks is a long time to be banished to my room, but it's not entirely awful.

Weston and I *aren't* over, never will be. Even if we have to wait until I graduate. Even if we had to wait a lifetime. It's just not possible that a world exists where we aren't together or waiting to be together.

And what's more, he's finding himself, I think. He's realizing that other people care about him, that he has friends willing to do whatever it takes to help with his grades, his life.

I'm glad he's learning this, that we're *good* or whatever, but I still wish I could fast-forward through this part, could press a button and have him by my side.

Because it's not unbearable, but it's *lonely*.

Dad's knock is softer than usual, and I almost don't hear it from where I sit, in the far corner of my brain.

"Come in," I mutter, and when the door doesn't open I say, more loudly, "I said, *come in*."

Jenny's head peeks around the door and I groan.

"Oh," I say. "What do you want?"

Jenny nods her head toward the bed. "Is it okay?"

I gesture for her to sit, flopping back down on my pillows. "Do what you want?" I ask. "We prisoners have no rights."

She perches on the edge of the bed, carefully, like the wrong move might make me go ballistic.

Which I guess is fair. I'm kind of crappy, as far as older sisters go. I might be crappy as far as daughters go, too.

"You can *sit*, sit," I tell her, patting the middle of the bed.

"Thanks," Jenny says, but she only scoots forward another inch or so. "Can I tell you something? And can you promise not to do anything yet?"

I'm not going to promise that, and she knows it, because she holds my eyes and continues. "Weston is in the living room."

I'm up like a shot, and Jenny immediately stands to block the door.

"Weston. *My* Weston?"

"Anna, *shh*. Yes. But let me tell you—"

I don't want to shove her, but I want her to *move* so I can get out to him.

"*Anna.*" Her voice is so unnaturally serious, so . . . grown-up, that I stop. "I'm *trying* to help you," she says.

Now that I know, I can hear the low strains of Weston's voice, of Mom and Dad speaking.

But nobody is yelling.

Nobody sounds they like might be getting thrown out of the house or smothered with their own jacket.

"Weston came to our school today," she continues. "I guess some of the seniors were there to try and get us to join band? Anyways, he was super nice, even when I told him I would rather die than be in band. He said we looked alike, you and me, and he was just . . . nice."

"He *is* nice," I say.

"He likes you, Anna. Like, really, *really* likes you. Like, loves you probably."

"But that doesn't explain why he is *here*," I say. "And what did you have to do with it?"

Jenny doesn't blink. "Oh, I planned it all out. When it was time for the seniors to leave, I told Weston to drive by my school after three and I would miss my bus and he could bring me home out of the kindness of his heart."

"You did *what*?"

Jenny raises an eyebrow, and I don't know what genetic gift allows *her* that ability, but not me. "You're not the only liar in the James family," she says. "Only I'm better at it than you. Also, have you been in his car? Have you noticed that it smells like salad?"

"But why wouldn't you have just called Mom and Dad if you missed your bus?" I ask. "Or me, for that matter."

She shrugs, her expression unchanging. "Oh, my phone is dead."

I narrow my eyes. "You have one of those rechargeable battery cases, don't you? Your phone is *never* dead."

Jenny shrugs again. "Also dead," she says.

"So, you lied to Mom and Dad about your phone being dead and organized this grand plot just to get Weston here." I pause a beat. "Why?"

It's an unspoken agreement, Jenny and me. We're too different. Everyone says so. We can love each other, be ready to die for each other, but we don't actually *like* each other. We don't go out of our way to do nice things for the other.

It's just not what we do.

But now I'm looking at her, like *really* looking, and she is . . . older. Somewhere along the way, she grew out her horrendous bowl-cut bangs, her face thinning out to reveal bone structure beneath the roundness of childhood. Her eyes are not as innocent.

And I wonder what I've missed with her, if it was age, not personality, that cut such a jagged edge in our sisterly bond. Maybe we're more alike than I thought and I just . . . missed it.

"I did it for you," Jenny says, and she sounds surprised that I have to ask. "And because I like him. He doesn't have any brothers and sisters. Did you know that?"

"I did know," I say, and I can't keep the awe out of my voice. "Thanks, Jenny."

"You're welcome," she says, smiling. "I like him better than you, so it works out."

Jenny and I must look too innocent when Dad comes to fetch us, because his face goes from carefully composed to exasperated when he sees us on the bed pretending to be consumed in a game of Uno.

"Yeah, right," he says. "Like you haven't been plastered to the door for the last twenty minutes."

"What was that, Father?" Jenny asks, her voice high and affected.

"Yes, Papá," I say. "We are but passing the time whilst we wait for news from town. I do ever so hope that Netherfield Park has let at last. It will so please Mother."

"Living room," he says to me. "Jenny? Your bedroom, please. *With the door shut.*"

Jenny groans, but she's already got her phone out, her thumbs flying as she responds to a string of texts on her very charged, very not-dead phone. The Uno cards stay scattered on my bed.

Dad tugs on Jenny's hair as she passes and flicks my ear as I follow close behind, eager to be in the same space as Weston.

"Be cool," he says quietly.

"I'm *always* cool," I say.

But I'm decidedly uncool when I turn the corner of the living room and see Weston, straight-backed and stiff-looking with his long legs jutting out from where he sits by the fireplace.

My fireplace. On a *Thursday afternoon.*

His eyes light up when he sees me, but the rest of him is unmoving as I ignore Mom's heavy stare and sit beside him, our bare knees brushing.

"Hi," I whisper.

"Hello, Anna," he says.

Mom and Dad are mirrors across from us, sitting on the edge of the sofa and looking at Weston and me like we're being interviewed for a job for which we are woefully unqualified.

"We would like to thank you again," Dad says to Weston, "for helping Jenny home."

"You helped Jenny home?" I ask, but my voice must be too falsely surprised because even Weston gives me an *Are you serious?* look.

"That's enough, Anna," Mom says.

"*Sorry,*" I mutter.

"We *are* grateful, but that doesn't excuse weeks of lying to us." Mom turns to me. "You're still in trouble."

I'm about to argue that I wouldn't have lied in the first place if I had thought they would give Weston a fair chance, but Dad silences me with a look.

"But Weston has told us everything," Mom says. "How he helped you pass your duet playoff and how you helped him with his homework and . . . Well, we're not saying you still wouldn't have been punished, but maybe we can . . . maybe we can start over."

"Start over?" I hedge. "In what way, exactly?"

"We were right to punish you," Dad says, "and you were wrong to lie. But we weren't entirely fair to Weston here, either. Or you." Dad comes to stand in front of us, clasping Weston by the shoulder. "I'm sorry," he says. "And I'm sorry that it took Jenny interfering to hear you out. We should have done that in the first place . . ." He turns to me. "For both of you."

"I'm sorry, too," I say. "I hated not telling you."

Mom must realize how heavy the room feels, because she isn't frowning when she asks, "So what *have* you two been doing when you were supposed to be working on projects?"

Weston doesn't give my face a chance to redden. "Four-wheeling, mostly," he says. "But we really did work on the duet and homework quite a lot."

"Still do," I pipe up. "The duet is more than ready for regionals, though. And Weston plays the piano, you know. He has the same teacher as Andy."

Weston is still not totally at ease next to me, his spine a little too straight and his thumb rubbing my hand too quickly to be comforting, but he relaxes when I ask him to stay for dinner and Dad says it's a perfect idea, Mom's small frown disappearing quickly.

Jenny drags in the computer chair for Weston to sit in as we bustle around, bringing chicken fingers and bowls of gravy and salad to the table.

It's weird how *not* weird it is for Weston to be reaching over Jenny to help make room for the salt and pepper shakers. After weeks of him being a secret, you would think there would be a period of adjustment, of waiting for him to fit in.

Weston might be cautious, his smile slow in a nonpirate, hesitant way, but the pirate smile is there when I peek at him while Dad prays to bless the food, one of Weston's hands in mine, the other in Jenny's.

This must be what it is like when people say a weight has been lifted from their chest, because I feel so much *lighter*, like this is how it was always supposed to be, with Weston beside me, trying to diplomatically say he shouldn't get a vote in tonight's rare Thursday family movie night, since he only just arrived.

I think it's hypothetical, his vote, until Dad asks Weston what kinds of movies his family watches and Weston evasively says, "We haven't watched movies together in a while."

Mom's eyes flick to me and down to her plate, but then she's back to it with Jenny, arguing that Weston should side with them and choose the psychological thriller they've been dying to watch.

"Nobody wants to watch that," Dad says.

"You mean you and Anna don't want to," Mom argues. "We have a tiebreaker now," she says, gesturing at Weston, "and if he's going to stay for movie night, he should have a say."

Weston clears his throat and says to me, "I'm beginning to think your mom is only inviting me to stay so she can watch the movie she wants."

Jenny taps his shoulder. "I also want to watch it," she reminds him, "and Anna probably does, too, even if it's just because it's got that cute guy in it that she likes."

"I do *not*," I say. "Y'all are insane if you think Dad and I are voting for anything other than the new rom-com on Netflix."

The rest of dinner devolves into each side of the table making their case to Weston about why their movie is a better idea and Weston slowly, so slowly, smiling his real smile for them, the *my* Weston smile.

When it's time for him to go—*"One movie night doesn't mean that rules and curfew have gone out the window, Anna Lynn"*—Weston has solidly won Mom's heart by voting for the psychological thriller, despite Dad's and my protests; has thoroughly examined my room (door open), with its coffee cups of pens and Christmas lights strung on my headboard, decreeing it *"so Anna"*; and has eaten his weight in microwave popcorn, playfully fighting with Jenny over the kettle corn seasoning shaker.

"Still don't want to run for the hills?" I ask him, when we walk out to his car. "They are a lot."

Weston laughs, a little louder than is warranted. "They are," he agrees, "but I like it. Plus, there are no hills around here."

"You'd have to run pretty far," I agree.

The words are barely out of my mouth before he kisses me, a sweet, lingering touch that I know he would deepen if we weren't on my driveway and if we were sure my parents weren't watching.

"What was that for?" I ask.

He tilts my head up with a finger beneath my chin. "Same sky," he says.

"Same sky," I echo. And because the world is finally spinning on its axis and my parents don't hate me and somehow, despite everything, I get to keep my family and Weston at once, I reach up to kiss him one more time.

Later that night, Mom comes into my room without knocking, pausing in the doorway when she sees me lying on my back, typing on my newly returned phone above my face.

"Texting Weston?" Mom asks.

"Yeah. He just got home."

"Good," she says. "Glad he made it back safely. You said his mom lives on the outside of town?"

"Yeah, but he's staying at his dad's in Bloom tonight," I tell her. "I think it's actually closer?"

"Like you wouldn't know," Mom says, her voice two parts teasing and three parts stern.

She hasn't moved from the doorway, so I set the phone down.

"You can come sit, Mom," I say. The dark room is crowded with the words we aren't saying, the ones she wanted to tell me earlier but wouldn't in front of Dad or Weston or both.

She sits on my bed, patting my leg where it's stretched atop the comforter. "I like him, Anna."

"You would have liked him weeks ago, if you had given him a chance," I say.

Mom sighs. "That's my fault. But you have to understand, when you're a parent, you want to keep your children safe. If you hear of anything that could hurt them, you do everything in your power to keep it from reaching them."

"But I told you he wasn't that way," I tell her. "And right

from the beginning, you wouldn't listen. You wouldn't even try. You wanted to believe Mrs. Anderson and whoever else because of a stupid rumor about a stupid tree that he didn't even kill."

"I know."

"But *why*? Why wouldn't you listen to *me*? I never lied to you, not before. And the only reason I *did* was because I . . ."

The words bottle in my throat.

"Because you love him," Mom finishes.

"Yeah," I say, because there's no denying it. "I really do, Mom."

"I know," she says.

I play with the edge of my comforter. "You don't think it's stupid or that we're too young or it's too soon or something?"

"Anna, you have always known exactly what you want and what you love. My opinion doesn't matter."

"It does, though," I say, and it's true. So many of my shadows have formed because I'm afraid to disappoint her or Dad. "I mean, I'll love him either way, but it would be *nice* to know you liked him, too. That you don't think . . . whatever it is you think of him."

"I think he's a very nice young man," Mom says. "It's obvious he cares a great deal for you."

"But?"

"No buts. I like him. I could have done without the lying, but that's more on you than him."

"It is," I say. "He felt worse than I did that I was lying."

Mom's lips quirk. "Not sure if that's a vote for him or just a mark against you," she says, her voice teasing. "But he *did* vote for my movie, so I'll let it slide."

We're quiet for too long after that, both of us getting lost in our heads.

"Who would you *want* me to date?" I ask. "Like, if you had to pick, who would you have chosen?"

"Oh, Anna—" she starts.

"Don't *Oh, Anna* me," I say. "It wasn't Weston, that much I know."

"I didn't *know* Weston," Mom says.

"Yeah, but admit it: You wanted me to date William or Andy or someone like that."

"I wanted you to date someone who would treat you the way you deserve," Mom says. "I wanted you to be safe and happy and whole."

"I'm those things with Weston," I feel the need to point out. "It just sucks, because nobody ever wants to look past his jacket or weirdness or *whatever* it is that makes people not want to be his friend."

"He's a little off-putting," Mom admits. My face must be *horrendous*, because she adds, "He doesn't mean to be, Anna, but he . . . he has a lot of wounds. You can tell. And sometimes people with wounds are unpleasant to be around. Sometimes they lash out."

"*Or*," I counter, "they are less likely to hurt others because they know what it's like to be hurt."

Mom is quiet, so I add, "Different isn't always bad, Mom. Different is . . . different can be *so, so good*."

I didn't know Mom had a slow smile, too.

"I'm sorry, Anna," she says, "if I made you feel like you had to lie to me."

"I'm sorry I didn't tell you," I say. "But also, maybe not? I have a feeling he's always going to side with you, and Dad and I are never going to get to watch a rom-com on family movie night again."

She shoves my leg.

"Whine about it to your boyfriend, but don't stay up too late. There's school in the morning and a game tomorrow night."

"And regionals soon, and the talent show next week. I know, I know," I yawn.

"Love, love, love you," Mom says.

"I love, love, love *you*."

And I do. Even if I disobey and stay up far too late texting Weston.

chapter 23

weston

Anna and I are still in our talent show finery when we un-
load our bags from the trunk of her parents' car. Her heels
click against the cobblestones of the roundabout drive of her
grandparents' lake house, and her long blue dress whispers at
her ankles as it's tossed in a light wind.

I'm pinching myself that I'm here, that after a week of
not-that-awkward dinners with her parents and even-less-
awkward weekend lunches with both Mom and Dad, I've
been invited to a family weekend getaway.

"It's only a couple hours away," Anna told me excitedly at
dinner, after her parents—begrudgingly, I think—said I was
welcome to join them after the talent show. "But it's three
stories and there's a tree that grows up through the top porch
and a lake and . . ."

At some point, I stopped listening, too absorbed in watching her eyes sparkle with excitement as she told me about her grandparents' tree house, as she called it.

I watched her tonight, too. Andy called me out on it when we took to the little stage in the cafeteria to play our piano trio for the talent show. "*Dude*, watch your hands, not the girl." But it was impossible to focus on the catered food or the talent performances or how the cafeteria had been transformed into something resembling a fine dining establishment when Anna was dressed like *that*.

Even in the low gleam of the lampposts lining the street, she's beautiful, almost ethereal, light shining through the gauzy bits of her blue dress. I'm especially grateful for the low light when our arms tangle, when she leans past me and the sleeves of my jacket, which she stole, rubs against my bare forearms.

"Your bag is *crushing* mine," she says. "What the heck did you bring?"

"Gaming console," I tell her. "For *King's Reign*."

"Afraid you'll be bored?" her dad asks, sliding around us to grab a handful of pillows they brought from home for Mrs. James. "Would have thought you'd want first go at driving the boat tomorrow."

"It's just in case I can't sleep," I tell him. "Or if we need a distraction when you're inevitably outvoted for movie night and the thriller gets too bloody for you and Anna to handle."

"You can't *leave* during family movie night," Anna says, having finally dislodged her duffle. "It's against the rules."

"Well, can we watch a movie tonight?" I ask her. "Or is that going to run too close to curfew?"

"There isn't a curfew at the lake house," Anna says. "Right, Dad?"

"Ask your mother."

It's almost midnight, but when Anna begs her mom to let

us stay up to watch a movie on the couch, she's met with little resistance, especially when I pipe up that Jenny should watch, too.

"She *can't* watch with us," Anna says, and Mrs. James looks ready to argue, until Anna adds, "She'll say we can't watch a Christmas movie, and I want to watch *You've Got Mail*."

"*You've Got Mail* is *boring*," Jenny hollers from downstairs. "I'm going to sleep."

"*You've Got Mail* isn't a Christmas movie," Mr. James's voice says from afar. "And I'm going to sleep, too."

Anna's mom laughs. "Sounds like we're all tuckered out. Just make sure you turn off the TV and kitchen light before you go to sleep," she says. "Good night, you two."

After she leans down to hug Anna and kiss her on the cheek, Mrs. James comes toward me. I think she's coming to hug me, too, and she does, but then she leans down and kisses *my* cheek, too.

"Good night, Weston," she says.

"Good night, Mrs. James," I say.

Anna, who's on her hands and knees, flipping through a binder of DVDs kept beneath the TV, missed the exchange.

"She kissed me on the cheek," I said. "Did you see that?"

"She *likes* you now, remember?"

We must fall asleep on the couch before the movie is over, because the next thing I know, Anna's dad is standing above us, gently shaking me awake in the dark.

"Weston," he whispers. "Bagels. It's time for bed."

Anna mumbles something and tightens her arms around me, which I gently loosen.

Mr. James must see this, because he smiles and says, "She did that when she was little, too. She never wants to move after she falls asleep. She can sleep anywhere, if you let her, and she clings to whatever's closest."

"I know," I whisper, and because his smile reminds me so much of Anna, I find myself saying, "She does this on the band bus. Sometimes I think she's going to cut off my circulation."

"Well, we can't have that," Mr. James says with a quiet laugh, leaning down to shake Anna. "*Bagels.* Bedtime."

When she finally rouses enough to move, Anna looks up, and she's *my* Anna. Christmas sock Anna. The other half of my duet Anna.

"Tell Weston good night," her dad says.

Still half asleep, Anna leans forward and kisses me square on the lips. It is *not* a gentle kiss, and certainly not one we should be having in front of her *father*.

"Good night, Weston," she tells me. "I love, love, love you."

Everything inside me softens.

"I love you, too," I tell her. "But you have to go to sleep."

"Was asleep," she mutters, getting to her feet. "Could still be asleep."

She holds the handrail as she goes down the stairs to the room she shares with Jenny, but she's wobbly enough that I ask her dad, "Is she going to be okay?"

His eyes are thoughtful when he looks at me. "She is better than okay," he says, patting my shoulder. "Good night, Weston. You'll forgive me if I skip the good-night kiss."

I laugh. It's the kind of stupid joke *my* dad would make. They'll definitely get along when they finally meet.

Saturday is an endless golden day of cruising around the small, private lake in a very nice boat and of roasting hot dogs over the firepit. I send a picture of the sun shining off the water to the joint text I started for Mom and Dad and me when they came to our game last week. They both respond, Mom with emojis, Dad with a gibberish of letters I take to mean he is jealous.

Jenny and Mrs. James claim they want to do a puzzle after lunch, but that lasts for about five minutes before they wander to their rooms for a nap.

"I'm not tired," Anna says, and her dad agrees.

"Y'all want to go to the square in town? It's small," he says to me, "but it's got a few little shops and one of those fancy Popsicle places."

"*Popsicles*," Anna says, and it's decided.

The town square *is* small. Even on the weekend, there are hardly any cars as we pile out of the Jameses' van and into the sunlight.

The "few little shops" end up being an antique store, a place that says it's a boutique but looks like an extension of the antique store, and a tiny bookstore that is probably closed.

It isn't much, but Anna and her dad roam through the antique store like it was made for them. They crawl through each booth, moving aside old tins of cocoa and bottles of Coke that might be vintage or might be from the corner store we passed on our way into town.

"What are you looking for?" I ask Anna.

Mr. James answers. "We're looking for treasure," he says. "It could be anywhere."

"You have to pick a best in show," Anna says, holding up a metal Slinky to show her dad. He shakes his head. She puts it back on the shelf next to a stuffed rabbit missing an eye. "And if it's not too expensive, we buy it."

"Twenty dollars or less," Mr. James says.

"It's the rules," Anna adds.

The best in show ends up being a pair of ceramic snail salt and pepper shakers. Someone has glued googly eyes on their eyestalks, along with tying a note around their necks that says, "Salt and Pepper are better together, just like us! $12 for both or $15 a piece. You choose, mortal."

"This one is missing the stopper on bottom," I point out.

"We're not going to use them for salt and pepper, silly," Anna says. "They're just going to be little snail friends on a counter or a shelf or something."

"Little snail friends that are constantly watching you," her dad agrees, carrying them to the checkout counter, which is just a white folding table at the front of the store. "I'm going to put one of these in Anna's backpack to remind you both that I am *always* watching."

"*Dad*," Anna says.

"*Bagels*," he mimics, but they're laughing.

That night we end up watching another thriller that Jenny and Mrs. James want to watch, and Anna hides under my arm for the entire last half of the movie.

It's becoming easier to see, a future with Anna and me, a future of coming to the lake house with her family on weekends and going fishing with her dad, of tubing in the lake with Jenny and letting Mrs. James bully me into helping her with the impossible puzzle on the big wooden table. A future where my parents share a text message and maybe *me*, one where we aren't together, but we're not exactly apart, either.

There's a restful lump in my chest, something I haven't felt in a long, long time, and it takes me a minute to realize it's contentment. My grades are fine—or will be. Band is fine. My parents are fine.

Anna is here. She's not going anywhere.

My biggest worry is that I might need to invest in another jacket, because I'm not sure if I'm ever going to be able to tell her no when she asks to wear mine.

chapter 24

Cℓ

anna

When my grandparents bought the lake house, it was like my family had stepped into one of those TV shows where people drive golf carts more expensive than cars and wear pastel shorts and shirts.

It was magical, a jump away from reality for a weekend at a time, where we could pretend that nothing mattered except how fast we could get the tube to fly across the water.

"Someday," Grandma said, while we sat on the second-story wraparound porch, "you girls can bring your kids here. And your kids' kids here."

"I don't want kids," Jenny said fiercely. "I want to have a bunch of dogs and snakes and birds."

"And you, Anna?" Grandma asked with a laugh. "Do you want dogs and snakes and birds, too?"

"I want everything," I said. "I want it all."

Sunday morning comes too soon at the lake. It always does.

"One *more*," Jenny begs, and even though the car is loaded and Mom has already made Weston and me go through the house to triple check that the lights and electronics are turned off, we head to the dock for one last boat ride.

Mom, Dad, and Jenny are at the front of the boat, so I lean against Weston near the stern, his arm draped casually around my shoulder, his aversion to touching me when my parents are nearby finally dissipating.

"Don't look now, but I think the James family might have accepted you as one of their own," I say.

Weston laughs, and tucks a bit of loose hair behind my ear. "The Ryans are fond of you, too. Nanny has asked *twice* when you'll be back to play at her house. She refuses to put away the army guys."

"Your aunt told me at the talent show that she's going to start stocking Dr Pepper in the fridge for me," I say. "She also said she has more of your childhood toys than Nanny and that she's very mad at you for not bringing me over for a visit."

"All in good time," Weston says, still laughing.

"Because we have nothing but time?" I ask.

Weston's pirate smile is devastating. "*Yes.*"

On the car ride home, Weston, Jenny, and I take turns reading aloud from Jenny's required book for school. It's the story of a brave mouse with too-large ears who feels different, which I worry might be too on the nose for Weston, but he throws himself into making silly voices for all the characters, which even eye-rolling Jenny adores.

When we get back, Weston stays for dinner, and then until curfew, when Dad teasingly reminds us there are still rules, and we have school tomorrow.

I walk Weston to his car, our breath mingling in little puffs that float in front of us. I can tell he's tired, but he kisses me thoroughly. They're at his car all the same.

"I need my jacket back," he murmurs against my lips.

"It's mine," I say, pulling it tighter around me.

"You can have it back tomorrow."

"For the whole day?" I bargain.

"For the whole day," he promises. "Though neither of us will need it, since Mr. Brant is going to march us into the ground to prep for next week."

He begins working the sleeves from my arms one by one, like I'm a little kid.

"I love you," I say. "Even though you suck at picking movies, and you kept mixing up your mouse voices."

When he's worked the jacket off me, he kisses me again, his eyes laughing as he pulls away. "I'll try to do better next time."

He's so different than the boy I barged in on in the practice room the first week of school. His hair is longer, a bit darker than I thought it would be, still blond, but curling around the tips of his ears, the back of his neck. His eyes are still indescribable, but they don't squint at the corners as often.

I like happy Weston.

"My Weston," I murmur into his jacket, leaning forward for one last hug.

"My Anna." He smiles into my hair.

I tap his jacket as we pull apart. "All day tomorrow, remember."

"Promise," he says, still grinning. "Tomorrow, it's yours."

The last thing I manage to do, before the sun and the boat and the weekend of grinning so much it hurts claims me for sleep, is send him a text of the stars and our version of good night: Same sky.

chapter 25

∾

weston

chapter 26

anna

It seems wrong to wake up this happy on a Monday, especially when this week is going to be heck on wheels, chock-full of practices and cramming sessions before the contest on Saturday. Everything is perfect, but not perfect enough. We will be fine-tuned within an inch of our lives.

I roll over to text Weston but panic when I see the time.

I'm *late*. Like, an hour late for practice and still not out of bed.

I'm going to need a whole new pair of running shoes to work *these* late miles off.

My case hits my doorframe as I scramble out of my room, trying unsuccessfully to pull my last shoe on *while* moving. I run past Jenny's room, ignoring the low sound of her crying. She's probably got her hair stuck in the straightener again, or one of her friends didn't like a photo she posted online. *Where's Weston when she's being unreasonable?*

He's at band practice. *Not* owing a million late laps. That's where.

I round the corner to the living room and stop short.

Every light is on: the overhead fan light, the two little matching table lamps Dad found at a garage sale and Mom painted a matching forest green. One of the shades is slightly dented from when Jenny and I knocked it over while playing with a bouncy ball when we were kids.

We never have all the lights on.

Ratio's gaze is trained on the lamp shade's blemish until I walk into the crowded living room. His eyes snap to mine like magnets.

His is the gaze that I meet, even though Mom, Dad, Jonathan, and Pastor Collins and his wife are crowded onto the couches.

Everyone looks somber, and the room is eerily quiet except for Mom's sobs.

Ratio flinches when Mom's crying grows louder at the sight of me, her tearstained face somehow becoming alarmingly redder.

"Oh, sweetheart, I'm so sorry," she tells me. "So sorry, so sorry."

It's frightening how quickly my brain puts together the pieces.

Ratio and Jonathan are here.

Pastor Collins is here.

There is one glaring omission, and I know.

I know.

If he was in the hospital, I would have been woken. Rushed to his side.

If he was hurt or sick or injured, I would have been told.

But the cavalry has arrived, the people here to pick up the pieces of what hasn't broken yet.

"Bagels," my dad begins as he stands up, and for the first time in my life he pauses to catch a shuddering breath before he continues, "come sit down."

I don't want to hear what comes next.

I don't want to sit down.

My eyes frantically jump back to Ratio's steady face, begging him to tell me the clanging in my bones is not true, that everybody's got it wrong.

He shakes his head ever so slightly, and I know.

I *know*.

Time slows. Stops.

It's like a superhero movie, where the heroine is so fast that everyone else appears frozen. I am free to wander from person to person, examining their every move, their every expression.

Jonathan with his concerned eyes frozen somewhere between my mom and Ratio; Dad with tears he doesn't know how to process carving out paths over his cheeks.

Distantly, I hear Jenny's crying, suspended on a low sob.

I decide I'm going to let the pain come. I decide I'm going to shoulder as much of it as I can.

The world spins back into motion.

"What happened?" I ask Ratio. Dad opens his mouth to answer, so Ratio doesn't have to hold the burden of telling me. But Ratio stands and quiets Dad with a touch of his hand.

"Car accident," he says. "On his way home last night. Instant. No pain."

"Where?" My voice is a croak.

"The pumpkin patch road."

I nod. "Okay."

There's nothing else to say. "Thank you for coming," I tell Jonathan and his family. "That was really nice of you."

"Anna," Mom says, and her hiccupping sobs are so forceful that my name comes out wrong and slurred. "I'm so, so sorry."

"It'll be okay, Mom," I say. "I'm going to step outside and get some air, if that's all right."

My voice sounds hollow, but not broken.

Nobody stops me, nobody responds. Pastor Collins is rubbing my mom's shoulders. Ratio and Jonathan silently follow me out the front door, onto the cold, brown lawn that is already curling in on itself in anticipation of winter.

My hands are itching with energy I don't know how to use, so I start to unwind the Christmas lights that Dad always puts up too early from the tree. After a beat, Jonathan and Ratio step up to help me, unquestioning.

"This sucks," Jonathan says.

"It's fucking bullshit is what it is," Ratio says.

And something about the way he says it, the vehemence of it, the unexpectedness of it, makes me snort.

"You wait until he's gone to prove you're a mere cursing mortal," I joke.

They laugh. I laugh.

And then I'm on the ground, and it's not at all like the stories where a character says they don't know who is making the high-pitched keening noise. *I'm* making this noise. Me. The sound stuck somewhere between a plea and a broken, broken cry.

"Fucking bullshit," Jonathan agrees, squatting down to brush the hair back from my face.

"We're late for practice," I say through my tears. "We're going to be in so much trouble."

"You don't have to go to school today, Anna." Ratio's drum major voice is on, the authoritative one. I wonder if he can speak Weston back into existing.

I wonder if he's already tried.

There's a whispered argument, sharp staccato bits from Ratio and Jonathan.

"What?" I ask, pulling myself together enough to stand. "What are you saying?"

Jonathan shoots Ratio a look. "Everyone's at the band hall. Everyone. We can take you, if you want to go."

"But you don't *have* to go," Ratio tells me. "It's only if you—"

"I want to," I say. "I . . . I don't want to be here."

The thought of going back into the house with Mom and her sobs and Jenny with her closed bedroom door and steady Dad being so unbalanced is more than I can handle. More than I can shoulder.

Ratio sighs, and something about the way he moves his hand to rub his face makes me think of Weston, and I'm barely able to bottle the tears.

"Let's go," he says, and we do, the three of us piling into Ratio's car and none of us saying a word during the ten-minute drive to school.

The band hall is full of people when we arrive: band kids and nonband seniors and parents and teachers. There's a table set up with coffee and doughnuts. Nobody seems to care that there's food in here, a novelty. Nobody is touching any of it.

I'm loosely aware of Mom and Dad arriving and trailing behind me, watching me as I am passed from one well-meaning set of arms to another. It is made abundantly clear that Ratio and I are *guests of honor*, that we are the ones that everyone wants to be near.

"I don't want to be here," I whisper to Dad.

"We can go," he tells me. "Whatever you want, Anna. Whatever you want."

I want to beg him to take me away somewhere, anywhere that isn't here, where so many faces are looking at me like I am something to be pitied, reminding me that *I am someone to be pitied*.

But wherever I go, I realize, is not where I want to be. Because *he* won't be there.

And maybe it's going to hit me in pieces, I think, and maybe this is a part of it: There's nowhere on earth that I can go, no plane or train or boat or four-wheeler that will let me reach Weston.

Which seems so profoundly wrong. My brain is arguing with me, insisting that someone is mistaken and he's not *here* but that he's somewhere, and if I can just figure out how to get there, we will be together.

I decide to stay in the band hall, but I do not go to class. Eventually, my parents take me home, but it feels like a movie with bad transitions. One minute I'm in the band hall, the next I'm sitting on the edge of my bed with my door closed. I can hear Mom quietly sniffling in the hallway, Dad's murmurs of comfort.

I don't know how long I sit staring at the phone in my hand, at Weston's contact information, wondering what will happen if I call it, wondering if he'd answer.

When she was younger, Jenny would be scared of storms and come running into my room to share my bed. I almost always told her to go away. She would look at me with huge sad eyes in the light of the hallway night-light, her doll dangling from her hand, and she would ask one more time: *Please.*

And I would almost give in. Almost. But I would tell her I needed sleep, that she needed to grow up.

I was a jerk.

Jenny is much kinder than I am. Always has been. When I open her door sometime after two in the morning, the hall light slicing into the darkness of her room, she sits up in bed and looks at me with eyes that look like mine, a face that looks like mine.

"Can I sleep with you?" I ask.

She doesn't say anything. Doesn't ask any questions. She just scoots over in her twin-size bed, pressing herself against the wall, and I close the door behind me.

We don't say anything the rest of the night. But when I finally fall asleep, only to wake up with snot and tears pouring out of me, Jenny strokes my hair as we both cry onto her pillow.

chapter 27

anna

Ratio comes to pick me up the next morning to go to Weston's mom's house to discuss the funeral arrangements. Mom and Dad want to come, but I tell them they have to let me out of their sight at some point, that Ratio is the most careful of drivers and nothing will happen.

"We just . . . be careful, Bagels," Dad says. And he hugs me long and hard, like I'm going away forever instead of for the afternoon.

I let him squeeze me, even though every time someone wraps their arms around me, I can only think that it's one more hug separating me from the last embrace I'll ever get from Weston.

"Skipping school?" I ask Ratio as I climb into the front seat. "How very Weston of you."

Something twitches in Ratio's jaw, his eyes trained on the

road. "Don't go back to school yet," he tells me. "Don't go on social media, either."

"Wasn't planning on it," I say. "But why?"

"Just. Don't."

Ratio is not Weston. He is under no obligation to be honest with me, to tell me the truth when I ask for it. But I'm going to ask anyway.

"Tell me," I say. "I can take it."

"They're *memorializing* him," he says, almost hissing. It's the closest to anger I have ever seen him. "Everyone is crying in the hallways and putting up handmade posters of how much they're going to miss him and how much he meant to them."

I snort. "They're pretending they gave a sh—shit when he was alive?"

The word gets caught on my tongue, but I push it out. There is a cursing deficit in the world now that he's gone. I should try and fill it. And who's going to punish me? Who is going to dare tell me I'm not old enough, that I haven't felt the brunt of the world enough, to decide which words are bad or good?

"*Yep*," Ratio says, and that's all he says.

Part of me wants Ratio to unleash, to cry, to throw something, to crack apart at the seams so that we can compare scars. But he won't.

It's what makes him such a good friend, his steadiness and unshakability. It's what someone like Weston needs—needed—Weston with his moods and abstract thinking that could plummet the sun into the ocean.

I wonder if he can hear my thoughts, if being dead means you're incorporeal and can slip into the minds of those you love.

"What do you think heaven is like?" I ask Ratio.

His answer is fast. "A lot like here," he says. "I think there's still work to be done, but it's work you're perfectly suited for, that you enjoy. I don't buy that it's a bunch of harps and angels and stuff. I think God is there, your soul is there, and that's enough."

"You think Weston is clocking in on some heavenly time card?"

Ratio's laugh is small but genuine. "Weston is playing music," he says.

It's a stupid thought, a trite one that will receive no confirmation in any sermon. My ideas about God and church and what any of it actually means are running through my hands like water, and I am left with the undeniable truth, the impossible reality, that Weston *is* somewhere. He didn't disappear.

And I too believe—have to believe—that wherever he is, he is playing music.

There are three other cars parked in front of the house when we pull up. I recognize Pastor Collins's green van, Mrs. Ryan's Prius, Hank's work truck.

"Is it just us?" I ask.

"Guess so," Ratio says.

Weston's parents and Pastor Collins are already at the table when we come in.

The chair Weston sat in the night I met his mom and she made us dinner is glaringly empty, boxes of photos stacked on its seat.

"Hey, kids," Hank says, standing when we come in. He's crying, his beard damp when he kisses the top of my head.

Dianne isn't crying, but her eyes are swollen beneath her carefully applied makeup.

"We have the service pretty well set," Pastor Collins says, sliding a yellow legal pad between Ratio and me. "But we wanted to see what you two wanted to contribute. There's no pressure. Weston's parents just want to make sure you have the opportunity to say your good-byes in the service if you so choose."

The pad lists the order of the service, but even though the words are familiar and worn, I can't read them because I can't believe this is real, that we are sitting around a table to talk about Weston Ryan's funeral.

Family processional
Opening prayer
Hymn
Hymn
Ratio?
Hymn
Anna?
Sermon
Closing hymn and family escorted exit
Pallbearers

Ratio clears his throat. "I would like to play a piece on the piano," he says to the table. "If that's okay."

"He would love that," Mrs. Ryan says. "*We* would love that."

She and Hank are holding hands atop the table, Hank's thumb rubbing over Dianne's knuckles in the same way Weston's used to rub over mine.

I look away.

"Anna?" Ratio asks. "What do you want to do?"

Everyone is looking at me, but I am staring at the pictures of Weston spread on the table, the knickknacks and bits of him set up like a messy shrine. I recognize some from our afternoon at Nanny's house. A few of the army men are scattered atop the photos, the war on kindness wilting beneath the onslaught of grief. There are restaurant napkins piled here, too, and I wonder if I should clean them up, but then I see they're covered in bits of writing and doodles.

I can't answer their question about what I want to say at my boyfriend's funeral, because suddenly my mind is far away, scraping together a list of things he's touched, things of his I have hidden away in drawers and backpack pockets and on band folders.

"His jacket," I say suddenly. "Where is it?"

The question makes Hank's eyes water again, but Dianne's gaze is steady when she meets mine. "The funeral home said it was in too poor condition to be returned," she says, a small hitch in her voice.

"It's still there?" I ask, and suddenly nothing else matters.

"I guess so," she says.

"Anna? The funeral?" Ratio's touch on my arm is light, centering.

"I'll speak," I say. "I'll . . . I'll write him something."

Pastor Collins nods as he takes the legal pad back. "Good," he says. "That's settled."

He says more. But I don't hear it. Ratio nods. Hank nods and cries. Dianne nods.

I probably nod, too.

But my mind is far away, swinging back and forth between the concrete culvert on the little country road between my house and Weston's and the funeral home where the jacket, *his jacket*, is waiting for me.

The man behind the funeral home counter absolutely does *not* want to speak with me.

He has on a three-piece suit with a collar tight enough to make a saint curse, a scowl that I think is meant to appear passive and grave, and suspiciously blond hair that doesn't quite match the deep lines around his eyes and lips.

He tells me the jacket is ruined, in a tone that suggests he will resort to telling me he burned it himself if I don't get out of his lobby.

"We did everything we could," he says. "But some things cannot be saved."

"But where is it?" I ask, my voice testy. "I don't care what it looks like; I'll take it."

I wish I were brave. I wish my voice was strong and my posture commanding, but I'm broken and everything about me reeks of desperation. I haven't showered in two days because I am convinced that I can still smell Weston's scent if I jerk my head quickly from side to side. My clothes are wrinkled from leaning against walls and hugging what feels like the entire town of Enfield as they drop off casseroles and cookies. My breath smells like the small tub of yogurt Mom all but force-fed me yesterday, a grotesque production reminiscent of "Here comes the train . . ." that ended in tears—hers, not mine.

My boyfriend is dead, and my God, could somebody *please* just get me his damn jacket because I can't think of it lonely and unworn any more than I can think of Weston's body lying somewhere in a refrigerator, irrecoverably preserved in death.

It's the closest I've come to losing control in public since my tiny universe collapsed in on itself, and the Suit must sense this because, with a long-suffering sigh, he leaves through a large wooden door and returns minutes later with a black trash bag, holding it out to me by the drawstrings.

He hesitates when I take it and says, "You'll want to send it out to be professionally cleaned. I . . . I wouldn't open the bag."

For a moment, he looks almost human. But the emotion sinks back into the mask of the suit and then he appears bored, idly straightening the already pristine stack of pamphlets on top of the counter in a gesture of dismissal.

And though I didn't expect it to smell like it does—musky and destroyed—I cradle the bag against me like an infant as I walk back to my car and try desperately not to think about the grave being dug somewhere behind me.

Mom and Dad are furious that I drove myself to get the jacket after Ratio dropped me off at home.

"You *know* you aren't allowed to drive right now," Mom says. "You know this, Anna."

"But why?" I ask. My keys clank angrily against the hall table. "When am I going to be allowed to drive again? Are you going to take me to school, drop me off, pick me up like I'm five? I'm grieving, not an invalid."

"Don't raise your voice to your mother," Dad says, and his words make us pause, because this is a line from a different play, one where the biggest transgression is coming home late or lying about where I'm spending my Wednesday nights.

It's too normal.

We're crammed in the narrow entryway when my stomach growls audibly.

Mom and Dad's eyes drop to my belly like they can see through it.

"You're hungry," Mom says, and her tone is caught between relief and something else. "What do you want?"

I want Weston.

I'm not hungry, but Mom and Dad look so hopeful, so concerned, that I use my lying powers for good. I owe them that much.

"Can we get Fixin' Burger?" I ask. "The chicken strips with gravy?"

They leave to get the food together, after asking repeatedly if I want to go, if there's anything else I want, but I insist that I'm going to shower. To rinse off and feel more human.

They leave in a state of near elation, and I feel guilty for causing their grief to double with concern for me.

I do rinse off, but only enough to wet my hair as proof that I showered, when they return. They'll be back soon. I don't have much time.

I take the jacket out of the bag, not caring that it's ripped in places, stiff, and not at all like I remember, and I slip it on over my arms and cry.

I cry so hard that I hiccup. I cry like my tears might bring him back.

I cry because I pray to the God of whatever heaven, of whatever hell, that Weston could still feel my body heat in these sleeves when he took the curve too fast, that in the end, part of me was with him.

I pray that it was quick. Instant. No pain.

When Mom and Dad come back with Fixin' Burger, I've returned the jacket to its bag and dried my eyes.

I manage to eat one chicken tender, a couple of French fries, enough to make them smile a little, to breathe a sigh of relief.

Later, I turn the fan on in the bathroom when I throw it up, so they don't hear.

chapter 28

∼೨

anna

The night before the funeral, I do the thing Ratio told me not to. I go online to see what people are saying.

The first photo on my feed is of Weston playing his mello-phone. It is poorly edited and with too many filters, the words "RIP Our Favorite Trumpet Player" scrawled on the bottom, posted by a nonband kid whose name I barely recognize.

There's a private group that I've been invited to: Weston Ryan Memorial Page.

Darin started it, which I doubly hate, because I *know*, wherever he is, Weston is pissed.

I click anyway. There are at least a dozen comments and posts. Variations of the same thing: So sorry he is gone. Can't believe it. His poor parents. I'm going to miss him.

But there's a name I recognize from the string of drunk texts, a picture of a girl with choppy blonde hair, beside a lengthy post:

My best friend Meghan's dad was his mortician. And i was telling her how everyone was
joking about how he was probably buried in
his leather jacket. he always wore the leather
jacket.and if you described him by the coat
they'd know who he was. She said she's gonna
ask her dad tomorrow if he was buried in the
jacket. Sorta creepy . . . gosh i miss this kid

Another post, this one a day later:

HE was NOT buried in his famous Leather
Jacket, shockingly . . . my friends dad was the
mortician. I guess his parents kept it? I can't
imagine anyone else having it.

I don't have the energy to be angry at the voyeuristic crap
pretending to be grief. I don't have time to wonder why people
like her get to be alive when people like Weston have to die.

I don't have time to feel badly that I would not hesitate
to press a button if it would force them to trade places, even
if the girl's profile picture is of her and a younger girl about
Jenny's age. Her sister, probably.

I don't care.

I close the laptop. Take out my journal instead.

I stay up most of the night, my brain flipping between exhaustion and chaotic energy. I flip aimlessly through the black
journal for a while, trying to conjure the words that will make
everything right when nothing is right, at all.

It's one in the morning when my phone lights up and Jonathan's name flashes across the screen.

"Look," he says when I answer, "it's you and Ratio. I
get that. I dropped the ball somewhere along the way and

stopped going to the fort and ... You don't know what I'm talking about. But I knew him. *Knew* him, knew him. And I know you did, too, and I ..." Jonathan lets out a long sigh that hitches into a sob. "I miss him. And I knew you'd get it."

I look at my journal, an idea forming in the back part of my brain that should go to sleep.

"Want to do something stupid?" I ask. "Like, really stupid?"

Jonathan's voice is not the least bit concerned. "Of course."

In the end, we invite Ratio. I consider warning him about Jonathan's mood, letting him know that Jonathan feels left out of the inner sanctum of Weston rememberers, but it turns out I don't have to.

We all pull up around the same time, killing our headlights so they don't shine in the cluster of houses and wake Weston's grandparents, or his dad, or his aunt and uncle. When we get out of our respective cars, Jonathan and Ratio come together and hug, not saying a word. It's not a side hug, or a handshake that turns into a lean, but a full-on, arms-wrapped-around-each-other hug.

They say something, but I can't hear it through their muffled embrace, can only see their breaths rising in the icy air.

When they break apart, their eyes are red, but they're half-smiling.

"Weston has turned you into a troublemaker," Ratio says, looking at me.

"I think you're right," I say.

"What a legacy," says Jonathan.

"He'd be so proud of you," says Ratio.

There is enough sincerity in his voice that I force a smile. Just for him.

We walk together to the workshop, pushing the big four-wheeler and one of the tiny manual ones out to the road.

"Does the little one even have headlights that work anymore?" Jonathan asks.

"Does it matter?" I ask.

It doesn't.

We ride until our fingers chill and freeze to the handlebars and our noses and ears turn pink, until we almost—but not quite—forget that Weston isn't riding alongside us.

chapter 29

༄

anna

The funeral is exactly what you'd expect: lots of crying, lots of hymns, lots of people nodding at me somberly as I pass, my arm linked tightly with Ratio's.

Ratio plays two pieces on the piano.

I stand in front of a crowd, open my little black journal, and read what I don't remember writing early this morning, when I snuck back into the house after we ran the four-wheelers down to empty.

It has crossed-out parts. At one point, I went on a mini tirade that involved the words "I hope your fucking Memorial Memorial Tree was worth the rumors that hurt a boy who did nothing. I hope the new one grows big and strong and then falls and smashes all the cars around it, and I hope they're expensive."

But I stick to the program and say words about eternity and love and grief that feel hollow and wrong even if they are true.

Weston's parents sit next to each other, holding hands and crying, nodding as I speak. Weston's casket looms before me while I read, a sleek expanse of black lacquer and silver clasps with a spray of flowers atop it that seem garish and out of place.

My words echo in my head that night, when I'm too antsy to sleep but too tired to do anything else.

I should have noticed more at the funeral. I should have taken in the picture of him in the huge, awful, ornate frame beside the casket, should have found where my parents were sitting to check their reactions, Jenny's reaction. Last time I saw her, before Ratio picked me up to go to the church, she was holding her schoolbook that Weston and I had read on the way home from the lake house. I don't even really remember sitting through the service, standing for hymns and sitting when my mouth was done forming words.

But I remember the look on Ratio's face when he played the piano, the long, long glance he cast toward Weston's casket before he took a deep breath and began.

I remember that I looked away after that.

I sit on my bed for a long time, ignoring the stars on the ceiling and instead trying to look beyond them to the shadowy, hazy, heavenish place Weston is supposed to be.

If he's hovering somewhere as a ghost, haunting me, he's invisible.

I wish he'd come back to haunt me. I asked his parents if we could include one of my glow-in-the-dark stars in the casket—which was closed at the reception and the funeral—and they agreed. I wonder if he can see it, where he is.

I wonder if we're still under the same sky.

The real funeral comes on Friday.

I grab the old pink plastic tub from the laundry room, the one that has been vomited into by my sister and me more times than I care to remember. Years of washing and rewashing have left the inside a faded pearl and the edges cracked with age. They pinch my fingers as I tote it from the kitchen sink to my bedroom, blue Dawn soap mixed with water sloshing from the sides.

The jacket is laid out flat, arms stretched wide atop a carefully laid pallet of beach towels that have witnessed sandy Florida trips and hair-dripping pool parties but never the stiff embrace of a dead boy's jacket.

The arsenal of sponges and rags I collected from beneath the kitchen sink watches somberly as I carefully position the tub beside the jacket and begin to assess the damage.

I suppose part of me entertains the great hope that the jacket cannot actually be Weston's. That some cosmic mistake is playing out and will soon be resolved. I see the bit of leather torn at the waist, the buttons missing from the left cuff, and hold on to the hope, even though I know a terrible thing must have occurred for Weston to let something this severe happen to his jacket.

To me.

I wash for an hour, maybe two. I scrub at mud that has soaked into the right breast and hardened, and a grotesque mixture of dried blood and mud, until the water turns gray and the soap bubbles fade into sludge. My fingers wrinkle from the water, and still I scrub.

Maybe he'll return to claim his jacket, his emblem, if only I can get it clean enough. Maybe this is a catharsis that my body needs, like craving bananas when your body needs potassium.

Whatever the reason, I don't want anyone else to do this, don't want some stranger touching what's left of the boy I love.

Or maybe I need something to do with my trembling hands.

I'm sitting folded against my bed, the jacket stretched out once more to dry, when there's a slight knock on my door.

"Come in," I say, already hating the *God is in control* or *Time heals all wounds* crap I'll get from my parents.

But it's not Mom or Dad. It's Ratio, his suit and tie from yesterday replaced with a faded junior high band shirt and jeans.

"Anna," he says in greeting.

"Hey," I say. I gesture at the jacket. "Sorry. I would have put this away if I had known you were coming over."

"No, I'm glad you didn't. Is it weird to say it's good to see it again?"

I don't respond, *can't* respond to this.

"You know why I'm here," he says. Ratio sits next to the jacket and almost involuntarily goes to touch it, but then stops short. He lets out a slow breath before meeting my eyes. "We need to talk about tomorrow."

Saturday. Contest. The duet. What I wouldn't give to have my performance be my biggest concern. What wishing well needs my coin, what bargain do I have to make to go back in time?

"What about it?" I ask.

Ratio is watching me. "It's your call, Anna. Nobody expects you to go, but the choice is yours."

"The band is still performing?"

"Yes."

"Without him?"

"Yes."

My breathing is uneven. "And you're . . . you're okay with this?"

He runs his hands through his hair, and it reminds me so sharply of Weston that I feel a little faint. I wonder how much of Weston is trapped in Ratio and vice versa. I wonder how much of Ratio Weston took with him when he left.

How much of me.

I want to beg Ratio to comb his fingers in his hair again, so I can memorize the look of it. And suddenly I know with heart-dropping certainty that a little piece of my soul will forever live outside of my body, roaming the earth for any sign of Weston, even a whisper.

"The band has worked too hard," Ratio says, his drum major voice slipping into his tone and just as quickly slipping back out. "Weston would want us to play," he says quietly. "You know he would."

I do. I know the boy whose jacket is laid bare next to me would absolutely want to see if his music, if the band's music, was good enough to go to state. He would sit next to me on the bus, tap out our duet on my fingers, and sneak a kiss for good luck on my palm before we took to the field. It would mean everything to him.

So I am as surprised as Ratio when I say, "No."

He blinks. "Really?"

"Really."

There's a long silence as we both contemplate my answer.

"You're surprised," I say.

"Yes," he says. "It doesn't seem like you."

I shrug. "I don't know who I am anymore."

He says something else, but his words flow over and around me. I say nothing in return.

Eventually, he sighs and leaves. I hear him talking quietly to my parents, but I can't make out what they are saying, and I don't bother trying.

I trail my hands over the damp jacket.

chapter 30

anna

When my alarm sounds, I rest for as long as I can in the moment between being asleep and awake, where I can *almost* pretend Weston is still here.

I pretend that we're going to the contest today, excitedly talking on the bus about our chances of making straight ones, of nailing our duet and impressing the judges. I pretend that we are debating whether or not Weston needs *another* band meme T-shirt, which of course he will buy anyway.

I pretend that I'm not pretending, but the alarm's insistence claws at my ability to hold off the inevitable, so I roll over to shut it off and sit up in the realization that Weston will not be on the bus today.

And I won't either.

Then why did you set the alarm? I can't tell if my brain is taunting or pitying me. *Why bother waking up so early if you aren't going?*

I crawl to the foot of my bed and lie down on my stomach so I can reach down and trail my fingers over the jacket. It's slightly damp. Still cracked and not right and . . . *his*.

I'm still his.

Feeling stupider than stupid, I whisper to the jacket, "What do you want me to do?"

Neither the jacket nor its owner replies, but I know their answer.

When I walk into the band hall, the room grows quiet, everyone pausing to stare.

It's not an unfriendly stare, not even a *curious about the girl with the dead boyfriend* stare, but it's heavy all the same. I stand in the open doorway with my duffle bag over my shoulder, Weston's travel shirt, which he accidentally left at my house after the lake house weekend, tucked next to my marching shoes, my hairbrush. The shirt is in a ziplock baggie, sealed tight, to preserve the smell.

Lauren meets my eyes from where she sits on the floor. A memory from the funeral, blurry around the edges, pops into my head: Lauren's face, blotchy red from crying, her leaning against her mom in the pews, both watching me read from my tearstained pages.

She wasn't at the graveside. I didn't expect her to be, but I was sad not to see her.

I expect her to come over to me, but she doesn't. She looks back down and whispers something to Olivia.

If I didn't know what true pain felt like, her dismissal would hurt, but nothing compares to the way a slightly damp, abandoned leather jacket rubs at my thoughts.

"I thought you weren't going to show up," Andy says, appearing at my side.

"Me, too," I say.

Around us, the room amps back up to its usual too-early noise levels, contest nerves and sleepiness battling for the volume controls.

I catch more than one person trying to hear what Andy and I are saying.

"You don't have to be here, you know," Andy says, his voice low so only I can hear. "Mr. Brant said we were playing without you two, that we would keep the duet silent."

"Oh," I say. "Maybe we still should?"

Andy shrugs. "You could just come and watch. You don't have to play."

I don't have to hear Weston's voice to know he would shove me into the lake if he found out I threw all of our hard work out the window.

It can't be any scarier than a four-wheeler in the dead of night, I think, and I hope the quip reaches him, wherever he is.

"I'm playing," I say, and I'm not sure if I'm telling Andy or Weston.

I expect to sit alone on the bus. I sit in the middle of the seat to communicate this. Everyone who passes pats my arm or gives a sad little smile, but nobody tries to sit. Nobody dares.

Until Andy plops down with an irreverence that would be outrageous if it weren't so blissfully distracting.

"I'm glad you stayed. It saves me from having to sit next to Olivia and hold her millions of bobby pins."

"I have bobby pins, too," I remind him, and it's such a normal, pre-Weston conversation that I'm taken aback.

"Don't think that just because you're sad you get to pick all the music," he tells me, handing over one of his earbuds.

I'm already sweating when we take the field, the snare drum tapping out a steady beat for us to march to our places.

I know from countless hours of watching videos of our

performances that this part looks like a shock of orange cloth being rolled out onto a meadow of green, our bright orange uniforms and white plumes bleeding onto the field. As we hit our marks, we march in place, waiting for those farther back on the field to find their places.

Pure habit makes me check Terrance's and Samantha's marks, too. They've hit them correctly, and though we are absolutely not supposed to talk on the field—especially at contest—Terrance nearly breaks my heart when he meets my eye and says, "You've got this."

Samantha's nod is barely detectable, even with her plume and shako. "He'd be so proud, Anna."

"Thanks," I whisper. I need their words to keep me rooted in what I am about to do.

The whole world is in slow motion when we turn to face the stands, the judges' box, the drum major podium.

Even through the bright sun, I can see Mom, Dad, and Jenny sitting just above my line of vision, Dianne and Hank beside them. Mom must have gotten my text and hustled everyone out the door to get here on time.

I take a deep breath, and the announcer's voice booms.

"The Fighting Bearcat Band of Enfield, under the direction of Nicholas Brant, would like to dedicate today's performance to Weston Ryan, a mellophone player and beloved member of their band, who passed away this week. His duet at the end of the second movement will be kept silent in his honor. Our hearts go out to you, Enfield. Best of luck."

The announcer pauses as the news ripples through the stands. The crowd of onlookers and members of other bands—some in uniform, some out—look toward each other, at us, and to the empty space where Weston should be.

"Drum major: Is your band ready?"

Ratio, who practiced the required drum major salute for weeks—a complicated series of hand motions that ends in a sharp salute toward the judges—stands at strict attention, arms by his side, purposefully unmoving.

When he realizes that Ratio isn't going to salute, a breach in protocol I had no idea he was planning, the announcer reads his final order: "You may begin your performance for the UIL Region Twenty-Five Marching Band Contest."

And then it's just us, forty-two kids in our orange and white uniforms, the sun beating down and making the turf beneath our feet smell faintly of tar and the sweat of the performers who came before.

We are a link in a chain that extends as far as the eye can see in either direction.

We are one band. Weston was just one piece of us.

Before Ratio puts the whistle in his mouth to count us off and start the mechanism that is this marching show, he meets my eyes, and there is a mix of pride and determination and fathomless sadness that both makes my stomach turn and fortifies me.

It's a look just for me.

It's a look just for *us*, the us left here to figure it out in Weston's absence.

Ratio blows the whistle and claps his hands.

"Band horns up and—"

"*Up!*"

And we are moving. I find myself strangely focused on the music, my placement, my marching. It would be normal, except that as I'm marching, the thoughts I've been too afraid to look at square in the eye are floating around me, gossamer in the wind.

What if Weston and I hadn't had a duet together? Would

he still have died? Would I care, beyond the pain of losing a fellow band member, the cruelest of breaks in routine but nothing more?

And I ask myself, if I had a button to push, one that would take me back in time to ask someone else for help, would I press it?

But as the opener ends and we begin our fluid transition into the production number, I glance across the field to where Weston should be but isn't, and I know my answer.

I would play a thousand duets alone before I would forget Weston Ryan.

When our duet comes, I think about what he said about the call-and-answer, how he was insistent that this was the key to unlocking my full duet partner potential.

I remember what Mrs. Itashiki said, lecturing me about not relying on someone else to play my music, how I needed to play around the silences.

And it's like the entire band falls away, though I feel their gazes, their aura of concern pressing at my back, as I play the very first note alone.

Part of me wants to insist that this is a solo now.

But I play it like a duet, like someone else is playing with me.

I play through blurry tears, letting the silence where he should be caress my ears, my cheeks, my neck.

And just when I've decided that these are the twenty seconds on which I will build what comes next, when I've decided to allow the loss of him into the inner chambers of my heart, a bird, plain and brown, lands on the field, not six feet in front of me.

He sings to me, his little sparrow song. At first it clashes with my notes, running up against them, but then he seems to understand the silences, and he sings to fill them.

I wonder if it's him, if it's Weston's way of letting me know that somewhere in this world or the next, he is still near.

I decide I'm okay with not knowing.

And then the production number is over, and the fast-paced, fast-marched closer springs into life. Ratio is on the drum major's podium, his eyes intent as his arms fly to keep time, bringing his hands down with the beat as if he can will the sound of the band to be on tempo with the sheer force of his movements alone.

Terrance and Samantha orbit around me in perfect time, our heels hitting the ground and rising again in perfect synchronization, our saxophones holding the melody with the flutes, the clarinets, and passing it back to the brass.

When it's finally over, when the last staccato note fades into the sky, there is a long moment of silence, a willful hold, a refusal to let this performance go without some acknowledgment, some recognition that this was not just about us or the competition or even the music.

I think it must be Ratio's doing, but then I see Mr. Brant step forward, a shako in his hand, and when Ratio gives us the order to march off the field and solidify into a line to exit the stadium, Ratio marches against us, carrying the shako in his hand.

When he comes to me, he murmurs, "About-face," and so I do, marching beside him as he carries the shako. Ratio asks Jonathan to join us, too, and together, the three of us march against the moving lines, three stones breaking up the waves of marchers.

Everyone is off the field when we stop to leave the shako in the dead center of the fifty-yard line. The Enfield band looks at us from their perfect rows along the sideline. I see one or two people remove their shakos.

Above us in the stands, everyone is on their feet, silently bearing witness.

I don't know how long we're going to stand here, Ratio and Jonathan and me, but then it begins.

It starts with Bloom, with their drum major clambering to stand on a bleacher seat, drawing the attention of the whole crowd, her drum major cape flapping behind her.

"Bloom! Atten–*shun!*"

The Bloom band snaps their feet together, instrumentless hands going up to triangle in front of their faces. She does a sharp, official about-face toward the field, standing with her hands folded behind her back, her chin high.

The other bands, watching from the stands, begin to follow in a jagged wave, the drum majors and band directors bringing everyone to attention as Ratio and Jonathan and I stand dumbfounded next to the playerless shako with the plume gently fluttering in the wind.

The parents, the onlookers, and quite possibly the judges in the box, based on the feedback that blares through the speakers, all stand. A silent watch, bearing witness.

"He would just *love* this," Jonathan murmurs to us, and Ratio snickers.

"It's probably best he's not here to see it," I say under my breath. "His head would be too big to fit into the shako anymore."

"His head would be too big to fit onto the *bus*," Ratio says.

The bands are still at attention as I pick up the shako and the three of us march off the field.

For a moment, there is a stretch of nearly complete silence. It doesn't last.

The next band takes the field.

The stands are once more filled with chatter and the munching of concession stand food and squeaking of seats.

And there's the yelling when they announce that Enfield has finished second and will be advancing to area next week, which should make me happy or sad or *something*, but I only feel satisfactorily hollow.

It's not entirely unpleasant.

On the way home, Andy takes the window seat and falls asleep on my shoulder. I let him.

chapter 31

❦

anna

It's Christmas break, and it has been five weeks since contest.
The ache in my chest has not so much lessened as it has become a part of my everyday life. One minute I'll be hanging
my T-shirts in my closet or eating a piece of Christmas chocolate, and the next I'm crying.

Not always, though. Most of the time I can carry on with
household chores and snacking without looking like a sob-
bing lunatic, but when the tears come, at least they don't scare
me anymore.

At least I know they'll pass.

Because I didn't know in those first weeks if they ever
would.

Late one night, there was a moment, when I was in bed and
the stars on my ceiling had already dimmed their lights, that I
started crying and didn't think I'd stop.

That particular time was a little more understandable, at least.

Because the Fighting Bearcat Band advanced to area, but we placed one spot away from making it to the state finals. There were no sing-alongs on the band bus home. Only the occasional sniffle.

But it didn't matter as much to me anymore, not going to state.

I just wanted to go home. To lie under my stars and my blankets and in my nest of pillows and Weston's jacket. I didn't need to go to San Antonio to march another silent duet.

But when I got home that night, when I crawled into bed, the tears came hard, and I wondered if, wherever he was, Weston was disappointed in me for *not* caring, for not trying harder.

It was the last time I cried that hard.

I almost miss it, though, the crying. Which is weird. At least I had something to *do*. Now I feel like I'm waiting, but I don't know for what.

I thought it was for marching season to be over, but it wasn't. When Mr. Brant passed out the concert season music, handing the first chair French horn part to Ratio and the second chair to Darin, I felt nothing. No relief. No grief. *Nothing.*

And I thought maybe I was just anxious, waiting for school to go back to normal, for people to stop looking at me, but that happened much faster than I thought possible. The handmade signs came down from the lockers. The lunch lady started accepting my quarters for ice cream instead of waving them away with a tearful smile. The teachers stopped pulling me aside to say "Don't worry about the assignment" or "Just do what you can." Terrance and Samantha stopped whispering around me, like their volume would have somehow been offensive to my delicate sensibilities.

Some days it feels like only Ratio and I remember that everything was different just two months ago. Jonathan shows up on the margins, too, when he isn't busy with college applications and quartets for the spring concert competitions, but his eyes aren't haunted like Ratio's, like mine. Not in the same way.

Ratio has become something of a staple at our house, which Mom and Jenny love. They shower him with affection and food, and we all pretend that we can't see the negative space around him, the place Weston is supposed to fill.

I'm not surprised when there's a knock on the door one cold afternoon and there is Ratio, standing on my porch, with his thin frame covered in layer after layer of long-sleeved shirts, a knit cap on his head and a thinly wrapped present in his hand.

"Merry Christmas," he says through the glass door.

"You're a week early," I tell him, as he wipes his feet on the mat and slides into the entryway. "You just missed the rest of them," I say. "Grocery store."

"You didn't go?" he asks conversationally, but I know the way he is looking at me. It's the investigative look. The *Is she okay?* look.

I shrug. "Didn't feel like it."

"Lucky for me," he says. "Because I wanted to give you this."

The package is slim and bendy, some kind of paper. The wrapping is red and gold, the corners sloppily taped. A yellow rubber bracelet with Weston's name and a tiny French horn on it peeks out from his myriad sleeves, Ratio's version of a leather jacket. His haunting.

"Thank you," I say. "Should I open it now?"

Ratio nods. "Careful, though. It's obviously paper, so don't tear into it or anything."

Something about the way he is standing, the way his head is cocked slightly as he watches me gingerly lift a piece of tape, rings the Weston bell inside me.

But I forget about it when I open the package.

I forget about everything.

In my hand are two sheets of music. "Full Flight" is scrawled at the top of the first page, with "Weston Ryan" printed in the top right-hand corner.

I'd recognize the handwriting anywhere.

I don't start crying until I see the words, the subtitle beneath the title: "For my Anna."

"It's piano music," Ratio tells me, as I look dumbly down at it through my tears. "His mom found . . . It's . . . it's not finished."

"I don't care," I say. "I don't . . . Can you play it for me?"

Ratio is too good to say anything but yes, and even though his house is closer, we go to Dianne's. It feels wrong to play this on a piano that isn't Weston's.

Weston's mom is back to traveling for work, and when we text to ask if she's home, she says she's not but that we are welcome to let ourselves in with the key beneath the mat.

I shoot a quick message to Mom and Dad letting them know I am with Ratio and grab my keys to lock the door behind us.

"The jacket . . ." Ratio says, and his voice catches. "Do you want to bring it?"

And I do, spreading it gently on the console between us.

We talk about everything and nothing on the car ride to the outside of town: Ratio's college applications, how he wants to play music for the rest of his life, how all the things in my notebook seem different now, how they feel too big and too small to be important.

How everything forever will be arranged around Weston.

"Is that stupid?" I ask. "That I think this is a forever kind of thing, even though he's gone?"

Ratio shakes his head. "Did I tell you what his grandpa said to me after the funeral? After I played?"

"No."

"We talked about how we used to play music together, Weston and me. And then he asked me what I planned on doing, and I said I was working to become a professional musician. He said that was good, and that from now on, I couldn't only work for myself. I had to work for Weston. I had to catch his stars, too, since he wouldn't be around to catch them."

"Catch his stars," I say. "I like that."

I wonder if his grandfather knows about the star I slipped into Weston's casket.

When we get to the house, I step out onto the gravel and stop, remembering what it was like to look up at the grand old Victorian for the first time, my heart thumping hard in my chest, knowing I was skipping school with Weston.

I look toward the platform, the tree house, and Ratio follows my gaze.

"Want to go?" he asks.

"I want to hear this," I say, holding up the music.

His smile is crooked and pensive. "Me, too," he says.

He takes a long time to settle at the piano, reverently lifting the lid and adjusting the bench so that it's the exact distance he needs from the pedals.

I'm already crying a little, watching him gently take the two sheets from my hand and arrange them on the stand.

"Can I . . ." I stop, take a shuddering breath, squeeze the jacket in my hands like a stress ball.

"What is it?"

"Can I sit at your feet while you play?"

I want to explain, want to tell Ratio why, but we have an understanding, Ratio and I.

He's not going to ask me to explain.

"Of course," he says.

I worm the jacket over my arms and sink to the carpet beside the floral couches, the winter-gray light trickling through the windows. I lean, gently at first but then with intention, against Ratio's knees.

"Okay?" he asks.

"Okay," I say. "*Okay?*"

Ratio's answer is a deep breath, and the music unfolds around us, a breathtaking swirl of music that starts at the bottom of the piano and works its way to the top in long runs of eighth notes. When it reaches its great height, when the sky is open and the clouds are below, you can see the sparkling sun.

The joy is so bright, it hurts. The relief and hope are so tangible, I half expect to turn around and see Weston standing beside us.

Because it's for me, but it's *my Weston*, our Weston. The music is so devastatingly him, his fingerprints touching each note.

And just as the music crescendos once more, just as it moves to the next part of the song, Ratio stops, and my ear tries desperately, *desperately*, to hear what comes next.

But I can't.

"Play it again?" I ask him.

And he does.

The second time he finishes, Ratio doesn't move, the last notes hanging in the air like a lingering, uncertain farewell. When he releases the pedal, they float out of the room, ringing into the far corners of the house that watched Weston Ryan grow from a little kid with hands too small to cover an octave into a grown teenager on the cusp of adulthood.

"Maybe it's not incomplete," Ratio says quietly. "Maybe it's a duet. Maybe we're supposed to finish it."

"But how?" I ask, my voice also hushed. "*How?*"

"The same as the Kaua'i 'ō'ō: We keep calling. We keep

playing our part, even when we're not sure if anyone else is listening."

"The *what*?"

"You didn't see it, the day we were here to plan the funeral?"

"See what?"

Ratio gently steps around me and disappears upstairs while I wait beside the bench, running my hands over the cool surface of the wooden foot. He returns with more paper, this time typed and in a plastic protector.

"It's a report he wrote," he tells me, as I flip through the pages, "that he left on his bedside table for some reason. His mom had it out with a bunch of other stuff. It's about this bird that is probably extinct. There was one remaining male left for a long time, and researchers found it and . . . Well, you can read it for yourself."

And so I read, and like the music that Ratio has just played, I can hear Weston in these words, his loneliness. It's crushing to read about a bird so desperate to find one of its own kind that it rushes toward the researchers when they play its call.

I'm wondering why Ratio thought it was a good idea for me to read this, until I reach the last paragraph:

> Scientists know that the Kaua'i 'ō'ō's song is a duet. You can hear the spaces between its calls in the surviving recordings. The spaces are where a mate should answer. Even though he had not heard the call of his mate in a long time, the last Kaua'i 'ō'ō did not lose hope. He kept the silences open so he could one day hear them filled. Maybe his mate wasn't dead. Maybe she was lost in the hurricane and someday they would be together and the duet would be complete.

"'Full Flight,'" I whisper. "Like the birds."

Ratio doesn't cry, but his eyes look heavy, like he might be considering it.

"You were the other half of the duet in every way, you know."

"I don't know," I say. "I think we both were. *Are.*"

"Are," Ratio agrees. "We are."

We look at the report in my hands, the jacket lying beside me.

"Can you play it one more time?" I ask him.

He does. And this time, when he plays, I imagine all the ways my voice can fit into the music, how my life is mine and always will be, but maybe part of it can be for Weston, too, a way to honor him. A way to remember.

If I were Queen Victoria and he were Prince Albert, I would build a statue. I would name every street after his favorite things. I would make the world remember him along with me.

But I'm not. He's not.

We're just Anna and Weston.

Maybe that's enough.

That night, when I get home, I eat dinner with my family. I eat all the food on my plate and suggest a game of Apples to Apples. My parents keep shooting each other looks of relief to see me laughing at adjectives and teasing Jenny. I sit next to Jenny on the couch when we watch a Christmas movie.

I live. I smile. I remind myself that grief can't have me and that I still have work to do, stars to catch.

And when the night comes and I'm in my room alone, I take out the black journal, and I begin to write.

About Weston.

About me.

About everything he was and could have been and everything that I will be.

I'm nowhere near finished when my eyes begin to droop and my fingers fall heavy on the pen, but I have time. I'll write more later, because that's what I do.

"Same sky," I whisper, as I begin to doze off, but I purposefully wait a moment before succumbing to sleep, in case there's an answer.

I'll keep playing my half until there is.

Epilogue

I learned how to love Weston when I was seven years old, ten long years before duets and my junior year of high school, in a section of a pet store whose tank occupants had no legs, no cuddles, and—if the Bible stories were to be believed—no morals.

Dad sidestepped and nudged me forward when the pet shop man took a snake from its tank.

"Go on, Anna," Dad said. "It's all right."

It did not seem all right, but I wanted Dad to be proud, to squeeze my shoulders and call me his little firecracker, to call me brave. So I extended my shaking hands.

And then the little snake was in my palms, curiously weaving his way around my fingers, his tongue flickering in and out. My eyes raked over his tiny black scales and the little bands of teal that circled him like the spools of ribbon he was named for.

He felt like mine. I brought my hand to eye level and murmured, "I love you, little friend."

When it was time to go, I cried.

We came back a week later, after my begging wore Dad down, and the pet shop man deposited a ribbon snake in my hand.

"This isn't him," I said.

The man barely paused. "They're all the same, darlin'."

But he wasn't the same, not at all. I would never stop thinking of my lost friend.

When I come home from the final football game of my senior year, it's late, and the house is silent. Mom and Dad and Jenny are asleep, and after a hot shower, I recline in bed and stare at the stars on my ceiling. I count. I beg them for sleep.

I wish I could text Weston; the impulse has never died off. I wish I could tell him about how the football team won the state championship or how Ratio flew down from college to be there for my final game.

Mostly, I wish I could tell Weston how putting my saxophone away at the end of the night—the last time I would pack it up after a high school football game—felt too significant to bear, how I half imagined it wouldn't feel so final if he were still here.

Sometimes I still look at my phone and wonder why I haven't heard from him, what he's doing, if he's excited about the newest edition of *King's Reign*—and then I remember. But before the shadows can catch me, I write.

It helps.

When I'm too tired, like tonight, I'll flip through my journals, my finger tracing line after line of memories and thoughts and questions, pictures I've taped on pages, doodles of things I've seen or dreamed.

At the end of each journal, I've glued the same thing on the inside back cover: a tiny photo of "Full Flight: For my Anna."

It's nearly too small to be legible, the notes the size of

pinpricks, the treble clef an uncooked macaroni. But I know what it is. I know what it *means*. It means I have to keep going. It means I have to keep writing, keep living, keep pushing the shadows away.

Because it's what Weston would tell me to do. It's what *I* want me to do.

A piece of driftwood bursts forth from the ocean of my brain, a thought constantly returning with the tide: *I wish he could* know. *I wish I could know that he knows I did this, that I wrote about us.*

Wishing only gets me so far when I'm this tired. When I realize that journal flipping is not going to lull me to sleep, I take out my phone to scroll through an endless feed of GIFs and memes and videos.

A photo of a bright yellow and black bird catches my eye, and my breath catches as I scramble to sit against my headboard.

"Breaking: Hawaiian Birds Believed Extinct Found Nesting," the headline says. "Kauaʻi ʻōʻōs Still Endangered, but No Longer Extinct."

My thumb aches from how hard I thump it against the screen.

"It's a huge breakthrough for the scientific community," the ornithologist who discovered the birds says in her video interview. "We're thrilled. That we found a nesting pair when we previously thought there were none left in the world is monumental."

The voice-over talks about how the birds were thought to be lost, how the last Kauaʻi ʻōʻō was, in fact, the *second*-to-last Kauaʻi ʻōʻō after the species had been declared extinct in the early seventies, until the last male was found in 1984.

"This goes to show that nothing is an absolute in nature." The ornithologist grins. "It gives hope to some of the other lost species. Maybe the end isn't always the end, right?"

I watch and rewatch the video, pausing to stare at the clip of the mated pair sitting side by side on a tree branch.

I know it's not scientific to give emotions to birds or whatever, but they *look* in love. They *look* like they know they're lucky to have found each other, to have beaten the odds.

But my favorite part of the video is the end. You hear an excited gasp from the scientist, the fumbling rustle of a camera, and the first ever recording of the entire Kaua'i 'ō'ō duet in its entirety, no missing voice.

Neither half of the famous duet is silent. Both birds—impossibly—are still *here*. They are playing the music that humans were arrogant enough to think they could decree gone forever.

I'm not sure if the God of Enfield and football and heaven lets citizens of the afterlife check their social media messages, but in case he does, I send the article to Weston's KingOfMello handle.

"Same sky," I type beneath it.

There is no unnatural presence or warm, fuzzy feeling when I send the message. The glow-in-the-dark stars don't fall from my ceiling. My skin doesn't prickle with some heightened awareness of a world beyond my own. But the leather jacket I pull from my closet and tuck beside me when I lie on top of my comforter feels a little warmer, and for now, that is enough.

It's enough to know that the duet isn't over and that tomorrow the sun will rise over our same sky. It's enough to know that there are a thousand and one things that I can be, that the world is full of possibilities, and Weston would want me to chase down as many as I can.

When I finally close my eyes, the glowing stars still shining on the backs of my eyelids, it feels like the silence before a deep breath, the moment before another piece of music begins.

It feels like Christmas in my chest.

It feels like opening a brand-new journal full of blank pages waiting for my pen.

It feels like the beginning of a very long and good story, and I swear I hear birds singing outside my window as I fall asleep.

Full Flight

for my Anna

Weston Ryan

Acknowledgments

As always, my eternal gratitude goes to my fantastic agent, Thao Le, for being the very best of humans and the BEST agent. If I thought I could get away with writing your entire acknowledgment in all caps, I would.

A million thanks to Vicki Lame, not only for editing the heck out of this book with so much kindness and expertise, but also for letting me pester you across all the internet platforms for advanced copies from your list of fantastic authors. I am so, so honored to be among them.

There aren't enough ways to say thank you, but the Wednesday Books team is fantastic, and I adore them. Special thanks to Angelica Chong, Kerri Resnick, Alexis Neuville, Sarah Bonamino, Brant Janeway, Jennie Conway, and Jessica Katz. You have made every part of my publication journey a joy.

The best part of being a writer has been all the fellow

readers and authors I've tricked into being my friends along the way. Thank you for putting up with my endless GIFs in your texts and feeds, for cheering on my stories, and for letting me cheer on yours. I gave up writing a list, but I love you ALL. Special shout-out to Ash Poston!

Cassie Gustafson, you'll always get a full paragraph because you have to deal with more GIFs and phone calls than anyone ever should. Thanks for helping me be brave both in writing this story and in life. If magical capes and flying whales were real, I'd come and visit you every day.

To my family, so many parts of this story would be impossible if not for your unwavering support, your love, and your near-constant teasing. Thank you for making the bright parts brighter and the dark parts bearable. Also, to Scott, for sharing his headphones and not getting rid of me in the years since, and to the entire Ramos family for always being a soft place to land. I miss you all more than an entire book could say.

Extra shout-out to Cathy, the Dierks, and the Nalls. The movie nights, your love, and your inclusion of an awkward sixteen-year-old girl and only-slightly-less-awkward thirty-something have quite literally changed my life. Thank you.

To Eddie and Henry, who both make me smile more than should be humanly allowed. I'm so lucky. Thanks for letting me run away to fictional worlds, but know I'll always come back to the one that has you in it.

And finally, for one last time in print because I am nothing if not a sentimental old fool who still doesn't feel like she did you justice, to Michael. Thanks for letting me borrow your music for this story. I did what I promised you I would do: I answered. I hope you can read books where you are. I hope you like this one.